WELCOME TO PARADISE

BOOK 1 THE RESORT SERIES

LISE GOLD

Edited by Claire Jarrett

Cover Design by Neil Irvine

Que tus sueños te lleven a la vida que te haga feliz
Let your dreams guide you to a happy life

— UNKNOWN

1

"*H*ey, pretty lady. Why don't you put that phone down and come join us in the pool for an aqua aerobics class?"

"No, thank you." Lisa shook her head, avoiding the young man's gaze. Manuel's voice was annoyingly animated as he tried to persuade her to get in the pool for the third time that day. She knew his name because he had the equally annoying habit of talking about himself in third person, and the only reason he kept bugging her was because so far, she'd been the only one to turn down his invitation for an 'ab-tastic' class. All the women along the poolside swooned over him, but she would not jump on the Manuel train. Not now, not ever.

"Come on, I know you want to. Ab-tastic Manuel gives the best workouts; you'll feel amazing after." He flexed his muscles and Lisa could not resist an eye-roll before she shot him a glare.

"Will you stop bugging me? I've asked you nicely three times now. I don't want to get in the pool, especially not with you, and if you don't leave me alone, I'll go and speak to your manager."

"Of course." Manuel stepped back and held up a hand, seemingly just now grasping that she really wanted to be left alone. "I'm sorry if I overstepped." His tone was genuinely apologetic, and Lisa noticed the sideways glances from other hotel guests. She had an idea of what they were thinking; *How can anyone be grumpy on holiday in Paradise?*

The thing was, she wasn't on holiday, and although the hotel was called Paradise, it was far from exotic or even pleasant.

Hotel guests jumped in the pool when Manuel blew his red whistle, and Lisa put her phone under her towel to shield it from the splashing water. After the lockdowns in the UK and around Europe, people were desperate for human contact and so craved any opportunity for interaction, even forced fun. She was pretty sure a couple of the holiday makers deliberately jumped in right in front of her, and although she normally wouldn't care what rowdy and tipsy English tourists thought of her, right then, she felt judged and that wasn't a nice feeling.

Lisa demonstratively got up from the sunlounger, put on her shorts and grabbed her phone, her suntan lotion and her towel. Then she walked past Manuel, who was yelling inspirational quotes from her end of the pool, without giving him a second glance and headed for the bar. A drink might calm her down, even if it was the cheap, watered-down all-inclusive kind. Again, eyes followed her, and she wished then that she could just disappear into thin air.

They think I'm by myself because I'm too miserable to hang out with. Truthfully, she was miserable; even two months in Spain couldn't change that. *Forget it*, she told herself. Most of the guests would leave at the end of the week, new people would arrive and hopefully by then, everyone in the animation team would recognise her as the woman who didn't want to participate in mass fun.

"Rum and Coke, please," she said in a forced, chirpy tone to make up for her earlier outburst.

"Rum and Coke coming right up." The man made a show of pouring the rum over ice, spilled half of the Coke over his wrist and on the floor, then added a pink umbrella and a pink, glittery straw.

"Thank you." Lisa took a sip, pretending to scan the premises so she wouldn't have to talk to him. Benidorm was a strange place. The town being so popular with the English, it didn't feel like she was abroad at all, yet it was nothing like London either. Well, the sunshine was nice, she had to admit that. It certainly wouldn't have been this sunny in London, especially during June. After only four days there, her tan was already deep, and her long, blonde hair had even paler streaks running through it.

"How long are you staying?" the bartender asked.

Lisa smiled through a clenched jaw. She'd had this conversation with a couple of bartenders already, but she hadn't met this one yet. Looking away clearly didn't help and she was starting to realise that it didn't matter what she tried; the staff were trained to entertain their guests, period. "Two months," she said. "Maybe three, depending on my situation."

"Your situation? Well, that certainly doesn't sound like a bad situation."

"I suppose so," was all Lisa could think of to say, and looked over her shoulder when she heard heavy breathing.

"Another beer, mate," the man who had come up behind her said to the bartender. "Actually, make it two. One for me and one for the missus." His face was bright red from the sun and sweat was dripping down his hairy chest. When his eyes met Lisa's, his mouth pulled into a grim smile, exposing chipped, yellow teeth. "Hello there, beautiful."

"Hi." Lisa stood up, took her drink and waved her orange wristband at the bartender to show she didn't have to pay for it. "Thank you. Have a good day." Talking was the last thing she felt like doing and apparently her small, stuffy room was the only place she could escape the curious questions from the staff and unwanted flirtations from drunken guests.

Crossing the wide, paved square that led to the hotel's back entrance, she downed her drink in one go and placed it on one the glass collection stations, regretting she hadn't ordered another one.

Paradise Hotel looked like a building lifted straight from the old Soviet Bloc. It was a dirty shade of off-white, rectangular and tall, and whoever designed it had crammed as many rooms into the building as possible. To make up for the basic accommodation, they'd planted palm trees around the two big pools outside and placed two tiki bars on the premises, assuming that would be enough to justify the name. It wasn't the only hotel of its kind. On her walk last night, she'd seen many cheap all-inclusive hotels with similar exotic names lining the beachfront of Benidorm. 'The Pearl of the South', 'The Grand Mermaid', 'Emerald Bay' and 'Premier Sunset'—a smaller hotel that was entirely blocked from the sun by Paradise Hotel—all had the same worn-out look and eighties architecture.

Going on the cost of her room she'd expected her accommodation to be basic, but nothing could have prepared her for this. The lift rattled loudly as it went up, but with most guests spending the day outside, at least it didn't stop twenty-four times on the way to her floor. Even with her mask on the smell of mouldy carpet penetrated her nostrils, and with no air-conditioning in the corridors, she held her breath while she rushed to her room. She was grateful for the strict safety measures though, and the hotel guests all seemed to adhere to the rules inside the building, wearing masks in the communal areas and even gloves at the buffet. In her room, she quickly switched on the old air con unit that was stuck to her wall, its sides held together with duct tape. She could only be thankful it worked after hearing guests complain about their broken devices.

Her balcony doors led to a concrete base that was too small to hold the only rickety chair in her room, so she'd made a nest of the throw and her pillows to sit on. Compared to her beautiful South West London flat, which she'd given up last week, this looked more like a room in a halfway house, but she kept reminding herself that coming here had been the right decision as paying almost four-thousand pounds in rent a month just wasn't an option anymore. Nothing would be the same again, at least not for a while, and she'd have to somehow come to terms with that.

Sinking down in her nest, Lisa leaned against the railing as she opened her inbox for the tenth time that day. Surprised at seeing an email from one of her headhunters, she felt a tiny spark of hope.

'Hey Lisa,

I'm sorry to tell you that Levius Tech have decided to go with another candidate. Don't worry though, you've got this and I'm positive we'll find you something soon. Your CV is strong, but Levius felt that candidate 4 was better suited to their company.

Regards,

Cammie Peterson.'

"Fuck," Lisa muttered, sighing deeply as she flung her

phone onto the bed. She'd been willing to take a huge salary cut and lower her standards with *Levius Tech,* which was a joke compared to the super brands she'd previously worked for. When it rained, it poured. She was still waiting for a reply from another company, and she'd look for more jobs tomorrow. Surely, they wouldn't all turn her down?

2

*S*tella lowered her shades as she watched the blonde woman sneer at Manuel. Being on lifeguard duty meant that she could rest her legs for a couple of hours as well as keep an eye on the team from her chair raised six feet above the pool. Not that they needed much supervising. They were excellent at their jobs, but every so often, people were just not interested in their attempts to entertain them and that seemed to be the case right now. She made a mental note to ask Manuel about their exchange after the team meeting tomorrow and fixed her eyes back on the pool.

Even though this was an over eighteen resort, accidents happened regularly. Some guests got in the pool drunk, others fell asleep in the burning sun, then jumped in oblivious they had caught sunstroke. There had been heart attacks and strokes too, and she'd had to use the defibrillator twice since the resort had fully reopened again. Living an unhealthy lifestyle during lockdown, coupled with the endless supply of unlimited food and drinks in the resort, was a dangerous combination, but it wasn't her job to educate them. As the poolside manager, she had to make sure everything ran smoothly, that her team performed to their highest standards and that their guests were happy. And occasionally save someone's life when the on-site doctor couldn't get there on time. That too.

As Stella followed the woman with her eyes, she noted that she looked irritated as she stomped towards the bar and sat down with a huff. Drunk guests were annoying and difficult to handle, but angry guests were worse. This woman looked way too high maintenance to be holidaying here, and Stella suspected she'd complain about her team before the week was over. Not because they hadn't done a good job, but because some people couldn't help themselves; they complained about everything. Fair enough; the rooms, the food and the service weren't great at Paradise, but this wasn't the Shangri-La. This was a cheap and cheerful all-inclusive resort where you got what you paid for and all in all, their guests had a really good time.

Just as she'd expected, the woman ordered a rum and Coke. She'd probably tried the wine already and decided it tasted more like vinegar—which truthfully, it did—and that the lukewarm beer wasn't much better either. She could picture her at the buffet, grimacing at the colourless food that was tailored to the majority of their guests who had simple tastes; fish and chips, chicken nuggets, pie and mash, pizza and garlic bread. All beige and starchy.

Stella refocused on the pool. They couldn't afford any trouble as times had been hard enough over the past year. They'd been closed for eleven months over the pandemic and now they needed to make up for their losses. Barely surviving on the ten hours a week the staff got paid during the periods the hotel had been closed, many had looked for jobs in factories, farms or in other sectors, and she'd had to train twenty-one new people within three weeks as the decision from management to reopen instead of closing had come last-minute. Now, miraculously, they were at full capacity and it looked like they might be one of the few lucky businesses to survive.

She reached for her walkie-talkie as it crackled. "What's up?"

"It's Florence. We have a situation here at tiki bar one. Drunk man throwing a tantrum."

"Right." Stella sighed. "Can you come here and take over from me? Tell Dave to keep him there; I'll deal with him." Her physical break was short-lived, and although she had no trouble with the intense ten-hour days, it took some time to get used to being on her feet for so long again. She climbed down from her lifeguard chair and handed Florence her fluorescent vest. "Here you go."

"Thanks," Florence said, putting it on. "He's angry because Dave refused to serve him more beer. Good luck." She shot Stella a grin and chuckled. "By the way, it's payday today and the day shift is meeting up at that new tapas place for happy hour. Are you coming?"

"Sure, I'll join you." Stella shot her a smile and made her way to the bar. She wasn't a fan of the staff nights out, but they'd worked very hard and the least she could do was buy them a round. The woman was no longer sitting there with her rum and Coke; she'd probably left right after the drunk man had arrived. Curiously, Stella wondered why she was still thinking about her. Guests came and went, and although she was always friendly and pretended to recognise them, the reality was that she rarely did. This woman had only been here for a few days, and yet she'd noticed her every single day.

"Hi there. I'm Stella, the poolside manager. What's going on?" she asked, looking from Dave to the man and back. "I hear there's a problem?"

"Yes, we have a problem," the man sneered. "I've paid a fortune to drink whatever the hell I want, and this man is refusing to serve me." He held up his hand to show his all-inclusive wristband.

Stella crossed her arms in front of her chest and faced him, letting him know she wasn't one bit intimidated. "What's your name?"

"Pete."

"Okay, Pete. It's within our hotel's policy to refuse alcohol to guests if they are causing disruption or discomfort to others. You're being loud and obnoxious, so I think it's safe to say you've had enough for now."

"That's not up to you to decide," Pete yelled, leaning in.

"Keep your distance, please, Pete. You know the rules." Stella took a step back. "And yes, it is up to me, actually, so I suggest you go to your room, drink some water and sleep it off. Come back down when you've sobered up, and Dave will be happy to serve you."

"This is ridiculous!" Pete's wife said as she joined them. She was unsteady on her feet, her eyes red-rimmed. "Come on, Pete, put your T-shirt on. We'll go to Pit Stop; happy hour starts in twenty." Narrowing her eyes at Stella and Dave, she waved a finger in front of them. "And you two... expect a formal complaint tomorrow."

"Go ahead." Stella kept her cool as she took the coffee Dave handed her before making one for himself. Thankfully, situations like this didn't occur very often. "Complaints can be filed at reception."

Pete and his wife waltzed towards their sunloungers to pick up their bags, and Stella chuckled when Pete tripped on his way to the exit. There was no point getting worked up about it; in a couple of days, they would be gone.

3

_____

*D*inner was most bearable between six and seven pm, and although that was a little early for Lisa, at least the food wasn't completely stale by that point, and the dining area was still fairly quiet. On her first night, she'd made the mistake of going down at eight, and the place had been like a zoo. People throwing themselves onto the buffet, nowhere to sit, loud talking and shouting, and the cheesy nineties pop songs played in all communal areas had driven her to leave after ten minutes.

Now, it was mainly the cheesy music that tormented her ears, but she could deal with that. Scanning the food that was the same as every other day, her stomach was already protesting and screaming out for something fresh. Perhaps she should just go somewhere else tonight. After all, Spain wasn't expensive, and dining out one day a week wouldn't eat into her budget that much.

"What can I get you?" one of the chefs behind the long table asked her. "Today's special is spaghetti carbonara. Or would you like a bit of everything?"

Lisa shook her head as she knew exactly what that

meant. People who asked for 'a bit of everything' literally got that: chips piled onto pizza and pasta, topped with brown gravy that spilled onto the floor as they headed to their tables. "I think I'll just have this," she said, reaching for a piece of garlic bread with her gloved hand. "Thank you."

"Hey, you can't take food outside the dining area," he called after her, but she was already gone.

Lisa was pretty sure the staff all had their own ideas about her, and she suddenly felt an urge to get off the premises as fast as she could. The animation team thought she was a miserable git, the chefs thought she was a food snob—which admittedly, she was—and the housekeeping team probably thought she was boring for spending too much time in her room.

The night air did Lisa good as she wandered over the Lavante Beach promenade in search of somewhere to eat. It was warm and humid, but the sea breeze cooled her skin a little. At least out here she was anonymous, rather than 'that woman'. Soon enough, the staff at Paradise Hotel would start to wonder why she was spending months in a place she didn't even like, and why she wasn't taking part in the hotel's extensive social activities—she wasn't looking forward to the questions they were sure to ask.

The sun was lowering into the ocean, and she stalled for a moment to take in the sunset. The last beachgoers were leaving, looking tired from hours in the sun, but apart from families dragging towels, cool bags and inflatables along, the main stretch was fairly quiet. Lisa had already worked out the daily Benidorm routine. Most holiday makers had gone to their rooms by now, to take a nap and freshen up for the night ahead. Later, they would come out here to 'parade' as they called it, before attacking the buffets and enjoying more drinks at their hotels. It was a funny and alien concept to her, holidaying without any culture whatsoever. Spain was beautiful—she'd visited the country many times before —but this town didn't feel like Spain at all. To her left was the Mediterranean, to her right were numerous hotels, pubs —in the most English sense of the word—and supposedly Italian restaurants that served the same beige food she'd had all week. It wasn't pretty, but anything outside Paradise Hotel was a bonus by now, and Lisa decided to venture into the side streets, hoping to find an authentic Spanish restaurant.

As she found herself wandering through the old town, restauranteurs left, right, and centre tried to catch her attention. "Best pizza in Benidorm!" one waiter shouted. "Best value for money", another one said, then added: "Unlimited buffet!"

Lisa upped her pace, making her way through the network of streets filled with bars and restaurants. She didn't like to be hauled in and she didn't like to feel forced to join long tables with rowdy strangers. It was a whole new world to her, and she realised then how sheltered she'd been. Not sheltered in the traditional sense; her parents weren't strict or Victorian in any way, but she'd definitely always lived inside a comfortable, wealthy bubble of politeness and this was not a part of that life. She was not their kind, and they could smell it as they followed her with their judgmental stares. When she finally escaped the crowded streets, her anxiety rose to alarming levels, and she sank down on the pavement. *Six more weeks. How am I going to survive this?*

Taking deep breaths, she waited for the panic to subside as she held onto her chest. She rarely had panic attacks but her break-up, losing her job and months of worrying about paying rent and bills had made her vulnerable beyond belief. *Get a grip, Lisa. You've been all over the world, for God's sake. This is Benidorm, so calm the fuck down.*

When she opened her eyes again, the white noise finally faded, and she saw that she was in a quiet alleyway. Opposite her, gentle Spanish guitar music was playing from a small tapas bar where they were setting the tables for the night. It felt daunting to go inside in her current state, but at least it was quieter and sitting out here wouldn't get her anywhere either, and so she got up and peeked through the window.

"Buenos dias!" A tall waiter with a perfectly groomed goatee opened the door for her and spread his arms. "Our first customer ever."

Lisa managed a smile as she followed him into the restaurant that only held about a dozen tables. "Ever? I doubt that."

"It's true. It's our opening night." He rubbed his hands together. "We need to make a good first impression, and that means you won't find better Spanish food anywhere else in town tonight."

"That sounds good to me." Lisa sat down at the window table, after he pulled out a chair for her. The décor was rustic and basic and that was a welcome change after the neon-lit bars and kitschy restaurants she'd just passed.

"I'm Joachim. Give me a shout if you know what you want to order. That's our menu," he said, pointing to a blackboard. "We only have house wine, but it's good house wine."

"Thank you. Then I'll have a glass of red, please." Lisa scanned the board, mentally translating the dishes and already salivating at the look of it. "And can I have the Padrón peppers and a slice of tortilla to start with?" she paused, pursing her lips. "Oh, and a tomato salad and the grilled squid, please."

"Of course." Joachim wrote down her order and when he walked off, she heard him whisper something about a potential reviewer to one of his English colleagues. It made sense that he thought she might be from a magazine. She hadn't seen many people here on their own and with her dark jeans, white shirt and trainers, she certainly looked different from the rest of the British women, who wore colourful dresses with rhinestones and were smothered in make-up and novelty jewellery. She sat back and thought of her ex-girlfriend, Sandrine, who used to nickname her 'The Slayer', after the notorious food reviewer. But then again, it could work to her advantage today. If the waiter didn't ask her straight-up, then who was she to contradict his suspicions?

4

"Isn't it a bit early to eat?" Stella asked as she followed Manuel and eight other team members to Hostaria, the new tapas bar Manuel's cousin had opened.

"It's never too early to eat." Manuel waved at his cousin, who was smoking a cigarette outside. "Besides, this coño here was worried no one would show up, so he needs the place to look full. Drinks half price. Just tonight and only for us." He patted the man's shoulder, then stole his cigarette and took a drag before they hugged and exchanged some small talk.

While they caught up, Stella's eyes were drawn to the window table, where a familiar-looking woman was dining on her own. *Is that the grumpy woman from Paradise?* She didn't voice her thoughts, as she was worried Manuel, who had already consumed quite a few drinks, may crack a joke a little too loud, and official complaints about her team members was the last thing she needed.

"This is our bossy-boss, Stella," he said to his cousin, patting her shoulder.

"Hello, Miss Stella. I'm Joachim and this is my new bar."

"It looks nice." Stella shot him a smile and held out her hand to let Joachim squeeze it, even though she couldn't care less about male attention. "And it's really nice to meet you. Congratulations on your opening and thank you for arranging the staff happy hour." Her eyes shifted to the window again, drawn to beautiful Miss Grumpy. "Could we have a table in the back?" she asked, just to be on the safe side. The woman really was gorgeous, she decided then, and as she followed everyone inside, her stomach did a flip when her eyes met Miss Grumpy's for a split second. They were blue and intense, her stare as cold as a winter's morning, but there was also sadness in them, and something else she couldn't quite put her finger on.

Joachim, who had seen the brief exchange, leaned in and whispered: "I'm pretty sure she's a reviewer. It's cool, no?"

"Really?" Stella gave him a puzzled glance but before she'd had the chance to enquire any further, they were seated and Joachim began to serve everyone wine, followed by sizzling chorizo and bread with dips. It was the first night she'd been out with some of her new team members, and she told herself to forget about the woman and focus on her people instead. After all, in her experience, it was way easier to get them on board if they liked her. It had taken her years to build a well-oiled machine of staff members who always had each other's backs, and although everything had fallen apart, she knew she could do it again. Even if it would cost her a good chunk of her wages.

"Drinks on me tonight," she said, smiling at the party. "Now, why don't you all tell me about your day. Who has a funny story to share?"

There was always something amusing to report, and with most staff members being Spanish, they were even more baffled by the English hotel guests than their English colleagues.

"Someone peed in the pool today," a girl called Luciana said. "The new signs are big and clear, but there was still an accident and then the water went green." She laughed. "I love these new chemicals, but it's so annoying that everyone has to leave the pool for thirty minutes. It means they spend more time at the bar."

Manuel shrugged. "They did it before too, it's just that no one ever knew. And now..." He clapped his hands together dramatically. "Bam! Busted!"

Luciana burst out in laughter too, and they speculated about which guests may have committed the crime. The chemicals that turned urine green had led to a lot of hilarity when they'd first started using them, but now that the pool had to be cleaned more often, it was getting rather tiresome.

"I'll see if we can get some better signs with a visual," Stella said, turning to Luciana.

"As if that's going to help." Manuel rolled his eyes. "Everything changes, but one thing stays the same. The guests." He sat back and took a sip of his wine. "Although currently, there is this woman who's quite different from our usual crowd. She's hot. In fact, she'd be super sexy if she just smiled for once. I swear, that woman is miserable on every level and she even—"

As soon as she put two and two together, Stella kicked Manuel's leg under the table while her eyes shifted to the woman by the window, but it was too late. Manuel continued his rant of insults and the woman stood up, slammed some cash on the table and walked out.

"Wait, your food is ready!" Joachim called after her. "I can bag it up for you if you like..." He opened the door, but she was already out of sight.

"What the fuck, Manuel!" Stella shot him a glare. "I was kicking you. Did you not get the hint?"

"What hint?" Manuel frowned.

"The woman you were talking about was sitting right over there." Stella got up and sighed as she shook her head and gave Manuel some money. "Here, pay for the drinks and don't wait for me. I need to sort this out." Although she knew it was Manuel who should be apologising and not her, he was too tipsy to do that right then, and anyway, she was much better at smoothing things over than him. "Could you bag that food up for me please?" she asked Joachim. "I'll drop it off. I know where she's staying."

5

*A*nother panic attack. *Breathe*, Lisa told herself. *Just breathe.* Stumbling through the crowds yet again, she desperately tried to find her way out of the city centre. Finally running towards the beach, she was gasping for air as she sat down in the sand. Never had she felt so humiliated and so embarrassed in her life. She'd recognised some of the Paradise staff members, but it had been Manuel's voice that had made the hairs on her arms rise.

She'd told herself she was just being paranoid, but now she knew they really had been talking about her. *Miss Grumpy.* They'd even nicknamed her. And now she was stuck at Paradise with staff who hated her, even though she'd done nothing but beg them to be left alone. Her confidence crumbled, Lisa had no idea how she would manage to stay there. But what was the alternative? Move in with her parents and her brother? At least here she still had some privacy, some form of autonomy over her own life.

Needing to hear a familiar voice, she scrolled through her phone and called her friend Ebony, the only person who might have some sensible advice for her. Her parents would just tell her to perk up or come home and her brother, well, he had enough on his plate, and she didn't want to bother him either.

"Lisa?"

"Hey, Ebony." Lisa sniffed. "Sorry to call so late, but I need to talk."

"What's up, babe? You sound upset."

"I am. I really, really hate it here and everyone hates *me*."

"Babe..." Ebony sighed. "I'm sure no one hates you. You're one of the kindest people I know. Have you been drinking?"

"No. I'm just so... so fucking lost. Nothing is working out. I can't find a job, the staff are rude to me, the guests hate me, this town is just awful, and I don't fit in. I feel so self-conscious all the time." Lisa sniffed again. "I had two panic attacks tonight. I'm not sure if I can stay."

"Panic attacks? You haven't had those in years."

"I know. They've come back and they're bad."

"Then come home." Ebony paused. "No one is forcing you to stay there but consider giving it a little more time first. You've only been there for a week, and by next week there will be new guests, so everything will be easier."

"You must think I'm pathetic," Lisa said with a huff. "No one would ever complain about being on holiday."

"No, I don't think you're pathetic." Ebony chuckled. "I do think that right now you may be a little oversensitive and that's okay. The past year is just catching up on you. You haven't had an easy one and it takes time to acclimatise. But just wait and see; you'll get there."

"Miserable on all levels, that's how they described me tonight."

Ebony gasped. "They said what?"

"Miserable on all levels. I literally heard them talking

about me behind my back. The hotel staff that is," Lisa clarified.

"That's awful. You should file a complaint against them."

"I'm not sure that's going to benefit my stay long-term, so I'd better not."

"So..." Ebony paused. "*Have* you been disrespectful to them?"

"I don't think so." Lisa tried to remember if she'd been rude at any point. "Maybe I have, I'm not sure of anything anymore." She picked up a shell and threw it into the sea. "I'm sorry. I'm sure you have better things to do than listen to me whining. I just had to vent for a moment; I haven't had a conversation in seven days."

"No problem, babe. I'm actually on a date right now." Ebony lowered her voice and Lisa heard a door slam before the sound of cars in the background. "Sorry, I'm just going outside so he won't eavesdrop."

"No, don't do that for me. Enjoy yourself, I'll call you back tomorrow." On top of everything, Lisa now felt bad for interrupting her friend's date. After a long and difficult break-up, Ebony had been single for four years. She'd finally started seeing other people again and here she was, troubling her with her minor problems.

"It doesn't matter," Ebony said. "It's just an internet date and he's not all that. I'm only staying for a second drink out of politeness because he travelled quite a long way to meet me."

"Why? Does he look different from his profile picture?"

"No. He's tall and handsome and well dressed, but we don't actually have that much to talk about face to face. He was funny when we were chatting online but in real life, he's actually a little basic and he keeps checking himself out in the reflection of the window." She sighed. "But hey, he's better than the previous ones. I'd better give him the benefit of the doubt, maybe he's just nervous."

"Maybe." Lisa pulled her knees up and sighed. "Go back. Enjoy your night. I'll call you when I've perked up. You're right; I'm just feeling sorry for myself and I'm being a little dramatic."

"Okay. Have a cocktail, babe. A cocktail always does it for me." Ebony chuckled. "I'll speak to you soon, honey. Go to sleep, everything will be a little better tomorrow."

"I know. Thank you." Lisa hung up and put her phone back in her handbag, noting she'd never felt so lonely. She was in an alien world; a world where she didn't belong, with people who were different to her and rules she didn't understand. Behind her, she heard someone calling, but she kept her eyes fixed sternly on the horizon, hoping whoever it was would go away.

6

———

$\mathcal{B}$y the time Stella ran back in the direction of Paradise Hotel, with at least ten different dishes and a bottle of red wine that Joachim had thrown in as the woman had left way too much money, the boulevard was riddled with tourists, market stalls and hospitality representatives handing out flyers. If the woman was here somewhere, she'd never find her, and even if she'd gone back to her room there was still only a small chance that she'd be able to find out what room she was in. The reception team consisted of seventeen staff members, and with over two hundred rooms, they didn't know the guests personally.

She went down the promenade steps and continued over the beach, slowing her pace. Unsure why she cared so much, Stella narrowed her eyes as she scanned the beach. *There she is.* Spotting a figure in a white shirt sitting by the shore facing the sea, she approached her. "Hey, lady?" When the woman didn't answer, Stella closed the distance between them. "Hey…" A touch on the woman's shoulder made her turn around abruptly.

"What?" She looked up at Stella, then at the bags in her hands.

"You forgot your food."

"Thank you, but you shouldn't have bothered. I'm not hungry anymore."

Stella bit her lip as she lingered on the spot. This was not going the way she'd planned. "Well, I thought you might want it for later. There's a bottle of wine in there too." For a split second, she met the woman's dazzling blue eyes and almost drowned in them before she looked away again. "Can I sit with you?" she asked, then lowered herself in the sand when the woman didn't answer. "Look, I'm sorry about my colleague. That was very rude. I totally understand that you're upset and furious and that you'll want to file a complaint against my team."

"*Your* team, huh? That explains it. Are you trying to bribe me or something?"

"Not really. Unless a food bribe is a thing, but you paid for it, so no, I wouldn't class this as a bribe." Stella shrugged when her joke clearly didn't hit home. "I just want to apologise, that's all." She hesitated before she continued. "I'm Stella, the poolside manager at Paradise Hotel. And your name...?"

"Lisa." Lisa straightened her back and cleared her throat, but Stella could see she wasn't as confident as she made out to be. "You should tell your staff to stop pestering guests. It's annoying and it's making me feel..." She fell silent, then turned to look ahead again. "Never mind."

"I'm sorry. They're trained to get people in the pool now and then. To distract them from drinking at any opportunity. But I'll tell them to leave you alone. I promise."

"Thank you."

Stella opened one of the boxes and held it out for Lisa.

"Here, try a Padrón pepper. I had one earlier and they're really, really good."

Lisa looked like she was about to throw the peppers in her face, but instead, she reached out and took one, slowly chewing it as she gazed out over the water. Although there was a lot of background noise from the lively town, the rustling of the waves so close to shore made it feel peaceful here.

"Good, right?" Stella tried again.

"Better than the crap they serve at Paradise."

"Right. I agree with you on that." Stella chuckled. "Can I ask you something?" She got no reply but pressed on anyway. "Why are you here if you hate it so much?"

Lisa's lower lip started trembling and she wiped away a tear. "Because it was cheap, and I needed somewhere to live."

"Oh." Out of all the possible answers, Stella had definitely not seen that one coming. "Do you want to talk about it?"

"No, I don't want to talk."

"Okay." In need of something to focus on, Stella took a piece of bread from the bag and nibbled on it. "Do you want me to leave?"

"It's a free world, do what you want." A hint of regret flashed through Lisa's eyes as she turned to Stella. "I'm sorry, that was rude. But yes, if I'm honest, I'd rather be alone."

"Then I'll go." When Stella met her eyes again, she really felt for the woman. There was so much pain and insecurity in them, so much hurt, and she cursed Manuel for making it worse. Standing up, she placed a hand on Lisa's shoulder. "Listen, I know this sounds strange because you don't know me, but I'll be around if you ever want to talk, okay?" Stella had no idea why she'd just offered personal support, but it felt like the right thing to say. As she walked away without waiting for an answer, she could feel Lisa's eyes on her.

A message came in as she strolled back to the boulevard. *'We'll be at Mas Tequila later. Want to join us?'* It was from Vera, Manuel's friend, who sometimes tagged on during staff nights. They'd ended up in bed together a couple of times, and whenever Stella received a message from her involving tequila, she knew exactly what Vera was hinting at. Normally, she'd embrace the opportunity of no-strings sex, but after tonight's drama, she was tired and just wanted to crawl into bed. Perhaps it was for the better; at least she'd wake up fresh tomorrow morning and wouldn't have to deal with the awkwardness while Vera stuck around for longer than she was comfortable with.

'Sorry. Too tired. Rain check?' she replied.

'Nooo! Come out, I want to see you!'

Stella threw her head back as she laughed and slipped her phone back into her pocket. Vera had already been drinking, that much was clear.

7

"*P*ablo, you really have to stop waking me up so early," Stella mumbled as she turned over in bed. The brown and grey tabby was an early riser, and he was having none of her plans to sleep in. "It's seven am and you have plenty of dry food."

Pablo let out a dramatic cry and tapped her cheek with his paw. When Stella buried her face under the covers, he started pouncing on her, excited by the mysterious moving mass.

"Okay, okay. I'm coming." Stella groaned as she sat up, scratched his chin and gave him a kiss on his head. She hadn't had a lie-in since she'd rescued Pablo, but even so, he was still her favourite. "You're just greedy, you are."

Pablo jumped off the bed and headed up the stairs towards the kitchen, looking over his shoulder every few steps to make sure she followed him.

Stella laughed at his enthusiasm as she tied her dressing gown and opened the kitchen cupboard, the sound immediately attracting her other four cats. "Hey, Yeti." She bent down to greet her eldest, a fluffy, white cat. Then she patted

Smelly, her big, long-haired ginger male, and finally the two grey brothers who she'd found by the roadside when they were kittens. "Good morning, Chicken. Good morning, Tuna."

She made herself a coffee before she divided cat food over five bowls, put them on a tray and carried everything outside to the roof terrace that spanned half of the top floor. "Here you go."

Chicken and Tuna were less interested in breakfast today and wandered onto her neighbour's roof after a couple of bites. They preferred their favourite foods which they were named after, but Stella didn't always have leftovers from Paradise Hotel, so sometimes they had to do with the basics. Pablo however, managed to finish his own breakfast along with the leftovers from the others in record time, then jumped onto her neighbour's roof terrace. "Hey, where's my thank you?" she called after him. "Don't I even get my after-breakfast cuddle today?" The cat flap downstairs was barely used as they all preferred to wander the rooftops of the old town, along with dozens of other cats who lived around there.

The village of Altea was still sleeping, but Stella heard the owner of the café opposite talking to one of his staff members as they put their tables, chairs and parasols outside. The blue sky promised another sunny day and she expected it to get busy in town later as Altea was popular with day tourists who came to admire the cute, cobbled streets that were lined with flowerbeds, old white townhouses, and quaint shops and galleries. She walked to the edge of the rooftop, leaned over the wall and greeted the café owner, then sat down to sip her coffee while the town slowly came to life. It was just as well that she was up early; she could walk to the newsagent's as soon as it opened and get her newspapers before her favourite ones were sold out. Grateful she hadn't gone out last night, she cherished the tranquillity of her own company. Vera was a lovely girl, but they had never been more than distant friends with benefits. At twenty-four, Vera loved to party. She was cute and funny, and Stella had no doubt she was sleeping in some other woman's bed right now as she still lived with her parents. That didn't bother Stella. In fact, she kind of hoped Vera would find someone else to focus her attention on as she'd called her a little more than she was comfortable with lately.

The sound of a door opening turned her attention to the left. "Buenos Días, Benedicta." Stella waved at her old neighbour, who walked out onto the adjacent roof terrace with a laundry basket.

"Hola, Stella!" Benedicta, who still had her curlers in her hair, pulled down her washing line and started hanging her big, white undergarments while she mumbled something to Pablo, who was rubbing himself against her legs, hoping for another snack.

Benedicta was lovely and tended to keep mostly to herself, but Stella's other neighbours—a retired English couple—regularly invited her over their dividing wall to join them for sundowners when she was off work. She loved living here and although her parents had argued it probably meant that she'd never return to Seville, buying the narrow three-storey, two-bedroom townhouse was the best decision she'd ever made. With its exposed beams and bare walls, it had heaps of Spanish character, it was cool in the summer and the fireplace kept her warm in winter. The roof terrace that overlooked a quaint little square in the old centre of Altea was a bonus, and she found herself spending much more time up here than in the house itself. Her barbecue was set up in the corner, there was a dining table seating six, and she'd created a cosy seating area with an outdoor corner sofa, a coffee table and a large, square parasol that covered half of the area. She'd also installed a panel with a pull-down screen that served as a projection surface for when she had friends over for movie nights.

Even though her mortgage payments were fairly low, it hadn't been easy to keep up with the payments last year while Paradise Hotel was closed. She'd had to work odd jobs in food delivery and fruit picking, and she'd rented out her spare room to keep the roof over her head. Unlike many of her friends, she'd been lucky to get through it and she finally felt like she could breathe again. Because right now, having a job and a home was everything.

Thinking back to Lisa's comment about needing a place to live, she wondered what had happened to her. She'd seemed so low and hurt and lost, and even though Stella had apologised for Manuel and wanted to leave everything behind her now, she still couldn't seem to get the woman out of her mind.

She contemplated stopping off at work on her way to the beach to see if Lisa was in her usual spot by the poolside. *Why am I even considering this?* It was silly that she was still bothered by the incident; she was used to troubleshooting and did it every single day. This was no different.

8

_L_isa tapped on the link to another vacancy. The salary wasn't even close to what she'd earned before but still... she would need something soon, and beggars couldn't be choosers. Just as she was about to apply, a reminder popped up on her phone with a memory from exactly two years ago. It was a great picture of her and Sandrine, sitting in a fancy restaurant in Antigua. It had been their last holiday together, celebrating their four-year anniversary. Not much later, Sandrine had moved to New York.

An up-beat pop song started blasting through the speakers, announcing another ab-tastic class. Or perhaps it was a fit-tastic class, or a morning pool sing-a-long. Lisa sighed and noted that she felt even more self-conscious today. She'd never been insecure but recently, her confidence had plummeted to zero and she hated being the centre of any kind of attention. Deep down, she just wanted to be invisible, but being invisible wouldn't help her land a new job. With an oversaturated market, it was survival of the fittest and although she'd been top dog before, now, she'd have to take anything she could get. Because if she'd learned one thing from the current job market, it was that there was always someone better, smarter, cheaper and more capable out there. And they were all ten years younger than her.

Keeping her eyes on her phone, she expected one of the animation team members to lure her into the pool, but they left her alone. *Thank God. Their manager must have spoken to them. What was her name again?* Lisa couldn't remember, and although she'd kept an eye out for the woman today, prepared to apologise for possibly being rude, she hadn't seen her anywhere.

Aimlessly, she clicked on the picture that took her to more pictures in the same album. A snorkelling trip, white sandy beaches, great food and early morning swims. They'd been so happy back then. At least she'd thought they were happy. They had a great flat in central London, interesting friends, amazing careers, fabulous holidays... And Sandrine had given all of that up for a job. Not even *a job* in general. No, just a better job. Lisa had always known Sandrine was ambitious, she just hadn't expected her to put her career before their relationship. And here she was. Alone, no job and no home. A lot had changed in a year.

"Hey there." Lisa flinched as her eyes shifted to the poolside manager, who was standing next to her. "May I sit down?"

Nodding, Lisa pulled up her legs to make space on the lounger. "Go ahead."

"I just wanted to apologise again for last night. I really appreciate that you haven't filed a complaint yet and I sincerely hope you won't. Some of the team members are very young and they don't think before they speak."

"Thank you." Lisa's eyes met the woman's and she decided she looked sincere. She wasn't wearing her red shorts, white cap and white polo shirt today, but denim shorts and a grey T-shirt. Her shortish dark hair was combed back and the way she kept running her hand through it told Lisa she was nervous. "And I'm sorry if I was rude. I'd rather just forget about it; it wasn't even on the hotel premises, so I wouldn't dream about filing a complaint."

"I appreciate that. I've told Manuel and the others not to come near you again, although I know he'd like to apologise in person too." The woman gave her a sweet smile and Lisa felt a little more at ease with her now. It was so strange to talk to people again, after hardly speaking to anyone apart from Ebony and her family face-to-face.

"No need." Lisa smiled back at her. "What was your name again?"

"Stella. And you're Lisa, right?" Stella held out her hand to shake hers. "I hope we can start with a clean slate." She paused and regarded Lisa curiously. "How long will you be staying?"

"I booked the room for two months, but I might stay for three if I'm still in limbo."

"In limbo?"

"Well, I need a place to live, and in order to find a place to live, I need a job so I can pay the rent. It's a long story, I won't bore you with it."

"You're not boring me." Stella paused and held her eyes. "And I'm not working today, so I have all the time in the world."

"I doubt you'd rather spend your precious day off listening to me whining than hanging out with friends or chilling out on the beach." Lisa managed a chuckle.

"Are you kidding me? I'd love to listen to your whining," Stella joked. "Listen, I'm going for a coffee. Want to come?"

When Lisa hesitated, she put on her most charming smile. "Come on. This is not a pity invitation. I don't know why, but I have a feeling we'll get on if we're not confined to our manager-guest roles." She glanced ahead and waved at one of her colleagues, who was staring at them.

"Are you even allowed to privately mingle with guests?" Lisa asked, sensing Stella felt like she was being watched.

"No... But if you don't tell, I won't. My car is parked around the corner next to the supermarket. I can wait for you there."

"Okay, a coffee wouldn't hurt, I suppose." Lisa internally scolded herself for sounding so negative yet again. "I mean, a coffee would be nice."

"It will be better than the stuff they serve here, that's for sure."

"It can't possibly be worse than Paradise coffee," Lisa shot back at her, and she felt her mood lift. She was surprised at herself for accepting the invitation, but something about Stella cheered her up, and that was exactly what she needed. "Let me get dressed. I'll meet you there in ten minutes."

9

Stella had no idea why she wanted to spend time with Lisa so badly; she hadn't even meant to stop off at Paradise. It had been a subconscious action, but when she'd suddenly found herself parked close to the hotel, she'd decided to look for her anyway, because the quiet and reserved woman intrigued her. She was beautiful, stunning even, and Stella suspected her libido might have gotten the better of her again. Lisa was wearing a simple white summer dress and white Nikes, and her long bare legs looked enticing. *Don't even go there. You're punching way above your weight, not to mention she's a guest and probably straight.*

"Have you seen much of the area?" she asked, driving out of town.

Lisa let out a sarcastic chuckle. "Trust me; I've seen enough." She shook her head and held up a hand. "I'm sorry, I'm being negative again and I really need to stop complaining about everything."

"That's okay. Paradise Hotel and the tourist strip are far

from charming at first sight, but you'll come to appreciate it after a while." Stella laughed when Lisa remained silent. "Hey, I moved here from Seville and believe me, coming from one of the most beautiful cities in Spain it was a little shocking to me too. But I like it here now."

"Hmm..." Lisa seemed deep in thought as she rolled down the window. "How come your English is so good?"

"Eighteen years of working in tourism," Stella said. "And most of those tourists were British. I'm sure you've noticed you're not the only Brit here." She shot Lisa a sideways glance, then forced herself to fix her eyes back on the road. Lisa's long, blonde hair was blowing around her face wildly, and she kept tucking it behind her ear. "I started in a hotel in Seville when I was seventeen and moved here when I was twenty-five to work in a hotel not far from here."

"Do you miss Seville?" Lisa asked.

"No, not anymore. But I used to. I go and see my family every six weeks or so, so it's okay. It was harder when I couldn't travel, though." Stella paused. "Are your family based in England?"

"Yes, they live just outside London. My parents and my older brother."

"Are you in a relationship?" Stella knew she might be pushing it with the questions, but she just couldn't help herself.

"No."

"Sorry. Did I overstep?"

"No, it's not that. I just don't like to talk about my private life right now as there's not anything positive to say about it." Lisa paused. "You?"

"In a relationship?" Stella shook her head. "No. Some flings here and there but nothing serious." She didn't mention that she was gay as she didn't want Lisa to think that she was hitting on her. "I just haven't met anyone special."

"Hmm."

Stella looked at her again. Lisa seemed to do the 'hmm' thing a lot and she had no idea what it meant. It sounded like disapproval, but she didn't think it was.

"I'm sorry." Lisa turned to her. "I haven't really spoken to many people lately and I'm a little out of practice. I mean, not like this, in a social capacity. I've talked to delivery people and occasionally to my parents and my brother, but I've been very withdrawn, I guess."

"Lockdown?" Stella asked.

"Yes. And depression. I just didn't feel like speaking to anyone."

"Not even your friends?"

"I've only been in contact with one friend..." Lisa stretched her arm out of the window and let her hand drift on the wind. "She was worried about me and thought some sunshine might do me good."

"Maybe she was right."

"Maybe." Lisa paused. "Where are we going?"

"A little place ten minutes from here. It's where I like to have coffee and read the papers on my days off." Stella pointed to a huge pile of newspapers under Lisa's feet.

"Oh my God, I'm so sorry. I thought it was old rubbish." Lisa picked them up, dusted off the sole marks from her trainers and placed them on her lap.

Stella laughed. "No need to be precious about them; they're usually in a worse state when my cats have gotten hold of them."

"So many," Lisa mumbled, going through them.

"Twelve from all over the world to be precise." Stella winked. "I like to stay informed, but I hate being on my phone the whole time."

Lisa looked at her with interest. "Twelve newspapers, huh? You must be very informed indeed." She smiled. "And how many cats?"

"Five at the moment." Stella took a left turn and drove down towards the coast. "They come and go. I take on some of the stray ones and they tend to stick around."

"Five?" Lisa laughed out loud for the first time, and Stella felt weirdly proud for being the cause of it. It was an honest and lovely laugh and going on Lisa's reaction as she slammed a hand in front of her mouth, she suspected she hadn't laughed in a while. "I somehow have trouble picturing you as a cat lady."

"Yeah, well, even though I hate to admit it, I probably am. Do you have pets?"

"No. I've always wanted a dog, but..." Lisa fell silent and stopped herself. "No, I don't have any pets. I love animals, though."

"Me too." Stella steered her white Beetle into the curb and parked in her usual spot. "Sorry, no more personal questions, I promise. Anyway, here we are."

"This looks lovely." Lisa glanced over the pebbled beach and the small café built on a concrete platform right by the water's edge. The building was painted in a soft pink and covered in wisteria. Surrounded by palms and tropical plants, it looked like the perfect little hideaway. "Your local?"

"Something like that. It's nice to get out of town sometimes."

"It's beautiful. Do they have iced lattes? I haven't had one of those in weeks."

Stella smiled as she got out of the car and held open the door for Lisa. "Yes, they have the best iced lattes, and it's on me."

10

*T*he coastline was gorgeous and rustic here, with wild rock formations that rose from the sea and the waves splashing up against them, leaving a trail of cool condensation in the air. Lisa took in a deep breath, cherishing the tranquillity as she took in the premises. The cute coffee house blended in beautifully with the outdoor terrace that was laid with artisanal, patterned grey, soft pink and cream coloured Cristobal tiles. Natural pigments and materials were used throughout, from the fabric on the canopies to the cushions on the robust wooden benches, and light grey, linen curtains were blowing out of the open doors as Stella walked out with two coffees.

"Here you go." Stella put a huge, iced latte in front of her and handed her a straw.

"Thank you so much. Next one is on me." Lisa shot her a smile and took a sip, then searched for a pen in her handbag before she opened *The Times*. "Mind if I do the crossword?" She watched Stella run a hand through her hair again and wondered if it really was a nervous thing, or just a habit.

The wind had blown it into a messy do and she looked cute. A fleeting thought about Stella possibly being gay crossed her mind, but she shook it off as it seemed pointless to speculate. It wasn't like she was interested; she had way bigger things on her mind right now than women, and the last thing she needed was some fling that would turn highly awkward as they'd be seeing each other at the hotel every day.

"Go ahead. That one is way too difficult for me." Stella pulled the *China Morning Post* from the pile and flicked through it, then focused on an article that caught her attention.

Lisa turned to her crossword, surprised that Stella seemed to know exactly what she needed. This way, they wouldn't have to talk, and at the same time, it was nice to have the company. She hadn't done a crossword in years. Not because she didn't enjoy it, but because she hadn't taken the time to relax and allow herself to do something entertaining and pointless just for the sake of it. In the past years, there had always been work, commuting, social obligations, household chores, and all those little things that got in the way of alone time. Sandrine considered anything that didn't lead to a gain of some sort as a waste of time and without knowing, Lisa had taken over that mindset herself. Things were different now, she reminded herself. She'd had more than enough time to relax since she'd arrived, but having been so set on finding a job, she hadn't given herself any slack.

Hours passed while Stella read, occasionally making a remark about something in the news that led to a short discussion. Lisa asked her for word suggestions in return and it soon became clear that Stella had been underselling herself when she'd told her it was too difficult for her. It was a strange way of spending the morning with a potential new friend—barely talking—but Lisa felt at ease in Stella's company, and the serene setting calmed her.

There wasn't a cloud in the sky, and as it neared midday, it was starting to get very warm. She searched for a hairband in her handbag and pulled her hair up into a ponytail. "I'm so hot," she said, fanning her face.

"Yes, you are." Stella laughed as she put her newspaper down and used one of the three ashtrays the waiter had brought over to weigh it down. "Sorry, that was a dumb joke. But you are," she added, shaking her head and rolling her eyes as if cursing herself. "Want to go for a swim?"

"A swim?" Lisa blushed and nervously chuckled at the 'hot' comment that had come out of nowhere. Avoiding Stella's eyes, she glanced at the sea instead, not wanting her to see how much that had startled her. The idea of a swim with Stella suddenly seemed incredibly intimate, even though she knew she was imagining things. "But we don't have towels and it looks really rocky."

"We don't need towels; we can dry in the sun, and yes, it's rocky but I know where to go in. I've done it before." Stella pointed to the bikini strings that were tied together at the back of Lisa's neck. "I see you're already wearing your swimming costume and I have suntan lotion in the car, so you won't have to worry about that either."

"I have some in my handbag too," Lisa said, her heart beating even faster now. What was wrong with her? Why was she overanalysing a joke? And why was she suddenly thinking of Stella applying suntan lotion onto her back?

"Well?" Stella stripped off right in front of her, leaving her clothes on her chair, and Lisa tried really hard not to stare. She hadn't seen Stella in her swimwear; she always wore her Paradise uniform at work, and she hadn't been prepared for the indulgence of a hot woman in a bikini. Because if she was honest with herself, Stella was sexy as hell.

"Okay." She stood up, took off her trainers and stripped off her dress, conscious of Stella's eyes on her. *Nothing she hasn't seen before,* she reminded herself. "What about my handbag?"

Stella yelled something in Spanish at the barista, and he yelled back at her and gave her a thumbs up. "Sebastián will look after it." She started walking down the cement steps that led to the thin strip of shelled beach and gestured for Lisa to follow her. Her behind looked deliciously perky in the boy shorts. Her shoulders were definitely swimmer's shoulders; broad and muscular, and her arms were toned and strong. Lisa tiptoed after her, careful not to cut her feet on the shells as she stepped onto the beach, now admiring Stella's abs as she turned slightly to look over her shoulder. "This spot right here isn't too bad."

Lisa sighed at the cool water rising up her legs as she waded in. She hadn't been for a swim at the beaches by the hotel as it had always been so busy when she walked past. In this little bay though, they were the only people in the vicinity, apart from a couple of people at the café.

"This is heaven," she said, letting out a deep breath as she turned on her back and floated.

"I knew you'd like it." Stella grinned and swam closer to her. "It's not so bad here now, is it?"

"No, it's not so bad at all." Lisa straightened herself, her toes barely touching the bottom as she stopped paddling to wipe water from her eyes. "Thank you. I appreciate you taking me here, and for not pushing me to talk. I've had a really lovely morning."

"I'm just glad to see you smile," Stella said and swam away, giving Lisa some space.

"Me too," Lisa mumbled to herself. She turned on her back, inhaled deeply and let the sunshine wash over her.

11

*E*ven with the balcony doors wide open, the room was unbearably hot. Lisa had reported the broken air-conditioning unit to the service team six hours ago but so far, no one had come to fix it. That wasn't surprising. Problems seemed to be noted down on a long list rather than solved at Paradise. She silently cursed her choice of hotel once more, then reminded herself that this really was the only option she could afford. She was usually able to catch some warm water in the shower before eight am, but between nine and midday, there was no chance of a warm shower, and at night even less so. Not that she needed a warm shower. What she needed was to cool down.

Opening her iPad, she was grateful that at least the Wi-Fi worked as she sat down in her nest on the balcony. It overlooked the pool, which was closed now, and in the distance, she could see the sea in between the buildings and the trees along the promenade. From here, even the pool-side looked kind of nice at night, with the lights illuminating the water and the dark silhouettes of the palm trees rising tall against the sky.

"Stella," Lisa mumbled to herself. *What had she said her surname was again?* They hadn't talked much yesterday morning, but she'd made a comment about one of the crossword answers being her surname. *Castillo?* She typed it into the search engine, along with the name of the hotel and immediately, Stella's picture appeared. Her social profiles were set to private, but the hotel's website had a page dedicated to management, and there she was. Stella Castillo, poolside manager, thirty-five years of age. She'd worked here for seven years and according to the small piece written about her, she loved flamenco, good food and cats in no particular order. The latter made Lisa chuckle when she once again tried to picture Stella as a cat lady. She couldn't imagine her dancing flamenco either, as she'd only ever seen her in shorts and she was pretty sure a frilly dress wouldn't suit her. No, Stella seemed like a woman who played football or beach volleyball or...

"Hmm..." Lisa narrowed her eyes as she studied the picture again. Fuelled by curiosity, she opened YouTube and typed 'Stella Castillo flamenco'. Scrolling down, she eagerly searched for footage. There were thousands of videos of flamenco dancers, but none of them matched her name. Lisa shook her head with a sigh. Why was she even doing this? Sure, it was a welcome distraction from her twelve hours of job hunting a day but still, it was very unlike her to take such an interest in a woman. It had been years since she'd even been remotely interested in anyone. Well, apart from Sandrine, of course, but that had died out when her last hope of ever being reunited had vanished with a phone call. *I'm sorry, but I don't think this is going to work out after all.* The famous last words. Of course, Sandrine had met someone else, and Lisa had beaten herself up about being so oblivious ever since. All the signs had been there. The lack of contact and affectionate messages, Sandrine's obvious disinterest in what was going on in her life, and then there had been silence, mostly, with Sandrine only replying to Lisa's messages when something urgent had to be addressed.

And so, Lisa had lived in a strange limbo, half in and half out of the relationship, unable to move forward and unwilling to let go. She'd been alone in the flat and alone in the relationship, the only one who had still been making an effort. It was for the best that Sandrine had ended it; she knew that now. But then, it had ripped her apart and sent her into a numb state of deep loneliness with her confidence shattered and her mind constantly spinning as she tried to figure out what she could have done differently. She'd tried everything. She'd sent presents and nice messages; she'd been interested and engaged. She'd even thought about moving to New York, and she'd mentioned that to Sandrine. Because what was the point of being in a relationship with someone you loved if you couldn't be together? The latter had sealed Sandrine's decision, she suspected. Sandrine just wanted someone to keep her company when she felt like it, someone to bring to parties and business dinners, and that someone had to be a woman she could impress her friends and colleagues with. The woman in question had been Sandrine's colleague, and Lisa wasn't one bit surprised about that. As work was such a big part of her life, dating co-workers had always been her thing, and when Lisa couldn't play that role anymore, she'd found someone else. The betrayal had not only hurt Lisa deeply, but her sense of security, that was already dented from losing her job, had taken another hard blow. All along she'd been replaceable; as good as any other successful, attractive woman. Thankfully, she'd realised that and stopped dwelling, because she had more urgent things to focus on, which evolved around getting her life back on track.

She'd made a to-do list. It wasn't long and it hadn't seemed ambitious when she'd put it together, the list set as a screensaver on her phone. Written with the intention of giving her a boost, the effect had been the opposite; a looming reminder of what she hadn't achieved.

1. Find a job. That had proved bloody impossible so far.

2. Move into a nice flat in South West London. She could forget about that for now and was mentally preparing herself to move into her old bedroom in her parents' house.

3. Meet new people. Most of her friends were her and Sandrine's joint friends, carefully selected by Sandrine based on their wealth, interesting qualities or success. And frankly, Lisa wasn't interested in seeing any of them anymore. They hadn't called her to ask how she was after the break-up, or made any effort at all to let her know she was their friend too. Her only close friend was Ebony, and in a city like London where life was buzzing and exciting, where there was something to do every night of the week, it felt lonely when Ebony was away for work or busy with whoever she was seeing.

4. Be healthy and happy. The last point on her list seemed ridiculous in a place like Paradise Hotel, where the food was anything but healthy and the noisy guests challenged her mood every single day. No, ticking off the list wasn't going well. But despite everything, she did feel better than when she'd first arrived. And it would be naive to deny that Stella had something to do with that.

12

"*All* stocked up?" Stella rubbed the sleep out of her eyes as she glanced over the tiki bar.

"Yes, I'm good to go for the day." Dave tapped one of the fridges. "But as I told you, this one keeps giving up from time to time. There's only so many times I can fix it; it really needs replacing."

"I know. I've already asked for extra budget next month. Fingers crossed Mr Avery approves it." Stella perched on one of the high stools and sipped her coffee, ignoring the rattling noise coming from the fridge. Ultimately the budget was out of her hands and since she only had twenty minutes until guests would flood the poolside, she was going to enjoy every second of tranquillity while she could. Saturday mornings were busy, as most package holiday flights returned to the UK in the afternoon, and so everyone was desperate to swim, eat and drink as much as they could before they left.

"Mr Avery never approves anything anymore. This place is falling apart." Dave huffed. "I know times have been tough, but we can't run on a broken engine."

"True." Stella didn't know what to say to him. She'd spoken to their finance director five times but until the tour operating companies paid out at the end of the month, there was simply nothing in the pot. They'd never had this problem before as they'd always had a buffer from the constant stream of people. Now that they'd started from scratch after lockdown, it would take a while to build that buffer back up. "Let's hope it lasts for another twenty-nine days." She looked around, noting all the sunloungers were lined up in neat rows and that the pools were looking nice and clean. Manuel was dragging a bag of floats to the main pool, for his eight am fit-tastic class.

"Morning, boss!" he yelled.

Stella smiled and gave him a wave. Sure, Manuel's tact was a little off sometimes, but with an amazing work ethic and the enthusiasm of a puppy, she was grateful to have him on her team. Besides that, the guests genuinely liked Manuel as the men wanted to be him and the women swooned over him. Well, not all the women. Lisa most certainly hadn't. With her long, wavy blonde hair, slightly pouty lips, blue eyes, long, dark lashes and a seriously great body, Lisa was the epitome of femininity, yet she'd shown zero interest in one of the most handsome men in the vicinity. Not that she should; everyone had their type, and Lisa didn't seem like she was in the headspace to flirt in the first place. But then there was the way Lisa had looked at her while she'd stripped off her clothes at the coffee house. It wasn't the way straight women looked at her, so she wondered if maybe Lisa played on her team.

Finishing her coffee, she told herself to stop over-thinking things as she wasn't even supposed to take a personal interest in guests in the first place. Their peace was disturbed by two women who came walking towards them with towels in their hands. "Sorry, ladies, the pool doesn't open until eight," Stella said.

"No worries, we'll wait." One of the women held up a hand to greet her, then glanced around the premises with a beaming smile. "It's so gorgeous out here, we just couldn't wait to have a look around."

"Oh, have you just arrived?"

"Yes, we came straight from the airport and it's too early to check in, so we thought we'd just hang around here."

"In that case, welcome to Paradise. I can't open the pool gate yet, but you can come and sit here with us." Stella tapped the seats next to her and shot Dave an apologetic look. "Sorry," she whispered. "They look so happy; I didn't have the heart to send them away. I'll make them a coffee. You just sit and chill."

Dave shook his head and laughed. "It's fine, I don't mind. Another one for you too?"

"Yes please." Stella spun around on her stool and turned to the women. She wasn't normally so chirpy early in the morning, but for some reason she was in a really good mood. "Coffee, ladies? Lovely Dave here has offered to make you one."

"Thank you, Dave, we'd love a coffee," the voluptuous one with peroxide blonde hair said. Her sparkly purple sundress and matching shades had clearly come straight out of the packaging, and her hair contained so much hairspray that it didn't even move in the wind.

Her friend was dark haired, skinny and covered in floral tattoos, and she wore a pink velour onesie, the neckline also studded with rhinestones. "Only if it's no trouble," she added. "I'm Magsie, and this is my friend Carla."

"No trouble at all, and lovely to meet you, Magsie and Carla. I'm Dave," Dave said as he turned on the old coffee machine that made an awful noise as it spat out the dark brew. "So, what brings you to Paradise?"

"It's actually our first holiday together," Magsie said, slicking back her dark, shoulder length hair. "And it's Carla's first holiday ever."

"Ever?" Stella's heart welled at how happy Carla looked as she passed on a coffee to her before sliding one towards Magsie. She'd heard it before, but it still touched her. Paradise offered a cheap package holiday and this was many of their guests' first holidays. "Then I'm sure you'll have a wonderful time," she continued, stirring sugar through the bitter hotel coffee. "There's an aqua gym class this morning, if you want to join. The bar opens at noon for alcoholic beverages and Saturday is karaoke night, so you're in luck if you like to sing."

"That sounds amazing. Oh Mags, we're going to have the time of our lives this week." Carla put an arm around Magsie and gave her a kiss on her cheek.

"Have you been friends for long?" Dave asked, putting a plate of cookies in front of them.

"Four years to the day," Magsie said. "And I don't know what I'd do without her."

"That's sweet. How did you meet?"

Magsie hesitated, glancing at Carla for a moment, then continued when her friend nodded. "We met at a women's shelter in Manchester four years ago. We'd both escaped an abusive relationship and left our lives behind to start over with nothing but the clothes on our backs."

"I'm so sorry to hear that," Stella said.

"Yes, we've had some rough years, but we've come out all right, haven't we, Carla? And look at us now, sitting here in sunny Spain."

Carla returned Magsie's smile and squeezed her arm.

"Apart from my son Georgie, Magsie's the best thing that ever happened to me. We've helped each other through difficult times and now we just want to have fun."

"Oh, you will." Dave smiled. "How old is your son?"

"He's six." Carla opened a picture on her phone and showed it to them. "He's a good little boy and he probably saved my life. If it wasn't for him, I don't think I'd have the courage to leave my husband." She glanced at the picture lovingly. "He's with my mum while we're away. He loves his grandma."

"He's very cute." Stella turned to Magsie. "And you? Do you have any kids?"

"No, but I consider Georgie to be my stepson. We all grew close when we shared a room at the shelter, and we've been sharing a room ever since."

"You live together?" Stella asked. She wasn't worried about being too nosey. After working in hospitality for so many years, she had a sixth sense for who wanted to talk and who didn't.

"Yes. The shelter helped us get jobs at a warehouse and we moved into a flat together so we could share the rent. We're like a little family," Magsie said.

"The perfect family," Carla added. "Georgie is growing up surrounded by love and Magsie's like a second mum to him. We take turns looking after him because I work night-shifts and Magsie works dayshifts, and we've been saving up to come here since we got back on our feet."

"I'm honoured you decided to come to Paradise for your first holiday." Stella looked at them over the rim of her cup. It wasn't very often she had such personal conversations with guests, and she certainly never choked up while talking to them. Mostly, it was about the weather, about where to score the most handsome men in Benidorm, where to find the biggest and strongest cocktails or the best English pubs. The alarm on her phone pulled her out of her thoughts, and she put her cup down and stood. "I'm so sorry but I have to get to work. It was really nice to talk to you, ladies, and I sincerely hope you have a wonderful time here." She pointed to the sunloungers and winked. "I'll go open the gates now, so you'll have first pick. The row over there has sun all day."

13

"I'm sorry, darling. You weren't included in the candidate selection for the VC interviews." The headhunter—the fifth who had called Lisa with bad news this week—tried her best to sound regretful, but Lisa knew she didn't care as long as she got her commission in the end. "Again, it's no reflection on your CV or achievements. They just felt these people fitted their team better."

"I understand. What was their feedback?" Lisa kicked a pebble across the road before she crossed it. She'd been for an early evening walk and was just arriving back at the hotel.

"They didn't provide feedback, only the candidate selection."

"No feedback whatsoever? But I need to know what I have to work on in my interviews going forward?"

The headhunter cleared her throat. "I can ask, but they had over thirty very qualified people to choose from. It may take weeks before they come back to me with the interview notes, if they have them at all. Initial telephone interviews aren't recorded as thoroughly nowadays."

"Of course." Lisa sighed and sat down on the wall by the hotel's front entrance. The long evening walk had done her good initially, but this phone call threatened to send her into another sleepless and anxious night. "So, what do I do now? Are there even any more vacancies in marketing? Because I think I've applied for just about every job out there by now."

"I know. It's tough at the moment, but don't give up. You're very employable and you have a fantastic, successful work history. How about I call you as soon as something else comes up? In the meantime, don't forget to think outside the box. Perhaps look at different career paths, or taking a job abroad?"

"Sure." Lisa failed to stop tears from trickling down her cheek. Getting the job that she wanted had always been a given rather than a blessing, and she'd never thought she'd be in this position. So desperate for something, anything. "Thank you for your time. I appreciate it."

Dropping her phone into her handbag, Lisa covered her face in her hands and burst into silent tears. A hand on her shoulder startled her, and she quickly wiped her cheeks and straightened her back. "I'm sorry, I'm..."

"Hey, don't apologise. Would you like some company?" Through her blurred vision, Lisa saw it was Stella, who had sat down beside her. "I'm not going to ask you if you're okay, because clearly you're not..." Stella paused. "And I'm aware that I don't know you that well, but I'm here if you want to talk. If you don't, we could go for a walk or something?" She held up her car keys. "Or a drive? I've just finished my shift."

"I've just had my forty-seventh job rejection," Lisa said with a sniff. "I shouldn't be so emotional about it, but it's been a lot lately." She blinked a couple of times and removed the mascara stains from underneath her eyes.

"Why do you want to help me? I don't understand why you'd want to spend time with a depressed stranger."

"You're not that much of a stranger anymore," Stella said. "We went for a coffee, so that makes us acquaintances, I'd say. And as your acquaintance, I'd love to hang out."

Lisa managed a chuckle. "You're funny."

"See? I'm cheering you up already." Stella put an arm around her, and Lisa felt herself tense up. Maybe because she hadn't been hugged in so long, or maybe because Stella's nearness did something to her. She liked being around her more than she was willing to admit, and already, the phone call that had upset her so much didn't seem like such a big deal anymore. Allowing herself to relax a little, she leaned into Stella as she pulled her closer and squeezed her shoulder. It felt really good to have someone on her side.

"Drive?" Stella asked.

"Okay." Lisa stood up and wiped her eyes again, then ruffled a hand through her hair. "Where to?"

"Where do you want to go?"

Lisa bit her lip as she thought about that. "I don't know." She regarded Stella as they walked to her car. "Do you live around here?" Her hand shot up. "Sorry. Just to be clear; I'm not inviting myself over to your house. I was just curious, that's all..."

Stella laughed as she opened the passenger door for her. "That's okay, you can invite yourself over." She got in too and rolled down all the windows. "I live in Altea. It's a really pretty village not far from here. I think you'd like it. Want to see it?"

"*Are* there pretty villages around here?" Lisa asked as Stella turned onto the boulevard and passed Paradise's sister hotel, Premier Sunset, the vile dark purple building with its yellow entrance quite possibly the most unattractive piece of architecture she'd ever seen.

"Was that a joke? I didn't think you did jokes," Stella teased.

"I guess it was." Lisa smiled. "Okay, why don't you show me your hometown? But only if you were already heading there," she added.

"I was heading home, actually." Stella winked. "And I'd love to show you around, so let's go. We still have a couple of hours of daylight."

14

*A*ltea was busy, but a different kind of busy to Benidorm. Instead of loud pop music, bad karaoke and flashing neon lights, the town was filled with small, candlelit cafés and restaurants. Street musicians played Spanish guitar along the pretty promenade, and the charming town centre was lit by lanterns hanging from the front doors of the houses that lined the narrow, cobbled alleyways. There were flowerbeds on every corner and square, and the white houses all had flower-filled baskets under their windowsills and beautifully tiled steps that went up to their front doors. It had a happy, tranquil vibe to it, and Lisa could sense the excitement of the tourists who passed them.

"How do you cope with some of the guests?" she asked as they conquered a steep hill. "Two grown women were arguing over a sunlounger yesterday, even though there were plenty of others free. It was too ridiculous for words."

Stella laughed. "I've gotten used to it, and you'll get used to it too. But honestly, most guests are friendly and happy, and don't forget, these people don't go on holiday regularly.

It's their one trip of the year, sometimes only every two or three years. With so much anticipation leading up to it, they tend to let go more than the usual tourists I imagine you're used to seeing on your travels."

"Hmm..." Lisa felt a little ashamed now and was worried Stella would think her a snob. "Yes, I probably shouldn't be so judgmental."

"I don't blame you. Some of the guests are obnoxious and very annoying. I was judgmental myself when I first started working there," Stella said. "But the other day for example, I spoke to two women who were on a holiday for the first time in their lives. They told me they'd met in a women's shelter after escaping their abusive husbands; I can't begin to imagine what they've been through. And it touched me, you know? It was like a new start for them, the point where they knew things were really looking up again because they could afford to relax for a week."

"That is touching." Lisa fell silent for a moment. "You're sweet." She kept her eyes fixed ahead, conscious of that rosy blush that Stella seemed to bring out on her cheeks.

"Thank you." Stella cast her a sideways glance. "You're sweet too."

"You don't know that. I haven't been at my best lately."

"I think I have a pretty good idea; you're not that hard to figure out. And you don't have to feel bad about hating being in Benidorm. It's not for everyone and I imagine it wouldn't be your usual choice for a holiday destination."

"Certainly not; I'm not the all-inclusive resort type." Lisa looked around the quaint alley and smiled. "But Altea is somewhere I'd like to visit again."

"I'm not into all-inclusive resorts either," Stella said. "You don't get a real feel for a new place if you're locked between four walls. I like to eat local, get lost and go with the flow."

"You sound like the perfect travel companion."

"I am." Stella shot her a cheeky grin. "Maybe we should take a trip together."

Lisa didn't know what to say to that because even though it was a joke, she truly loved Stella's company. Stella lifted her spirits and brought back a spark in her she thought she'd lost.

Reaching the small park at the top of the hill, she found herself genuinely smiling for the first time in months as she took in the romantic atmosphere from above. The sun was low now, casting a yellow glow over the rooftops. "I like it here," she said, looking out over the town and the sea behind it. "It must be a lovely place to live."

"It is. I'm happy here." Stella's eyes met hers, and she held her gaze for long moments before she looked down at her feet. Lisa sensed she was nervous as a loaded silence followed. "Are you hungry? You're missing the wonderful and indulgent Paradise buffet."

"Does that mean you want me to leave?"

"No, not at all!" Stella shook her head and laughed. "You really have trouble taking a joke, don't you?"

"I'm just not used to human interaction anymore." Lisa grinned. "But I can definitely live without the Paradise buffet. Are *you* hungry? I'd like to take you out for dinner if that's okay. To thank you for being so nice to me." She felt herself blush again and internally cursed herself. "Unless you're busy?"

"No, I'm not busy but I should probably feed my cats," Stella said. "So why don't I fix us some food at home? The view from my roof terrace is just as nice as this."

"Are you sure? I can take a taxi back now and grab some food on the way..."

"Please." Stella briefly took her hand and squeezed it. It wasn't a flirty gesture, but her touch still brought a flutter to Lisa's core. "I wouldn't have offered if I didn't mean it."

"Okay. In that case, I'd love to. But let me at least get you a bottle of wine on the way."

"If you insist." Stella hooked her arm through Lisa's and they headed back down through an alleyway on the other side of the park. This one was lined with galleries and craft boutiques. Some of their art was displayed outside, and most had little seating areas at the front, where the owners or artists were drinking wine and chatting with potential customers.

Lisa stopped to look at the sculptures and paintings while Stella made small talk with the locals. "Why are there so many galleries here?" she asked.

"I suppose because it's a pretty town. The coastline and the light are beautiful, so a lot of artists have come here over the years and never left. Altea is actually known for its vibrant art scene." Stella pointed to a corner shop as they reached the end of the street. "You can buy wine there if you want. I live opposite."

"You live here?" Lisa looked over the pretty little square where a café, a small shop and a restaurant were housed. Along the back were two stone picnic tables where old men played chess under the light of lanterns that hung from big trees. "How dainty."

"Dainty?" Stella laughed. "How English."

Lisa shot her a smile over her shoulder and went inside to the wine. As she waited for the wine to be bagged, she glanced at Stella, who was standing outside. If she wasn't mistaken, there might be some mutual physical attraction between them. Stella wasn't her usual type; Lisa had always dated very feminine women, but for some reason she felt way more excited in Stella's company than she had with anyone else. The woman was most certainly sexy. A cute face with big, sparkling dark eyes, sun-kissed skin, a dazzling smile, shiny dark hair that fell over part of her dark eyebrows and an athletic body. She was the polar opposite to Sandrine, who always pranced around in high heels, knee-length dresses, styled hair and full make-up. Never a hair out of place, but no room for spontaneity either.

"Señora?"

Lisa was pulled out of her thoughts as the shop owner handed her the bag. "Oh... gracias." She took it and gave him a wave, still baffled by the way her mind kept going there. *Stop imagining things. She's just being nice.*

15

"Welcome to my pad." As Stella walked up the stairs ahead of Lisa, three cats immediately came running up to her. "Those little rascals are Chicken and Tuna, and this is Smelly." She picked Smelly up and carried him up the last steps.

"You really are a cat lady," Lisa joked. "And who is this?" She knelt down on the landing to pet a tabby and laughed when a fifth cat followed. "Oh, hello. One more."

"The tabby is Pablo, and the white one is called Yeti."

"They're so cute."

"They're naughty mostly, especially Pablo but yes, they're very cute too."

"So, you're the naughty one, huh?" Lisa said to Pablo as she stroked him. He stuck his head in her large handbag, then climbed inside and settled. "I can see that now."

Stella laughed. "Do you mind? He doesn't like to be picked up, but he's quite happy being carried around in any item he settles himself into."

"You're a funny one." Lisa scratched Pablo behind his ears and lifted her handbag from the floor, highly amused when he decided to stay inside. She straightened herself and shifted the now heavy handbag onto her shoulder as she walked into the long and narrow living room. The faded terracotta tiled floor was broken up with off-white hand-woven rugs. A rustic coffee table stood before a wide, white sofa and the white curtains in the window behind it had a delicate orange pattern woven through them. The artworks on the walls, the plants scattered around and the photographs on the wooden beam above the fireplace made it feel cosy and intimate. It was very tidy, she noticed, and apart from a pile of paperwork on the sideboard that stood against the other wall, there was no clutter. "Your house is just as cute as your cats. It looks so authentically Spanish."

"It's an old townhouse and I didn't do much to it when I moved in, so yes, I suppose the carcass is exactly as it was a hundred years ago. Downstairs is a spare bedroom, a bathroom, a utility room, and there's a small patio at the back. Up here is my bedroom, bathroom and living area, and my kitchen and roof terrace are upstairs."

"The famous roof terrace?"

"Yes. I tend to brag about it and I'm in my full right to do so because it's perfect." Stella walked ahead of her up the second flight of stairs and grabbed two glasses from a cupboard in the kitchen before she opened the double doors that led outside.

"Your view is incredible," Lisa said as she stepped out. "You're so lucky."

"No luck involved, just a lot of hard work," Stella retorted.

"I'm sorry, I didn't mean to insinuate that..."

"It's okay. Nowadays it's sad that I even feel that I have to justify having my own home, but you know... most of my friends haven't been so fortunate to keep their jobs."

"Yeah, I get that."

"Anyway..." Stella beckoned for her to sit down. "Let's talk happy things. Times are getting easier, businesses have reopened and the economy will restore eventually." She lingered on the spot as she looked Lisa over. "Do you like paella?"

"I do. But isn't that a lot of work?"

"Not at all. I have some in the freezer that I made last week. Pour yourself a glass of wine while I heat it up and make a quick salad, and I'll be out in a bit." She went back into the kitchen, took the paella out of the freezer and gathered some fresh parsley from a pot on her windowsill. Glancing outside, she noted Lisa looked a little more at ease now, with her long legs crossed in front of her. *Those are some legs.* Pablo had climbed onto her lap, and she was stroking him and talking to him in a soft voice as she sipped her wine. It was cute and endearing in a sexy kind of way. Women had to be animal lovers; that was a make or break for Stella. Not that it mattered; it wasn't like they were dating, but she liked to look at Lisa, that much was true. Despite Lisa's slightly low mood, she liked talking to her too. She had a soft demeanour about her, a vulnerability that Stella rarely saw in women.

Her phone lit up and she sighed when she saw it was Vera. *'Want to meet up tonight?'*

'Can't, I have company,' she replied, hoping Vera wouldn't press on.

Seconds later, another message came in. *'Are you with a woman?'*

Fuck, she's getting jealous now. Stella never meant for it to be anything more than casual with Vera, but lately she'd messaged her regularly. *'Yes,'* she answered because it was the truth. Vera didn't need to know they were just having dinner.

'I knew it. Never mind. I'll go find someone else to keep me company.'

Stella didn't know how to reply to that, so she didn't. She wasn't going to feel guilty about not showing up whenever it suited Vera and although she liked her, she couldn't see it going any further than where they were now. The whole casual thing had been easy for years but in a small town where most gay women knew each other it was getting harder and harder to keep it simple. Last time Vera has spotted her kissing someone, she'd thrown a tantrum, scaring her date away. Admittedly, the one-night stands were starting to get a little boring. The same conversations beforehand; just enough small talk for her to feel okay about diving into bed with a stranger, the awkward midnight escape when she used her cats as an excuse, and the fear of bumping into the ones who had weird fetishes on a night out were situations she could do without.

"Are you sure you don't need help in there?" Lisa called.

"No, just chill out, I'm almost done!" she yelled back, defrosting some king prawns to go on top of the dish. It dawned on her then that she hadn't cooked for a woman in years. *What has gotten into me?* The urge to impress Lisa suddenly overcame her then, and she went in search of some lemons to make her paella look pretty.

16

*L*isa sat down after she'd helped Stella clear the table and stared at her through the double doors. She wasn't sure if it was the bottle of wine they'd polished off, the natural, flowing conversation she didn't realise she'd missed so much, or the fact that Stella was seriously attractive that made her want to be near her. She just seemed so at ease in herself, so happy and carefree. *Not to mention that cute smile and sexy, tanned legs.*

"Milk? Sugar?"

"Huh?" Lisa startled, her eyes flicking away from Stella's legs.

"In your coffee...?" Stella arched a brow and smiled.

"Oh, just a bit of milk, please." Lisa returned her smile as she took the mug from her. "You have a wonderful home. I had a great time."

"Excellent. That's what I aim for." Instead of sitting in the armchair opposite like she had all evening, Stella sat down on the sofa next to Lisa. Although she held a respectable distance, their legs touched for a brief moment, and the reaction it caused shocked Lisa. Butterflies, shivers, a heat flaring between her thighs… "I thought you could do with a bit of distraction from all that job hunting."

"Yes, it's been good to take my mind off that for an evening." Lisa glanced down at their legs and Stella moved away a little as if she too, had felt it. She was still glowing, her core fluttering when she met her eyes. "I've had this never-ending stream of rejection and I'm trying not to let it get me down, but you know…"

"I understand." Stella nodded. "I've had several temporary jobs over the past year, just to pay my bills. I really missed my job and every time it looked like there was light at the end of the tunnel, there was a new outbreak, a new period of lockdown." She paused and regarded Lisa. "What is it exactly that you do?"

"I'm a brand builder. It's marketing related, just more of an overall package that includes branding, customer experience and culture."

"That sounds interesting."

"It's fun, and I'm good at it. But with so many companies struggling and so many unemployed, the job market has become saturated." Lisa sighed. "Add to that the fact that there are some really talented young and much cheaper people out there… The competition is killing. I'm willing to take a pay cut and I've already broadened my search— even into PR—but without result so far."

"And you've given yourself two to three months to find something while you're here," Stella concluded.

"Yes. London is a terribly expensive city to live in and I couldn't afford the rent on my flat anymore after my partner moved out. Staying here is much cheaper and since it's all-inclusive, I thought I could stretch my savings for longer. If I don't find anything by the end of August, I'll just have to move in with my parents and work in a pub for a while until I do find something. It is what it is."

"Right. And moving in with your parents wasn't an option before?"

Lisa shrugged. "I could have done that. But my brother has also moved back in with them. He's recovering from a car accident, so I didn't want to be in their way and besides, moving in with my parents at thirty-four is not on the top of my list, as you can imagine." Lisa took a sip of her coffee and sat back, still aware of their closeness. She was also hyper-aware of her arms and legs, as if they'd suddenly doubled in length and she had no idea what to do with them anymore. It was weird how Stella made her feel clumsy, and as she recrossed her legs and clung onto her mug with both hands, she hoped it didn't show. "I could always move into a shared house, but I'd just feel like a student again, like I'm starting all over, if you know what I mean... Most rentals, even house shares offer six-month contracts, and at least if I'm with my parents, it will hopefully be very temporary."

"Okay. And how is your brother now?" Stella winced. "I'm sorry, I'm getting personal again and I promised you I wouldn't."

"It's fine, the wine has chilled me out a little, and I actually don't mind talking to you. My brother is doing better every day, thanks for asking." Lisa noted she really was fine talking to Stella. "I know the past year and a half has been shit for everyone, so I try not to complain too much but admittedly, it's been difficult."

"Tell me."

Lisa hesitated. "Well, Sandrine, my girlfriend at the time moved to New York before the pandemic hit. The plan was that I would visit her, and that she would visit me, but we couldn't really meet up as travel restrictions came into place, and she didn't seem to mind that so much."

"Do you think she was seeing someone else?" Stella asked. The change in her expression when Lisa had mentioned the word 'girlfriend' did not go unnoticed.

"I know she was; she admitted it eventually. Then I was made redundant because like so many businesses, the company I worked for suffered from the impact of the pandemic. And when I couldn't talk about my job, it became very clear that we had very little to talk about in general. Sandrine always had this ridiculous idea of us being a 'power couple'. She liked the fact that we were both young and successful; her whole life revolved around her career." Lisa subconsciously licked her lips as her gaze lowered to Stella's mouth. She had beautiful lips; full, a little pouty, and she suddenly found herself wondering what they would feel like on hers.

"Sandrine sounds shallow." Stella held up a hand. "Sorry, I don't know her, but you deserve better than that."

"Yes, that's what I tell myself." Lisa smiled. "So then, my brother had the accident but he's doing okay now and learning to walk again. Hopefully he can return to work by the end of the year." Lisa could hardly believe that she was telling Stella all of this. It was like a dam had broken and now that she'd started, she couldn't stop talking. "Then, during the second lockdown I was unable to find a temporary flatmate to pay my bills, so I saw big chunks of my salary vanish every month." She sighed deeply. "And then Sandrine called me to tell me it was over."

"Fuck, I'm so sorry."

"Yeah, me too," Lisa said, fighting back her tears. "Even though looking back, I can see that I'm way better off without her. But at the time, I saw my future falling apart, and I became very distanced from life in general."

"Depression?"

"Yes. I didn't feel like talking to anyone and became isolated and depressed. Once the world started going back to normal, I knew I needed a change, not only because I couldn't afford to live there anymore, but also because I'd gotten sucked into a negative downward spiral. That's when Ebony, my best friend, gave me a kick up the ass and suggested I come here. Well, not to Paradise Hotel specifically, but she'd found these cheap all-inclusive holidays online and she said if I was job hunting, it would be more affordable and way more pleasant to do it while being in the sun."

"Your friend was right, even though you might not see that right now."

"No, I know she was right. I already feel way better than I did in London. But I've become insecure and paranoid and..." Lisa covered her face in her hands and shook her head. "Oh, God, why am I telling you all this?"

"Because you really needed to talk," Stella said. "Thank you for trusting me."

"Thank you for listening." As she met Stella's eyes, Lisa felt her pulse race. Stella's gaze darkened and she looked at her as if she wanted to kiss her, yet she didn't make a move. The silence and tension between them felt like an unspoken promise, and although Lisa could really do with some distraction, she was scared to make a move herself. What if she'd read the situation all wrong? What if Stella wasn't into women, or into her? "I'd better go," she said, getting up. Rejection had become her middle name and she couldn't handle another one, even if she simply wanted some meaningless fun.

"You don't have to go, you can—"

"No, I've kept you long enough." Lisa managed a smile and hoped she didn't look as flustered as she felt. "Thank you again. I hope you'll let me take you out for dinner to return the favour one of these days."

"I'll hold you to that." Stella got up too and lingered on the spot, then grabbed her phone from the table. "Could I have your number?"

"Yes, of course." Lisa noticed her hand was trembling when she took the phone and entered her contact information. "Message me so I have yours."

"I will." A smile played around Stella's mouth when she took her phone back, her eyes never leaving Lisa's as she slipped it into her back pocket. "There's a taxi rank at the end of the street. Just follow the road downhill."

"Okay." Lisa found herself staring again. Stella's lips looked so moist and plump in the flickering light of the candles. Swallowing hard, she brushed passed her and rushed towards the kitchen doors before she could do anything stupid. "Thank you so much for dinner, I'll let myself out."

17

"*What's* with the suits?" Stella asked Kira, Mr Avery's assistant, as they got out of the lift together.

"The suits?" Kira frowned. "Oh, the suits. Fuck. They're early." She glanced at the group of formally clad men waiting at reception, then straightened her skirt and blouse and turned to Stella. "How do I look?"

"Great as always. Why? Who are they?"

"They're from a hotel group." Kira leaned in and lowered her voice. "Potential buyers for Premier Sunset."

"Our sister hotel next door?" Stella frowned. "But they've just reopened."

"True, but they've had a lot of complaints apparently and they can't keep up with the maintenance. It will take too much investment to bring it back to a reasonable standard, so Paradise Group is considering selling it to them. That way they can put the money into doing this place up. They're just preliminary talks for now, though." Kira gave her a quick nod to let her know their conversation was over, then put on her most charming smile as she approached the three men.

Stella watched her interact with them. The twenty-three-year-old graduate had proven to be more capable than the generally sceptical, more mature members of staff had initially expected. She was clever, funny and able to interact with people from all social classes, and she'd been a lifeline for the managers since they'd reopened, putting in 'good words' for them with Mr Avery when they urgently needed funding. The men laughed as she cracked a joke before leading them to the lift that would take them to the top floor penthouse, where the Paradise Group office was situated. Stella had been there many times over the years and on her most recent visit, during which she'd presented her plans and anticipated hurdles for the season, she'd noticed that even the penthouse was looking worse for wear. The previously immaculate white walls and ceiling were now stained from leaks, and she'd spotted a couple of cracks too. The ocean-facing roof terrace where they'd enjoyed the occasional staff meeting was not immaculate anymore, but overgrown with weeds, and the slate tiles were mouldy. If the board of directors didn't have the budget to keep their own playground looking slick and pretty, then she suspected the situation must be bad, as selling off one of their hotels had never been part of the plan. Paradise Group owned seven hotels when Stella started working at Paradise and they now had eleven in their portfolio, all in and around Benidorm. She didn't have much to do with Premier Sunset herself; she was in charge of Paradise poolside and was rarely involved with their neighbouring sister hotel. But she knew people who worked there and was aware that a sale could lead to redundancies.

"What's going on?" Manuel whispered as she joined him at the bar for a coffee before starting her late shift.

"The group is thinking of selling Premier Sunset, apparently."

Manuel's eyes widened. "Fuck."

"I only just found out." Stella lowered her voice. "I suppose it doesn't concern my job, so they didn't have to inform me. And nothing's been set in stone according to Kira. They're just talks, for now." Her attention was spiked when she saw Lisa walking to the poolside, where she dropped down on a sunlounger with her iPad. When she took off her kaftan and started applying suntan lotion on her arms, legs and torso, Stella was unable to keep her eyes off her.

"Everything settled with Miss Grumpy now?" Manuel asked, following her gaze. "I'd apologise but you told me it was better to leave it so I—"

"Hey, don't call her that." Stella was aware that she sounded sharper than she intended. "I'm sorry. Yes, everything's fine. And you don't have to tread on eggshells around her as long as you don't try to make her join in with the 'fun'," she said, making quote marks in the air.

"I wouldn't dare." Manuel quietly whistled through his teeth at the sight of Lisa in a tiny black bikini.

Lisa glanced around as if she could feel someone looking at her, and when she spotted Stella by the bar, she waved and shot her a beaming smile.

"What the fuck?" Manuel turned to Stella when she waved back. "What did you say to her?"

"Nothing, we just talked." Stella didn't mention that she'd been hanging out with Lisa. She wasn't allowed to mingle with guests apart from in a professional capacity and she wasn't sure if Manuel would be able to keep it to himself if she told him.

"You must be one hell of a talker," he joked.

Stella chuckled and shook her head. "No, she's just really nice, actually. People aren't always what they seem at first glance." Apparently, she was a bad liar. Manuel studied her, then slammed a hand on the bar.

"You have the hots for her." His triumphant grimace would have been funny any other time, but right now, it made Stella blush profusely.

"I do not."

"Yes, you do."

Stella finished her coffee and got off her stool. "Be careful what you say, Manuel. This could get me into trouble." She relaxed a little and rolled her eyes when he jutted out his bottom lip and pulled an innocent face. "And not a word about the sale of Premier Sunset either. I assume they're keeping it quiet for a reason and I don't want anyone to spread rumours."

18

It was amazing what a little human interaction could do to one's spirit. The poolside wasn't as daunting today as it had been in the past weeks and Lisa even found herself smiling at a couple of people as she threw her towel over a sunlounger. She didn't recognise any of the original guests and suspected they'd all left by now. It was a chance to start over in a way, and she felt much more at ease, now that no one was watching her. Well, apart from some of the men, but she'd gotten used to that and ignored their stares as she applied suntan lotion to her legs.

She felt more optimistic and even a little cheerful, and as she spotted Stella at the bar, her face pulled into a smile as she waved at her. The woman had not only put her at ease, but she'd been a great listener. Normally, Lisa would worry that she'd been a burden, but she didn't feel that way with Stella.

Her eyes shifted to her phone as it rang, and she quickly dried her hands to take Ebony's call. "Hey, babe. Sorry I didn't call you back; I forgot."

"That's okay. How are you, honey? Feeling better?"

"A lot better, thanks. I was being silly the other night; it was nothing. Maybe I was just tired."

"Don't worry about it. I'm just glad you sound chirpy again."

Lisa took a sip from her water and poured some over her chest to cool down. "How was the rest of your date?"

"Oh, God, don't get me started on him. I ended up sneaking off after he confessed he was looking for someone to join him and his wife in the bedroom."

"What?" Lisa laughed. "He should have told you that upfront. It doesn't seem fair to tell your date you're married until you're on the actual date."

"Totally agree. Anyway... How's Benidorm today?" Ebony snickered as she drew out the word in a dramatic tone. "Are you fried yet? Are you daytime drinking?"

"Don't put any ideas in my head," Lisa joked. "Because that midday rum and Coke suddenly sounds very appealing."

Ebony's loud laughter rang in her ear and Lisa laughed along with her. "Are you serious? Rum and Coke? That's not something you'd normally drink."

"It's low-risk," Lisa said. "The beer is watered-down, the wine is poison and so is anything else grape related. How are you apart from the shitty date?" She sank back on the lounger, enjoying the sun on her face.

"I'm okay. Starting my new job tomorrow, so I'm excited. I might come and visit you for a long weekend if they'll allow me a day off."

"Are you serious? I'd love that." Lisa's face lit up. Over the past months, she'd told people she'd missed them, but those words had just been words. She'd been withdrawn and almost comfortable in her own isolation but after last night she felt a little sparkle of her old self again, and with that came the need to see her best friend whom she'd neglected. Ebony had been laid off too, but unlike Lisa, she'd managed to find herself a new job.

"Dead serious. Is it pretty there?"

"No." Lisa chuckled. "It's kind of like a cross between a playground—except the loud creatures running around screaming are adults instead of toddlers—and a village clubhouse. Oh, and someone peed in the pool the other day. There's this chemical they put in that turns urine green. My room is shocking to say the least and sometimes I sleep on the balcony because it's too stuffy in there."

"God, that sounds awful. It didn't look that bad on the website."

"True. I think they used pictures from twenty years ago. The hotel is basic at best, the food is terrible but there are nice places around here. One of the staff members showed me around and I was pleasantly surprised at how beautiful the area is."

"So, you're making friends?"

"No. Just someone who works here."

Ebony chuckled. "I know you, Lisa. You never bother to mention people unless they intrigue you in some way."

"Is that so?"

"Yes. You're not exactly a social butterfly and you don't throw yourself into new friendships. So, tell me about this 'person who works there'," Ebony continued in a mocking tone. "Is this person a *she*?"

"Yes, it's a woman but it's not what you think. Nothing's going on. I was just upset the other day because I kept getting rejection emails and calls, so she took me out for a coffee and I went to her house for dinner. She's cheered me up and I needed that."

"Still nothing on the job front then?" Ebony asked.

"No. And I've run out of marketing vacancies to apply for. I'm trying PR now, but I have even less hope for that as I don't have much experience in the field."

"Sorry to hear that."

"It's okay. I'm glad you found something; I really mean that. You're so good at what you do, and you were always my favourite colleague."

"And you were mine. Who knows? Maybe we'll get to work together again one day. I'll certainly put in a good word for you if they're looking to expand the team."

"Thank you, I appreciate that." Lisa followed Stella with her eyes as she walked towards the lifeguard chair on the opposite side of the pool and climbed up. She hadn't seen her sitting there before; she was usually in the chair by the other pool if she was on lifeguard duty. By now, she had a good idea of the staff's shifts. A ginger haired man usually sat in the chair overlooking her spot. It was funny how she had her usual spot herself, but she'd gotten used to the lounger in the corner that was always free as it got the least sun.

"Well, I'll let you know if I'll be able to visit but getting a day off shouldn't be a problem. We seriously need to get together; it's been too long. And you have a double bed in your room, right?"

"The double bed is questionable but for two or three nights, I'm sure we'll manage and I'm already looking forward to it," Lisa said, noting that Stella was looking directly at her now. Stella quickly glanced away when Lisa's eyes met hers and she shifted her attention to the pool, as if she'd been caught staring.

"Perfect. And then you can introduce me to 'someone who works there,'" Ebony added in a teasing tone.

"Ha ha, very funny. I'll speak to you soon and good luck

tomorrow." Lisa hung up with a smile and continued to apply suntan lotion, this time aware that she was sitting in Stella's line of sight. She felt strangely excited, knowing she was being watched and when she finished, she pulled out her hairband and ruffled a hand through her locks, making sure she looked as good as she possibly could.

19

*A*lthough she'd promised herself that she wasn't going to go there, Stella had done exactly what she'd been fighting for days. She'd texted Lisa. She knew it was a foolish thing to do. After all, she was going against her contract by having personal relations with a guest. But three days had passed since Lisa had been at her house and she'd thought about her non-stop. Texting was a big step; it meant a direct line of communication between them that was sure to blur the professional boundaries even more.

Stella was a sucker for blondes, but she couldn't recall ever having it so bad. She'd even taken over a shift from her colleague this morning, so she'd have an unobstructed view of Lisa. That was wrong too, of course, and even bordering on creepy, but Lisa didn't seem to mind being her eye candy. Now that she'd learned Lisa was into women, Stella was able to think of little else than seeing her again in private. It was a silly crush and not the first time she'd been charmed by a guest. But guests came and went, and Lisa wasn't leaving by the end of the week. And that made it both exciting and dangerous.

Now, she was waiting in her car on a corner near the hotel where she'd told Lisa to meet her after her shift. She'd had a quick shower in the staff quarters, changed into white shorts and her favourite shirt, and she felt like she was about to go on a date. Was this a date? And if it was, did that mean she was underdressed? There was no time to ponder over it as she saw Lisa approach in the rear-view mirror, and suddenly nerves got the better of her. The woman looked stunning in a simple, white off the shoulder summer dress. She'd curled her hair a little and it fell in bouncy locks over her shoulders as she walked with a sway in her hips. "Fuck," she muttered, staring at her.

"Hey!" Lisa bent down and smiled at her through the open passenger window before she opened the door and got in. She looked lighter, happier today, and as she took off her shades, Stella saw she had a twinkle in her eyes that made her even more attractive.

"Hey there." Stella felt her face pull into a cheesy smile as she started the engine. "Hungry?"

"Yes, but it's my treat." Lisa returned her smirk, then turned to look ahead.

"If you insist." It wasn't uncomfortable, but they certainly were in a weird space and that grey area between new friends and potentially something more physical was confusing. "You look beautiful," she said, deciding to take a chance. It wasn't something she'd say to a friend, and with that one simple sentence, she knew she'd established what was happening here. They were on a date.

"Thank you. You look great too." Lisa's cheeks flushed a pale shade of pink and Stella let out the breath she'd been holding. "I don't know any places around here, so you'll have to pick."

"No problem. What do you feel like?"

"Something Spanish. Something like that little bar that I stormed out of when…" Lisa bit her lip and winced. "Somewhere with nice tapas."

"Okay. We can't go back there though, as I can't risk being seen with you." Stella shot her a regretful look as she merged onto the coastal road. "Just in case my colleagues are there. I'm not supposed to…" she hesitated.

"Privately mingle with guests? Yes, you told me that. It's also why I didn't text you after you'd sent me your number, but I figured as you contacted me, you felt it was okay."

"Yes, I'm not too worried as long as we don't hang out in Benidorm." Stella smiled at her, relieved Lisa understood how important it was that no one could know about this. "But there's a nice tapas bar in Altea, if you don't mind going there again?"

"That sounds fantastic." Lisa stuck her hand out of the window and did that thing with her hand again. The way she let it fly on the wind was something only a child would do, and Stella found it adorable.

"Sorry, I'm not used to being in the passenger seat," Lisa said, drawing her hand back when she caught Stella looking.

"Don't stop. It's cute." Realising she was openly flirting, Stella chuckled to herself and shook her head. "Why are you not used to being in the passenger seat?"

"Sandrine didn't drive in the UK. She's originally from New York and only moved to London because of her job. She wasn't used to driving, let alone on the left side of the road, so whenever we went somewhere I drove, and I didn't mind."

Stella nodded. "Okay. Do you still have your car?"

"Yes, it's on my parents' drive as I don't have anywhere to keep it at the moment. I thought about driving here from the UK but there was no parking space at the hotel, so I figured it would be easier to just fly."

"True. Parking long-term is a problem at Paradise," Stella said. "It's a beautiful drive though, especially through Basque Country."

Lisa smiled. "So I was told. But for now, I think I like the passenger seat. It's a nice change. Refreshing."

"Good. Because I intend to take you out on more trips if you're up for it." Stella's heart raced as she glanced at Lisa, but she didn't seem fazed by her comment.

"I'll hold you to that, you know." Lisa winked. "Any chance to leave the hotel is a blessing. Especially if it involves you and the passenger seat."

20

*T*heir chemistry was undeniable tonight, and Lisa felt overwhelmed by a jumble of emotions that hit her one after the other, sometimes all at once. Nervousness, arousal and happiness caused her to be hyperaware of her surroundings and especially the company she was finding herself in. Stella looked gorgeous in a casual blue shirt, and her hair had a certain flair to it which made Lisa think she'd put a lot of effort into making it look effortless. She was on a date—or at least she thought it was a date—with a hot and exciting woman and all she could think of was where the night would end. Her legs freshly shaved and her hair styled in loose curls, she felt confident about how she looked, and it was clear that Stella liked her dress from the way she kept glancing at her shoulders.

The hole in the wall with three tables outside was called Miércoles, as it was only open on Wednesdays. Inside, the bar was crowded with locals and Stella, who knew the owner, had called ahead for him to hold a table for them. Situated on the outskirts of Altea, wedged in between a small supermarket and a tobacco shop, it was off the tourist track and the food was deliciously fresh and authentic.

"So, if you don't mind me asking… are you gay? Or bisexual?" Stella asked as they were feasting on a selection of freshly prepared Spanish dishes. Iberian croquettes with a spicy chutney, black aioli with nut bread, wild croaker ceviche, manchego cheese, Andalusian aubergine and octopus with violet potatoes crammed the table, only leaving space for two small plates and their wine glasses. The bottle of white wine they'd ordered was in the ice bucket next to them and their glasses were topped up each time the waiter came out.

"I'm gay," Lisa said, her heart skipping a beat at the turn their conversation was taking. Stella was fishing and that was a good thing. As much as she'd wanted to be left alone after their first encounter, she really, really wanted to talk now. "But I was a late bloomer; I didn't realise I liked women until my mid-twenties, and I've only had two girlfriends since, one of which was a serious, long-term relationship."

"With Sandrine?"

"Yes."

"So, you've only been with two women?" Stella looked baffled as she asked the question. "Or have you had flings in between?"

"No. I've only had sex with Sandrine and Bette. It's not that I'm against one-night stands or anything, it's just that I've been in relationships since the moment I knew I was into women, and that was when I developed a crush on Bette. She was a consultant I worked with briefly." Lisa laughed as Stella whistled through her teeth. "What? It's not that strange. A lot of people end up with their school sweethearts and never date anyone else."

"I know. It's just that you've been missing out. A lot."

"That's your opinion." Lisa locked her eyes with Stella's and Stella held her gaze for long moments. "What about you?"

"I've had girlfriends but nothing that long-term. My longest relationship was just over a year and it just kind of died out. I suppose we had fun together, but we figured we were better off as friends in the end. We're still friends." Stella sat back and rolled the wine around in her glass. "I just haven't met the right woman, I guess."

Lisa arched a brow, eyeing her boldly as she nibbled on an octopus skewer. She was feeling brave. Perhaps it was the wine, or perhaps it was her need to escape for a night. Stella brought her confidence back and that was something she clung onto for dear life because it felt good to have a little piece of herself back. "And you don't have lovers?"

"Lovers? I'm sorry, that just sounded so funny and old-fashioned coming from you with your British accent." Stella laughed and tilted her head, looking Lisa over. "Sure, I have lovers. They come and go." She licked her lips, and Lisa blushed as she shifted in her seat. "Perhaps *you're* in need of a lover. Are you?" Stella asked, mimicking a British accent.

"Are you making fun of my accent?" Lisa arched a brow and tried her best not to show how much Stella's words affected her. Sure, she was in need of a lover, especially if that lover was the attractive, funny and charismatic pool-side manager whose smile she'd been swooning over for days now. Before, she would have never flirted so openly with a woman unless she thought there was potential for a future relationship, but maybe it was time to do things differently now; to just act on how she felt rather than what she ought to do. All kinds of naughty thoughts flooded her mind as her eyes lowered to Stella's sun-kissed hands, then back up. "I'm pretty sure I don't have a squeaky voice like you just put on," she continued in a playful tone.

"You're right. Your voice and accent are cute and super sexy. I could never do it justice" Stella paused. "Aren't you going to answer my question?"

"Hmm... Am I in need of a lover? I suppose it's been a while."

"Is that a yes?"

Lisa let out a nervous laugh. "Depends on who the woman is. I don't just sleep with anyone."

"I think we've established that already." Stella's lips pulled into a smirk, and she leaned in too. "But I think you know exactly what I'm hinting at."

"Yes. I think I do." Lisa played with a lock of her hair, surprised at her out of character behaviour as she wasn't flirty by nature. Stella's smile set her on fire, and she took a long drink of her wine to steady her nerves and the constant state of arousal that was peaking to alarming levels now. Her head was spinning, her heart racing and her core was fluttering from the butterflies that made her mind wander to places she'd never been. "So, what do you suggest?"

Stella was calm and collected, the complete opposite to her while she helped herself to more food, seemingly in no hurry whatsoever. "Well, for starters, why don't you come back to my place for a nightcap after dinner?"

21

"*D*rink?" Stella asked, pouring them both a glass of red without waiting for an answer. She suspected Lisa might want a little more for liquid courage as she'd been quiet and adorably clumsy on the way home. It wasn't that she was trying to get her drunk, of course. The bottle they'd shared over dinner wasn't nearly enough to make them tipsy but as with all first times, everything was easier when relaxed.

"Thank you." Lisa seemed grateful to have the wine to focus on while she twirled it around in her glass, and Stella noticed her hand was trembling. Since they'd come back to her house, Lisa hadn't looked her in the eyes, and she was fidgety and restless as they sat down on the sofa on her roof terrace. Stella would never talk her into something she didn't want to do but she knew that wasn't the case with Lisa. The signs had been loud and clear. The flirting, the body language... "Hey there, Yeti." Lisa put her glass on the coffee table and stroked the cat while it circled around her legs and purred. Her smile came back then, and her shoulders visibly relaxed. "She's so cute."

"It's a *he,* actually." Stella picked Yeti up and put him in between them on the sofa.

"Oh, sorry, my little prince." Lisa scratched Yeti's chin as he crawled onto her lap and started kneading her, purring louder now.

"Strange; he's not usually drawn to people apart from me."

"Well, maybe I'm special."

"I can't argue with that." Yeti suddenly jumped at the sound of a door slamming in the street below, and ran off into the night, his white silhouette disappearing onto the neighbour's roof. "He's very skittish. Someone might have treated him badly; he was fully grown when I took him in, so I have no idea about his history." Stella shifted closer and put her own wine glass down. "You seem a little skittish too, if you don't mind me saying. I hope I'm not making you feel uncomfortable."

"No, you're not." Lisa bit her lower lip as she leaned into her, and Stella could feel her shiver as their shoulders touched. "I'm ..." she hesitated. "As I said, it's been a while."

"We can just talk over a drink and I can call you a taxi later. Or I can make coffee, if you want," Stella suggested.

"That's not what I want." Lisa turned slightly and smiled, her breath quickening as she lowered her eyes to Stella's mouth. When Stella didn't move, she ran a hand through her dark hair, cupped her neck and leaned in. "I've been thinking of kissing you all night."

"So have I." Stella's pulse raced at their closeness. Although she couldn't recall the exact moment she'd fallen for Lisa, the real seduction had happened long before they'd ended up here, she realised. She closed her eyes when Lisa's lips tickled hers, and the internal explosion it caused took her by surprise. She hadn't seen this coming;

not how intense it would feel, how overwhelmingly exciting it would be. From Lisa's soft gasp and the way her hand tightened at the back of her neck, Stella knew she felt it too. Just the light brush alone sent a flash of arousal between her thighs and as much as she wanted to pull her in and claim her mouth, Stella held back, letting Lisa decide where to take this.

A moan escaped her as Lisa pressed her lips harder to hers, then parted her lips slightly. She could hear her quickened breath and feel her arousal that mirrored her own. The thousand fantasies she'd had were condensed to a single moment in which nothing else mattered. Nothing but the need to explore her mouth. Their lips fitted perfectly, and the kiss was soft and vulnerable, almost innocent, at first. Lacing her fingers through Lisa's hair, the sweetness of her velvety tongue caressed Stella's own, melting something inside her.

When Lisa pulled away and licked her lips, the chemistry between them was explosive and Stella's imagination was starting to run away with her. Lisa's shy smile had faded and there was only desire in her gaze now. Only that look that told her this would be a long and memorable night. It was already memorable; Stella was sure their first kiss would stay etched in her brain forever. She reached out to trace Lisa's shoulder with her fingertip, stopping at the strip of fabric that ran over her upper arm. The heat and humidity of the evening air had settled like a blanket on her skin, emphasising her sweet and powdery scent.

Lisa's long lashes fluttered at her touch. "You make me crazy," she whispered.

"Likewise." Stella leaned in for more, drawn to Lisa as if she had no control over her actions. Lisa's lips sent her into a state of intoxication, and when she parted them again, Stella responded hungrily, tightening her grip. They fell into a passionate push and pull, a dance of limbs and lips.

Stella cupped her face, then let her hands roam down Lisa's neck and shoulders, playing with the elasticated neckline that would be so easy to pull down. With no bra straps showing, she suspected Lisa wasn't wearing anything apart from a pair of knickers underneath—a thought that had kept her occupied all night.

Lisa's hands explored her in return and soon, the kiss turned wilder. "God, this is good," she said as she backed away, holding onto her chest as it rose and fell rapidly.

"Mmm...." Stella gently nudged her down, and Lisa leaned back against the armrest of the sofa, exhaling deeply. Her dress riding up her thighs was a sultry invite, and she made no effort to pull it back down. When Stella caught a glimpse of her white underwear, she dropped her hand to her thigh and pushed up her hem as she caressed her skin. Right then, she needed Lisa as much as she needed air and water.

22

The bed was soft and smelled of fresh linen as Lisa lay down on top of the covers and looked at Stella. Her limbs were trembling, her nerve endings zinging, and Stella had left a trail of static sensation everywhere she'd touched her. The open window blew balmy wind into the room, soothing her skin that was damp from their heated kissing session on the roof terrace.

"You look like an angel in that dress," Stella said as she crawled onto the bed and steadied herself above Lisa on her hands and knees. Her eyes had a darkness to them, a sensuality that made her irresistible. With her shirt open, Lisa appreciated the view of her cleavage in the black crop top and her tight stomach as she ran her hands over it. As soon as she'd unbuttoned it, she'd begged Stella to take her to bed, knowing she wouldn't be able to stop once she started exploring her body.

"An angel? I'm not that innocent," she retorted, giving Stella a flirty smile to let her know her thoughts were far from pure. She wanted nothing more than for Stella to kiss her again like she just had. To claim her in any way possible because it made her body rage with lust. She wanted it all, and she wanted it now.

"True. By dawn, you'll be far from innocent." Stella looked at her while she ran a hand up her thigh and under her dress, and she smiled when she felt Lisa's muscles tense. "Can I take this off?"

Lisa nodded and lifted her hips, allowing Stella to pull down her underwear, then sat up and impatiently tore off her dress. She longed to feel warm skin against hers and as she pulled Stella's shirt off, she could feel her eyes burning into her naked body.

"I love your body." Stella's eyes dropped from her face to her breasts, to the thin strip of hair between her legs and back up. "You're so beautiful, you take my breath away." There was a subtle tremble to her hand when she brushed Lisa's hair away from her shoulders, and then Stella's mouth was on her neck and everything passed Lisa in a deliciously slow blur. The raw intensity of her lips; kissing, sucking at her skin, the soft scraping of her teeth, her hands on her breasts, burning her up like a touch of flame.

Lisa threw her head back and spread her legs so Stella could get in between them, sighing at the closeness. She dragged her nails over her back, then tugged at the sports bra until Stella raised herself and took it off. "Mmm..." The sight of Stella's small breasts caused a heat between her legs so strong she had trouble concentrating on the buttons of her shorts.

Stella bit her lip as she helped her wedge them down her thighs, taking her boxers along in the process. She kicked off the final garments and lowered herself on top of Lisa, her lashes fluttering when their bodies came together. Their legs tangled and their hands in each other's hair, their next kiss was like nothing Lisa had ever experienced.

The feel of Stella's body; firm and trim yet so soft and feminine, her weight that felt perfect as she weighed her down, her nipples, hard against Lisa's chest, her hips moving into her in slow, sensual thrusts. Her hands fisting her hair, her lips, her tongue, her deep breaths as if she tried to breathe in all of her. Then Stella's lips on her breasts, her teeth tugging at her nipple before she sucked it into her mouth. Her fingertips skimming her waistline down to the curve of her hips before moving to the inside of her thigh.

Lisa was squirming, moaning when she felt those fingertips land on her centre. Her touch was soft and careful, yet it felt like lightning had struck her, and her body filled with an electric energy that charged every cell until she couldn't possibly feel any more. Stella kissed her deeply while she slowly circled her clit, her touch firmer when Lisa begged her by lifting her hips.

"Is that good?" Stella whispered, lifting her head to look at her.

"Uh-huh." Lisa couldn't speak; her thoughts were white noise, her body a tumble of emotions and reactions that brought her higher and higher. The way Stella looked at her while she lowered her fingers and entered her was the sexiest sight she'd ever encountered. "Fuck. Yes!" Pulling Stella's face down, she kissed her fiercely, needing to feel all of her at once. The delicious fullness from Stella's thrusting fingers as she ground into her and her hungry mouth were making her delirious, and she was shocked by how intense it felt. A tornado of sensations washed over her, and she moaned louder, frantically circling and thrusting her hips.

Sensing she was close, Stella moved deeper, harder, faster, curling her fingers and hitting the spot that sent Lisa over the edge. Lisa clung onto her, one hand on Stella's back, her nails digging into her skin. Her other hand fisted her hair, and she held her as tightly as she could.

Everything became hazy then. Hazy like a dream in slow motion. The warm hand on her cheek told her Stella was watching her, but she couldn't manage to open her eyes until every bit of tension had left her body. When she finally did, a warm glow coursed through her at the sight of Stella's gorgeous face. Tiny beads of sweat were pearling on her forehead, her eyes were filled with desire and she looked a little smug, which made Lisa chuckle. "God, you're sexy, you know that? And so talented." She could still barely speak through her quick breaths.

"Am I?" Stella's smirk widened into a beaming smile, and she laughed when Lisa rolled them over and straddled her. "Well, so are you. Sexy, that is." She winked. "I have no idea if you're talented yet."

Lisa bit her lip and arched a brow as she leaned forward to brush her lips against Stella's. "Well, I guess you're about to find out."

23

"*Hey*, wake up." Sunlight was seeping through the bedroom window as Stella sat down on the bed and watched Lisa's eyes flutter open. She looked cute beyond belief, and her tousled hair and lack of clothing was a pleasant reminder of last night. "Do you want coffee?" she asked, placing a mug on the bedside table. Although she wanted to kiss her, Stella wasn't sure if that was part of the 'casual code'. She'd had plenty of one-night stands and over-thinking things was not something she normally did, but with Lisa she'd started second-guessing every step.

"Oh, God, I slept so deep." Lisa smiled at her and sat up in bed. "Why didn't you wake me earlier?" Her eyes suddenly widened when she saw Stella was already dressed in her Paradise Hotel polo shirt and shorts. "Should I be embarrassed? Did I snore?"

Stella laughed. "No, you didn't snore. And you don't need to get up; I just wanted to say thank you for last night before I leave for work. The door falls into the lock, so you can close it behind you. There's a direct bus to the hotel; it stops in front of the post office we passed last night." She hesitated. "Unless you want a lift? I can drop you off around the corner from the hotel, so my colleagues won't see us arriving together."

Lisa seemed to be mulling her offer over as she slowly awoke. "If I could get a lift that would be great," she finally said. "I can be ready in five minutes."

"Okay, no rush. I'm leaving in half an hour, so drink your coffee first."

Lisa smiled at her. "Sorry, I'm always a little out of it first thing; mornings are not my forte." The sheet fell down, exposing her breasts as she picked up the mug. She quickly pulled it back up, then chuckled and shook her head. "Not sure why I'm being such a prude; it's nothing you haven't seen up-close."

"Trust me, I've seen every inch of you." Stella's eyes stayed fixed on her breasts, Lisa's hard nipples now showing through the thin sheets. Her mouth had been there only hours ago, and she subconsciously licked her lips as she remembered Lisa's lyrical cries when she'd made her climax time after time. Brushing her hair behind her shoulders, she leaned in to kiss her forehead, and when Lisa looked up at her, butterflies took over her core. For the first time in years, she felt herself blush profusely. If she'd had it bad before, this was a whole new level and all she wanted to do was crawl back under the covers and make love to her again.

"Thank you," Lisa said. "For the coffee, and especially for you know..." she hesitated. "I had an amazing night. Mind-blowing, actually."

"Me too." Stella sat down on the edge of the bed and placed a hand on Lisa's thigh. "Maybe we could do it again?"

"Yeah..."

"Or if you don't want that, I totally get it," Stella hastily interrupted her. "Don't worry; I don't have any expectations.

We just had fun and... and I like you and..." She groaned in frustration at her inability to form a coherent sentence. How had they gone from a comfortable new friendship with natural interaction to this clumsy conversation? She was normally quite smooth. But then again, she was normally also happy to see her lovers go in the morning and with Lisa here, she really wished she could take the day off because everything was different with her.

Lisa shot her a shy grin in return. "No. I'd really like to do this again," she said softly. "If it's not too risky. I mean, I won't tell anyone."

"Okay." Stella nodded, failing to hide how happy that made her feel. Her smile was so wide she was worried her lips might crack. "And don't think I'm ignoring you when you're lying by the pool today because truth is, there will be a lot of things going through my mind when I see you. But I can't have anyone notice I've taken a special interest in one of the guests, if you know what I mean."

"Sure. I understand." Lisa leaned in closer. "And now that I know you're happy with this arrangement, I'm sure you won't mind if I kiss you again."

"I've been staring at your lips since I woke up," Stella admitted, then pulled Lisa against her and claimed her mouth.

Lisa kissed her back, deliciously slow and deep, causing a flash of intense arousal to shoot between her thighs. The sound of their moans filled the room again and Stella was pretty sure she'd be late for work if it wasn't for Pablo, who started pawing her. "Hey, stop it," she said with a chuckle, and lifted him off the bed.

Lisa laughed when he immediately jumped back on and settled between them. "Jealous much?"

"Only a little," Stella said with an eye-roll. "He's always

like that when..." her voice trailed off and she winced. "I'm sorry. I don't mean to insinuate that I have women over all the time."

"But you do?"

"Occasionally. I'm sorry, I—"

"Hey, it's okay. You don't owe me anything. We're just having fun here." For a split second, a hint of worry crossed Lisa's features, but she shook her head and smiled.

"Even if you're okay with it, I don't want you to think I'll sleep with someone else tomorrow because I don't want to," Stella protested. "I'm not *that* bad." She rubbed her temple and sighed. This conversation wasn't going well at all. Even though admittedly she did regularly have women over, she was certain that none of them would be on her mind after last night. She couldn't tell Lisa that though, because it would just sound like she was getting way ahead of herself. Her mind was a fog as she searched for something to say, but Lisa took her hand and pulled her back in.

"Why don't we just forget about this conversation?" She ran a hand through Stella's hair and shot her a mischievous look. "I like you and you like me and that's that. We've got at least ten minutes before I have to get dressed, so let's make the most of it."

24

The three men in suits were back today, accompanied by a fourth who was a lot younger. Lisa glanced at them from the poolside as they came out of the back door with a young woman she recognised, and she wondered if they were part of the management team. She'd seen them in the reception area before, but the way they were glancing around the premises made her think they were seeing the poolside for the first time. It seemed silly to wear suits in this weather, and she quietly chuckled when she saw one of them loosen his tie and pull at his collar. If they were management, there was a lot she'd like to say to them, but going on the state of Paradise Hotel, she suspected they'd become immune to complaints.

She turned back to her phone when a notification from the website she'd booked Paradise with came in. *'Would you please take a moment to rate your stay?'* The reminder came in daily and soon, she'd have to decide whether she wanted to prolong her stay or not in case Paradise would be fully booked in August. Upon arrival she'd never have considered it, but things were different now that she was having 'fun' with Stella. Not that she expected anything to come of it—in fact, she hadn't even considered something more serious—but it was good for her, she decided, as she'd rarely felt this alive and happy. Besides, she hadn't found a job yet and that was her one and only goal. Perhaps she'd be luckier in the coming weeks. New vacancies were opening again, and she'd widened her search to Scotland and Ireland.

Checking Paradise's availability, she saw that there were a couple of rooms free for the same price, but she still hesitated for a moment as her finger hovered over the 'book' button. She could move to another hotel, but from what she'd seen, they were all more or less the same in Benidorm and she liked having Stella to look at while she was out here. Finally, she took the decision, praying she wouldn't regret it as she booked the room. She'd done nothing but curse the hotel so far, but it was time to stop the negativity right here and now and just get on with it because so far, every day had been better than the previous one.

The review link came up again, and Lisa mindlessly pressed it and saw that Paradise Hotel had an average score of three-and-a-half stars which wasn't great, but it certainly wasn't as bad as she'd expected. Even more surprising; the majority of reviews were five stars. Then there was a batch of one-star reviews and a couple of two, three, and four-star ones.

Just out of curiosity, she scrolled to the five-star reviews first. 'Camilla G, Leicester. Unlimited booze, sun and fun. What more could you wish for? Had an amazing time here and the staff are lovely. We'll certainly come back next year,' the first one read. 'Miranda B, Luton. You get what you pay for so don't expect luxury. However, we had so much fun. Manuel from the animation team was a hoot and we made friends for life and can't wait *to return,'* another one said. Scrolling down, Lisa continued to the one-star reviews.

'Jack B, London. Due to house renovations, we were a little short on cash this year, so I suggested we'd try one of these all-inclusive holidays. My wife still hasn't forgiven me. The name of the hotel sounded promising but the harsh reality upon arrival was shocking to say the least. After a shabby painting fell off the hook, we discovered a hole in the wall of our room the size of a tennis ball and there were cracks around it as if someone had beaten into it with a sledgehammer. We could see the neighbours through it, and they could see us. As it was high season, there were no other rooms available, and they refused to give us a refund. The hotel's way of resolving the issue, was to place duct tape over the hole. The air con didn't work properly so we complained about that too. On top of all that, my wife is allergic to gluten and potatoes, and there was literally nothing she could eat. Even the salads were bulked up with pasta and croutons. We couldn't sleep from the noise at night so upon returning, we needed to take two extra days off to recover from exhaustion.'

Lisa laughed as she worked her way through the reviews, hugely entertained at the horror stories. When she'd gone through them all, she craved more as she hadn't had so much fun in a long time. Premier Sunset—Paradises' neighbouring hotel—was shown in the article along with a couple of other hotels in the area, and when she saw that Premier Sunset only had a two-star rating, she continued, eager to read what guests had to say about it.

'Edith L, Kent. The name of the hotel, if you can call it a hotel, is totally inappropriate. 'Black Hole' would have been more suitable. There's no sun as the hotel is standing in the shade of a much bigger hotel, and the window in my room wouldn't open. The beer was lukewarm, I wouldn't feed the food they serve to my dog, and the music was so loud I couldn't hear my own voice.

The carpet around the shower (yes, there was carpet in the bathroom!) was mouldy and I found a used condom under the mattress when checking for stains. I checked out after the second night and paid for a backpacker's hostel in Alicante, which felt like The Ritz compared to Sunset.'

'Peter M, Bristol. It took me three months to get rid of the fungal infection on my back after staying at Sunset. I also got a rash on my chest from the sunbeds, which faded after the staff told me to stop lying on them as some people were sensitive to the bleach that they use to clean them with. The bartender was nice but sadly, he had very little to work with as he was constantly out of stock. The rubbery microwaved lunch omelettes were full of eggshell and dinner was even worse. The electricity kept cutting out, leaving me in total darkness in my stuffy room on several occasions, so I had to venture into town to buy a torch. If you're thinking about booking here, let me save you from a horrible experience. Don't do it! You're better off sleeping on the beach. At least you'll have two of your primary needs covered: oxygen and light.'

"What's so funny?"

"Oh, hey, you." Lisa sat up when she saw Stella standing by the end of her sunbed. They'd agreed they weren't going to talk to each other here, but she clearly hadn't been able to stop herself. "I'm reading reviews," she said, turning her phone towards Stella. "Paradise Hotel and Premier Sunset. Do you ever read them?"

Stella rolled her eyes and laughed. "Don't get me started. I know it's far from perfect here and I actually agree with most of the bad reviews but let's face it; you get what you pay for."

"True." Lisa shot her a wink and continued in a hushed tone. "Well, I'm going to leave a five-star review and rave about the cute poolside manager."

"I appreciate that," Stella said, fighting a wide smile as she glanced around to make sure no one was listening in. "Hey, I was wondering... Do you want to come on a hike with me? I've got the weekend off." Lowering her voice, she added: "Please don't feel pressured. And tell me if I'm being too much."

"No, I'd love to go on a hike with you." Lisa batted her lashes, loving Stella's flustered reaction. "So, two days, huh?"

"Yes." Stella stuck her hands in her back pockets and shuffled on the spot. "You could stay over if you want."

"Hmmm..." The corners of Lisa's mouth curled up as she lowered her big, black shades over her eyes. Stella's proposal had aroused her immensely, but not wanting to come across as overly keen, she said: "That sounds nice. Message me where and when you want to meet."

"*I*'m sorry, guys, but I'm afraid I'm going to have to ask you to leave the poolside. We're closed for today." Stella looked down at the two women who had promised to pack their things and move away fifteen minutes ago. When she noticed one of them was crying, she kneeled down. "Hey, you're upset. Is there anything I can do?"

The strawberry blonde woman shook her head, causing tears to drip from her chin. "Thank you, but no one can help me." Mirroring her bleach-blonde friend, she started stuffing her suntan lotion and towel into her bag, then put on the bright orange dress she'd been using as a pillow.

"Are you hurt?" Stella pointed to a big bandage on her shoulder and upper arm. The skin around it looked red and sore. "If someone here hurt you, I can call the police."

"It's not that, it's..." The woman started sobbing again and covered her face with her hands. "Pull it off and show her," she said to her friend.

Her friend carefully removed the bandage and Stella suppressed a gasp when she saw the monstrosity of a tattoo covering most of her shoulder. A man's face was tattooed on her shoulder blade, and it wasn't a pretty face. His long hair and beard looked like they were blowing to the right, covering her upper arm in clumsy curly shapes, some crooked in places. One curl extended to under her armpit, making it look like she had a random patch of hair there. The eyes were all wrong; one looking up and the other down, and the teeth weren't aligned properly, giving the impression the man had three front teeth, instead of two.

"Whatever you do, don't tell me it's my own fault for getting a drunk tattoo," the woman warned Stella. "I've had at least ten people say that to me today and it's not making me feel better. I know I had too much to drink, and I asked for it. But come on; this isn't fair. It looks horrible and now I'll have to cover myself up for the rest of my life."

"Is that a family member, or your boyfriend?" Stella asked carefully, because she just had to know. She'd had a laugh looking at bad tattoos online before, but she'd never seen anything quite as terrible as this one.

"It's supposed to be Keanu Reeves," the woman's friend said, then added, "Sheila's a fan," as if that would explain the disaster.

"Oh." Stella tried to find a resemblance but there was nothing in the man's face that reminded her of the actor. Lost for words, she refrained from commenting on it. "Who did this?" she asked instead.

"Beni Tattoo. End of the strip." Her friend put on a pair of pink denim shorts and paired them with a crop top that barely covered her triangle bikini. "We walked past at two am after hitting the tequila at Pit Stop. They were just about to close but took on the job anyway. I got one too, but mine is a little more subtle." She removed a bandage from her ankle and placed her foot on the sunlounger so Stella could see it.

This time, Stella did feel an urge to laugh as it wasn't quite so drastic, so she bit her lip and avoided the woman's eyes. *'Benidorm. Been there, don that,'* it said in a cursive script. The spelling mistake in the basic sentence baffled her. "Was the tattoo artist drunk too?"

"I think so. I vaguely remember sharing the bottle of tequila I'd brought from the bar with them. There were two tattoo artists, and one went out to get more booze at some point. They said it was fine to drink in there because the parlour was closed. It took hours with that massive one of Sheila's, and by the time we left we could barely get in the cab."

"Oh my God... Did you pay them?"

"Yes." Sheila sniffed. "I checked my bank account this morning. Six hundred Euros I paid them. All my savings."

"And I paid a hundred and fifty," her friend added.

Stella took a moment to think it over. She wouldn't normally take action against local businesses who were fighting to survive after the pandemic, but this was criminal. "They're not allowed to tattoo you if you're under influence," she said. "I doubt they have a licence to stay open after midnight, and if they'd been drinking themselves, then you should definitely consider speaking to the police. At least they can help you get your money back and make sure this doesn't happen to anyone else." She shrugged. "Or you could check if you have a legal cover under your travel insurance."

"But we were drunk and—"

"It doesn't matter," Stella interrupted Sheila. "They shouldn't have done that. Not while you were intoxicated and certainly not while they were intoxicated, artistic interpretation of a brief aside."

There was some mumbling between Sheila and her friend as they discussed the course of action. "We don't speak Spanish," Sheila's friend finally said. "Do the police speak English?"

"Most of them do." Stella sighed. She hated seeing their guests so unhappy and whether they'd been reckless or not, this was unacceptable. There was a plausible chance that the police might just laugh at them if they didn't have a local with them, and that would make matters even worse. She wouldn't normally go out of her way after hours to help guests—her colleagues were more than capable to take over—but she doubted anyone was willing to deal with two grown women who had made bad decisions after too much tequila. 'No sympathy', was generally their running comment. "You know what? I'll take you to the station. They'll only come out here for emergencies, so I'll drive you there, and explain the situation."

"Really? Would you do that?" Sheila grabbed Stella's arm as if she were a lifeline, and although the police couldn't take away the weird face on her skin, Stella suspected getting her money back was better than nothing right now.

"Sure. Do you have any pictures you took at the tattoo parlour? A video, by any chance?"

"Yes. I have both. I'm Tiff, by the way," Sheila's friend said. Tiff scrolled through her phone and handed it to Stella. "I haven't dared watch it yet but please feel free."

"Thanks. I'm Stella. Poolside manager." Stella cringed as she looked through the pictures, one worse than the other. Sheila and Tiff in the chairs, clinking their plastic cups together, still happily intoxicated and blissfully ignorant of things to come. Sheila leaning against the backrest of a chair, while the tattoo artist held his tattoo gun in one hand and a shot of tequila in the other. Sheila looking cross-eyed, holding a bucket under her chin. *Oh, God.* Tiff holding up a piece of paper with the slogan that would be tattooed on her ankle, minus spelling mistake. Tiff biting her knuckle while one of the guys was tattooing her. Tiff pointing to Sheila's back in tears of laughter. Then finally a video where they spun around in the studio, showing off their fresh tattoos. In the background, one of the tattoo artists was drinking a beer, while the other filmed and commented.

"Are you sure we should show those to the police?" Tiff asked as she glanced over Stella's shoulder. "It's not exactly making us look innocent in the matter."

"Yes, this is evidence and trust me; the police here have seen worse." Handing the phone back, Stella straightened herself and gestured to the gates. "I'll be outside the front entrance in twenty minutes in a white Beetle."

26

"*L*isa! How's the Costa Blanca? Is this a good time or are you in the middle of bingo or karaoke with pensioners?"

"Fergi!" Lisa smiled at her brother's cheerful voice. He was always upbeat. Even through the very beginning of his recovery he'd been optimistic, never losing hope that he'd be back to normal within a year. "I'm okay, enjoying the sunshine. No karaoke or bingo so far," she added with a chuckle. "But the opportunities for that are endless here, so you'll be the first to know if I give it a go. How are you?"

"I'm good. Getting better every day; I made it down the drive and back this morning and I'm sitting in the garden as the weather's lovely here. Mum and Dad are driving me bonkers, but they mean well, so I try not to get worked up over Mum's constant fussing and Dad's repetitive stories about his time in the Royal Marines."

Lisa laughed. "I'm glad they're taking good care of you and I'm really happy to hear you're getting better."

"What about you? Will you be joining the household soon?" Fergi asked. "You mentioned it briefly before you so suddenly took off to Spain. It will be fun; we can fight over the remote control and break into each other's rooms. It's been decades since we did that."

"And subject myself to your heavy metal music and have you ratting me out every time I do something I shouldn't?" Lisa said. "As tempting as that sounds, I've actually booked another month here."

"Oh? From your messages, I got the impression the hotel was awful, and that Benidorm was awful."

"Well, I've changed my mind about a lot of things and..." Lisa hesitated.

"And what?"

"I've met a woman. It's not serious or anything, but let's just say she's made my stay a whole lot more fun, so I don't mind being here at all anymore."

"A woman?" Now it was Fergi's turn to fall silent. "I didn't see that one coming. Tell me about her."

Lisa glanced at Stella, who was going through some paperwork with the bartender. The urge to walk up to her, push her against the bar and kiss her was strong, but of course, she couldn't do that. Having eye candy while she relived their night was a welcome distraction, but she found herself doing little else than fantasising about Stella lately. "Her name is Stella and she's Spanish. She's the poolside manager here and I'm gawking at her as we speak." She turned her gaze skyward when her brother burst out in laughter.

"Sorry," he said, clearing his throat. "But that just sounds like the script for a cheap, lesbian porn movie."

"Can't argue with that," Lisa agreed. "She's seriously hot but that's only the icing on the cake. Stella is funny and kind and down-to-earth; she's taking me hiking on Friday."

"She sounds like the opposite to Sandrine."

"What do you mean by that?" Lisa twirled a lock of hair around her finger and fought back a grin as she caught Stella looking back at her. "You never mentioned that you didn't like her."

"I didn't want to say anything because she was your girl-friend, but you have to admit that she was a little high-main-tenance. Certainly not down-to-earth."

"I suppose you're right." Lisa sighed. "Looking back, I wasted years of my life with Sandrine. She moved on so fast, it's like none of it meant anything to her."

"Nothing's a waste, we learn from our mistakes."

"Sure. And when did you suddenly become so wise?" Lisa asked with sarcasm dripping through her voice. "I'm used to hearing things like 'Can I borrow some money?', 'Is your friend single?', or 'What's the correct way to eat a banana?'"

Fergi laughed. "Since my accident. And in case you're wondering; I finally figured out the correct way to peel a banana. You need to peel from the bottom and use the tip as a handle."

"Glad you've got your priorities straight." Lisa grinned. "When do you think you'll be able to get back to work?"

"Hopefully in a month or two. I'm aiming to walk to the bakers by the end of this month. As soon as I can do that, I'll contact HR and tell them I'm ready to be eased back into the office. They're not expecting me to return until next year, so they'll be pleasantly surprised. I never thought I'd say this, but I'm actually looking forward to working again."

"Huh. You always hated your job."

"Not anymore." Fergi paused. "How's the job hunting going?"

"It's not."

"Nothing interesting?"

"Lots of interesting jobs, they just don't want me." Lisa sighed. "I'm willing to settle for anything now. I can't stay here forever, and I really don't want to move back in with Mum and Dad."

"You'll figure something out," Fergi said. "Look at me. The doctors weren't sure if I would ever walk without a stick again, yet here I am, resting after conquering the driveway. It might have been a short stroll, but I'm walking."

"That's fantastic." Lisa winced. "I shouldn't be complaining about the job thing. It's nothing compared to your situation."

"Not true, everything is relevant."

"Hmm." Lisa followed Stella with her eyes as she walked past her. She shot her a subtle wink, and Lisa giggled at the flirtation. "Do you still have your flat?"

"No, I didn't want to pay rent while I wasn't living here, so I gave it up but that's fine. I'll find another place, maybe outside of London. I've had a lot of time to think about what I want, and I'd like to buy something in the countryside, providing the commute to work isn't too long. It's time for a real house and maybe even a girlfriend, if I can find someone who's crazy enough to date me."

Lisa frowned as she let his words sink in. She'd never thought she'd hear those words from her brother's mouth. Sure; he had girlfriends, but it never led to anything serious, and he'd never talked about grown-up things like buying a house or moving to the countryside. "You really have changed."

"Yes, I have," he said plainly. "I'm grateful for my life and that's the best place to be when starting over. So, don't fret about what you don't have, look at what you *do* have and create your life around it. If this woman makes you happy, go for it. Why not look for a job in Spain? Even if it's in Barcelona or Madrid, at least you'll be closer to her."

"It's a little early for that. As I said, it's not serious. Anyway, the job market here is even worse than in the UK."

"Then create a job. You're an expert, so why not start your own business?"

Lisa thought about that and realised he was right. There was no reason why she couldn't attempt to work for herself. She had contacts in all the right places, a wealth of experience and knowledge and she didn't need starting capital to present herself as a consultant.

"You're buffering," Fergi joked when she remained silent.

"I am. Frankly, I've never heard you talk so much sense and I'm looking forward to meeting the new and improved Fergi."

"You'd be surprised. I'm even thinking of cutting my hair short," he joked. "But seriously, Lisa, you make your own destiny. In life there's no such thing as luck, only hard work and determination. But if you love what you do, it will be a hell of a lot easier."

27

"*D*o you need a rest?" Stella asked. "I'm not sure making a woman walk for two hours just for a view is appropriate, even if that view is worth it in my opinion."

"No, I'm fine. It's really pretty here." Lisa shielded her eyes from the sun as she glanced up at the last bit of hill before them.

"Okay. But let me know if you get tired." Peñón de Ifach, also known as Calpe Rock, is one of the most famous sights along the Costa Blanca," Stella told her. "It would be a shame not to experience it when you're staying so close." The hike was intense, and she was glad they'd left early, before the heat of the day would kick in. They'd seen beautiful, rare plants and flowers, including wild orchids and brugmansia, and a falcon was circling overhead. Lavender grew along both sides of the narrow path they followed, attracting bees and colourful butterflies. Dotted over the hill were pine trees that grew horizontally on the slope; their trunks curling around their own base in places.

"As I said, I'll welcome any opportunity to get out of the

hotel and believe it or not, I love long walks, especially through beautiful landscapes." Lisa smiled as she turned to Stella. "Anyway, finish the story you were telling me. What did the police say about the tattoos?"

"Right." Stella adjusted her rucksack and pulled her cap further over her forehead. "They're going over to the tattoo parlour today to talk to the owner and said they would arrange for the ladies to get their money back. The damage is already done but still…"

"Won't they lose their licence?"

"They might. I'm not sure how close the owners are to the police. It's not really corrupt here, but it's not like in the UK either, so we'll see."

"I saw the woman with the big bandage by the pool yesterday. She looked pretty miserable; I was wondering what had happened to her."

"You should have seen it." Stella couldn't help but laugh as she shook her head. "It was seriously bad. It looked like some random weirdo on acid, inked by a drunk artist with very little talent for anatomy or anything else for that matter."

Lisa laughed along as she glanced at Stella. "You don't have any tattoos, I noticed. It's quite rare in this day and age."

"No, I'm all natural." Stella shot her a flirty look, fixing her eyes on Lisa's mouth. She wanted to kiss her badly, but early hikers kept coming from the opposite direction. They hadn't kissed this morning when Stella picked her up, perhaps because kissing was one of those strange things that defined the fine line between casual and something more and neither of them knew exactly how to behave in the physical sense now that they were just hanging out.

"That makes two of us. But maybe I should get my first

one before I return to the UK. "Benidorm. Been there, don that," Lisa joked.

"I promise I'll do everything in my power to stop you from waltzing into Beni Tattoo if you ever hit the tequila at Pit Stop," Stella retorted. "Although you having a drink at Pit Stop seems just as unlikely as the idea of you getting a ridiculous tattoo."

"True. There are many things I'd rather do than setting a foot in Pit Stop," Lisa said with a chuckle. "Last time I walked past there a woman was flashing her boobs at anyone who was willing to look."

"I've seen it so many times that it doesn't even shock me anymore. Do you miss London?"

"No, actually. I just miss a slightly bigger space, that's all. And a kitchen, I miss that too. I didn't cook very often, but now that I don't have the amenities, I find myself wanting to cook and I'm longing for a fridge to keep a good bottle of white wine. It's funny, isn't it? How we never really appreciate things until we lose them. My brother's accident made me realise I was lucky to have my health, and so my dreams are smaller nowadays. Before, I wanted a bigger flat in a nicer location, a better car and maybe another designer handbag. Now, all I want is a job, a social life and a place to live."

"It's a beautiful thing to realise you can do with less. It takes away the pressure." Stella put a hand on her back as they climbed the last bit of the path and gestured to the remains of an old wall on the top of the hill. "Calpe Rock used to be a watchtower—a vantage point to spot pirates and intruders. The crumbled walls date all the way back to the fourteenth century."

"Wow." Lisa took a moment to catch her breath as they

reached the top, then followed Stella to the edge of the cliff. "I can see why they used this place. The views are incredible."

"Yeah. It's quite spectacular." Stella smiled as she looked over the Bay of Calpe, the Mediterranean Sea and the magnificent shoreline that were a welcome reward after the climb. The cliffs were steep, and it smelled so good up here, where the sea breeze mingled with the rosemary, lavender and juniper growing at the top of the rock. When the only other two people up there started descending again, her core fluttered, and she hoped they would get at least a couple of minutes to themselves. "See that tiny little dot there to the east?" she asked, coming up behind Lisa as she pointed it out. Her chin rested on Lisa's shoulder while her hand snaked around her waist and, God, it felt good to have her close.

"Yes." Lisa shivered and leaned back against her.

"That's Ibiza. You can only see it on a clear day." Stella nuzzled Lisa's neck and inhaled against her skin. It was fine, she decided then, because Lisa's body language didn't lie; she wanted this as much as she did.

Lisa closed her eyes and tilted her head back, her breath quickening as Stella's hand moved up to her breasts. "Anything else you want to show me? I wouldn't mind if you continued pointing things out to me," she said in a breathless whisper.

Stella kissed Lisa's neck and gently nipped at her damp skin. "That's the Cape of San Antonio. It's at the tip of a pretty town called Xàbia," she said, turning Lisa in the other direction while she cupped her breasts and squeezed them. Feeling Lisa's arousal in her racing pulse made her ache with longing. "I'll take you there if you like."

"Hmm... You can take me anywhere you want."

At that, Stella chuckled, and she kissed her way down to Lisa's shoulder. "Then how about we have a rest up here and enjoy the view for a while before I take you to my bed?"

28

*L*ying lazily in Stella's arms, Lisa was glowing after what Stella had just done to her. She felt close to her, but most of all, she trusted her. The friendship between them, combined with their intimacy—not just the sex but also this, the sleepovers and holding each other for hours on end—had caused her feelings to grow faster than she'd anticipated. It wasn't purely casual anymore, at least it didn't feel that way. She hadn't planned on falling for her. This was only meant to be a bit of fun, a way to distract her from her worries, and she suspected Stella had flirted with her with the same intention. She didn't get the casual vibe from Stella anymore either. Now that she knew her better, she'd even go as far as to think that she'd fallen for her too, that the intense joy she felt when being together was mutual.

"I like doing this with you."

"Doing what?" Stella ran a finger up and down Lisa's belly, then moved up to her breast and cupped it gently, rubbing her thumb over her nipple.

"Doing nothing." Lisa shivered. "I'm not used to switching off, it's nice."

"Switching off looks good on you. Will you stay the weekend?"

"If you don't mind, I'd like that. Don't you have things to do?"

"Things can wait." Stella grinned and rolled on top of her. "Especially when there are much more fun things to do." She kissed Lisa slowly and deeply, causing her to go weak in all limbs.

"Yes, everything can wait." Lisa closed her eyes and sank into the kiss, once again surrendering to the delightful feeling of Stella's weight on top of her. She'd been in a constant state of arousal, a dreamy haze that made her feel light and carefree. Hands roamed freely as they ground into each other, interrupted by the occasional giggle when Pablo pawed them for attention. "Except Pablo," she muttered when his paw caught her eye.

Stella laughed, lifted her head to look at him, then let out a long sigh. "I'm going to do something I've never done before," she said in a humorous tone. She got up, picked him up from the bed and locked him outside the bedroom. A long and hurtful cry came from the hallway, and she shook her head and rolled her eyes. "Don't feel sorry for him; he's just being dramatic." Licking her lips, she climbed back on the bed and got in between Lisa's legs, then spread them apart. "Mmm... I'm hungry."

"You have a healthy appetite." Lisa marvelled at Stella's strong frame before her, then moaned when she bent forward and ran her tongue through her folds. Her warm mouth felt heavenly, and she bucked her hips, seeking more. Circling her clit with the tip of her tongue, Stella teased Lisa until she felt dizzy and delirious, all thoughts fading from her mind. Her centre throbbing, she begged her to continue but Stella looked up with a cheeky smile and made a spinning gesture with her finger.

"Turn around and get onto your hands and knees."

"What?" Lisa's breath hitched at her words and her heart started racing.

"Turn around. What are you waiting for? I'm not going to hurt you." The daring look in Stella's eyes was sexy as hell and Lisa was all too aware of how exposed she was as she did so. Stella's hand curled around her waist, then moved up to caress her breasts and pinch her nipples. Her other hand slipped between her thighs from behind and she ran it up and down Lisa's centre until she was squirming in her grip, and then entered her slowly.

"Jesus!" Lisa cried out as she pushed back against her.

"See? Nothing scary..." Stella took her in a tight grip and pulled her upright against her chest, her mouth sucking hard on Lisa's neck as she started fucking her. "You're so hot," she whispered in her ear. "So, so fucking hot. You have no idea what you do—"

"Yes!" Lisa threw her head back against her shoulder, basking in the tingling heat that spread through her core quicker than wildfire. Stella's hand roaming over her breasts and her belly, her lips on her skin, her teeth tugging at her earlobe and her fingers filling her up over and over turned her into jelly, and she could hardly keep herself upright. She let go and pressed herself into Stella's body behind her, spreading her knees further apart when her climax started building.

"Come for me, baby," Stella whispered in her ear, fucking her faster until Lisa exploded with a loud cry.

Lisa shut her eyes tight as her whole body tensed, and she ground her teeth so hard her jaw hurt. When the waves finally subsided, she breathed hard and let Stella take her in her arms from behind while her face nuzzled Lisa's neck. "I can't seem to get enough of you," she said with a tremble in her voice as her muscles relaxed and her heartbeat slowed again. Stella's heart was still beating wildly; she could feel the thud against her back.

"That's a good thing, isn't it?"

Lisa turned around with a grin, nudged Stella back and crawled on top of her. "It certainly is." She trailed kisses down her neck, then settled on her breasts to feast on them. She was obsessed with Stella's body, completely and utterly in awe of the way she moaned and moved when she used her mouth on her. Her body rolled and her eyes fluttered like she was in a trance. Moving down, Lisa could already feel the heat radiating from between her thighs. "I'm feeling pretty hungry too," she murmured, sinking her lips against Stella's warm wetness.

29

"Here's breakfast." Lisa put down a plate with scrambled eggs, a bowl with avocado and tomato slices and a basket with toast on the table. Pulling her shades down, she sat opposite Stella, feeling happy and content. The past two days and nights had been heavenly. They'd wandered through town, enjoyed late dinners and drank wine on the roof terrace while they watched the sunset. They'd gone back to Stella's favourite café by the beach to read the newspapers and do crosswords for hours before cooling down in the sea. The nights had been balmy and steamy, and she could still feel the physical aftermath of their morning sex. Now that Stella was going to work, it almost felt domestic to wake up early together. While Stella was in the shower, she'd snuck out to visit the local super-market, determined to do something nice for her.

"You're so sweet; you didn't have to do that." Stella helped herself to a piece of toast, scooped some of the eggs and avocado on top and shot Lisa an adoring look. "I appreciate it though; I never have breakfast before work, so this is a treat."

"Neither do I. But it's so lovely up here and we have time." Lisa returned her gaze over the brim of her coffee cup. "It's the least I could do. I had an amazing time with you, so thank you for that." She'd never made Sandrine breakfast before; Sandrine considered it a waste of time, and she was often quiet and grumpy in the mornings, cursing and groaning while she read her emails over black coffee. Looking back, Lisa had never enjoyed the small pleasures of life over the course of their relationship. Coffee in bed, an evening stroll or simply watching the sun go down together had been unheard of, but with Stella, she was soaking up every moment of the day as if it were her last and she'd happily make breakfast each morning just to see that dazzling smile on her face.

"I really enjoyed it too." Stella took a bite of her eggs and let out a content sigh. "You can stay another night if you want." She shrugged. "Stay as long as you want, I love having you here. Especially if you make me breakfast."

Lisa chuckled and shook her head. "Thank you, but I should go back to my room. I need clean clothes and my epilator."

Stella shot her a smirk as she reached under the table, lifted Lisa's foot onto her lap and stroked her leg. "No need. They're smooth as silk."

"Hmm..." The touch of her hand made Lisa's pulse race. "You need to stop that because you're turning me on again."

"Again?" Stella arched a brow. "I don't think I've met a woman with a sexual appetite like yours before."

"I could say the same for you." Lisa licked her lips as flashes of the past days hit her, one after another. Stella had been all over her; wanting her, needing her, exploring her, devouring her... Pulling her leg back and straightening herself, she did her best to park the juicy fantasies for later.

"But you have to go to work, so I won't tempt you." A flirty glance passed between them.

"You're right. I wouldn't get anywhere." Stella tilted her head and looked at Lisa, then dropped her fork, got up and walked around the table. She leaned over her, took her face in her hands and kissed her so slowly and sensually that Lisa melted in her chair. Stella's hands moved through her hair, raking through her blonde locks as quiet sounds of pleasure escaped her lips.

Lisa reciprocated, pulling Stella in closer as she basked in the warmth of her mouth and the touch of her tongue. Kissing Stella was better than biting into the juiciest peach, breathing in the cleanest air, listening to her favourite song and dancing her heart out all at once.

"What was that for?" she whispered when Stella pulled away and sat back down. Her eyes were hazy again, her chest heaving and the light ache between her legs had blown up to a throbbing sensation in a matter of seconds.

"Nothing. You're just impossible to resist." Stella bit her lower lip, chuckling at herself, and sitting back, she held up both hands. "Okay I'll stop. I have to show some people around this morning, so I can't be late."

"Who are you showing around?"

"Some potential buyers for Premier Sunset, they're from the Calvo Group. The hotel falls under our mother company and I've been asked to explain how the poolside team functions at Paradise. I have to get some takeaway coffees on my way in and pretend we've made it in our machine, just so they won't have to drink our disgusting brew."

"How ridiculous."

Stella chuckled. "Yes, that's what I said. Apparently, the board of directors is keen to sell as Premier Sunset isn't doing very well. It's in urgent need of renovation and the reviews have been so bad lately that they don't think it's worth investing in. It's not just the hotel rooms that need updating. The kitchen's been closed as the electrics weren't safe anymore, and the lifts keep getting stuck. I know some people who work at Sunset, and I don't want anyone to lose their jobs, but I suppose that's inevitable, when ownership changes."

"Sunset seems like a difficult place to sell. From the reviews I've read, it's got very little going for it," Lisa said. "The biggest complaint seems to be the total lack of sunlight."

"You're right. I imagine Paradise Group regrets buying it in the first place."

"Hmm…" Lisa mulled over that as she played with a lock of her hair. "Who is the managing director of the Calvo Group?"

"His name is Diego Calvo; I looked him up as I'll be meeting him today. He lives in Madrid but he's here regularly as his company owns several hotels in Benidorm."

"Calvo spelt C-A-L-V-O?"

"Yes." Stella frowned at Lisa's unusual interest. "Why? Do you know him?"

"No. I'm just curious, that's all." Lisa opened her mouth, about to add something, then shook her head and decided against it. "Never mind."

"Never mind what?" Stella asked. "Talk to me."

Lisa hesitated for a moment, then let out a long sigh. She wasn't quite sure what she wanted to say; the idea hadn't fully formed in her head yet. "I spoke to Fergi, my brother, last week."

"Oh. How is he?"

"He's okay. He managed to walk down the drive, and he

might even be able to go back to work soon, at least part-time."

"Okay, that's great. But what does that have to do with Diego Calvo?"

"Well… it's just that he said something that made me think out of the box," Lisa said. "Sorry, I'm being incredibly vague. I get like this when I have an idea; my mind won't stop churning and I get all distracted. Anyway, he suggested I start working for myself."

"That makes sense. In marketing?"

"Yes, marketing and brand building. I don't expect it to be easy to find my first clients, but I'm persistent and a hard worker, and even if I just try this in the interim period until I find a job, then I won't feel so useless. So, I'm thinking about options and potential opportunities."

Stella smiled. "And you're interested in Premier Sunset? Why? The sun isn't going to magically appear unless they tear down Paradise Hotel, so I don't see how brand building falls into that." She was clearly still confused as she tried to follow Lisa's train of thought.

"True. But when something is really bad, the only way is up, right? And I'm pretty sure I can help them with that. Do you think you can get me Mr Calvo's number?"

"I can ask."

"Thanks." Lisa picked up a slice of toast and absently nibbled on it. The excitement she felt after voicing her plan had taken away her hunger. "I'm going to have a look at a couple of places in Benidorm today, starting with Premier Sunset. Just to get my mind in the right frame."

"Does that mean you're planning on looking for clients *here*?" Stella asked, pouring herself more coffee from the pot. She filled up Lisa's cup too and leaned in over the table.

"Because I'd be really happy to have you here for a little longer."

Lisa felt a warm glow at her words. She hadn't necessarily thought of Benidorm as an option because of Stella. Or had she? The idea of staying had been unthinkable when she'd just arrived, but now, only a month later, Stella was the very reason she loved being in Spain. "I have to start somewhere, and I happen to be here now, so why not?" she said, deciding that answer was neutral enough not to give away how much she really liked her. It was too soon to tell Stella how she felt, but there was nothing wrong with looking at her options.

---

30

*P*remier Sunset was a funny place. Unlike Paradise Hotel, where the pool was heaving with people as soon as it opened in the morning, the pool here was quiet. That wasn't strange. Standing in the shadow of its big brother Paradise, it looked sad and a little murky. Lisa suspected the guests spent most of their time at the beach—which was only a short walking distance from here —in the mornings and came back once the bar started serving alcohol.

Determined to think outside the box—not only because she'd burned her way through all marketing vacancies and saw an opportunity here, but also because she desperately needed something to focus on—she sat down at the bar and ordered a coffee.

"Wristband?" the bartender asked. The name badge on his chest said '*Santos. Bar manager*'.

"I don't have one. I'm just visiting," Lisa said, handing him a five Euro note.

Santos seemed puzzled as to why she would choose to have her coffee here instead of at a café along the boulevard, but he took the money and gave her a wide smile when she told him to keep the change.

It was a sorry scene, especially as everything was so worn-out. Old, rusty sunloungers were placed along the long, narrow pool that was tiled with purple mosaic. Undoubtedly, it had been fashionable back in the nineties, but now it felt dated. The once white plastic tables and chairs under faded Coca-Cola parasols had turned a yellowish shade and there were no plants, just two palm trees and a patch of grass behind the pool area that was rather muddy. The bar was deserted, apart from two staff members who were sitting on the rickety stools on the opposite side, occasionally chatting to Santos in Spanish. If there was one thing that she'd learned from living in Paradise Hotel, it was that the British were single-mindedly focused on getting a tan while on holiday, so there was no reason for them to be here. The few people who did hang around—some sleeping on sunloungers and a couple perched on the flowerbed wall behind the pool—looked rather tired. She heard a man near her murmur something about the shitty Wi-Fi, but his female companion didn't answer as she was fast asleep on the lounger next to him. Fully dressed, her arm draped over the edge and her mouth was slightly agape, she looked like she'd fallen asleep here last night after hitting the bars. The music was way too loud for the subdued atmosphere, and all in all, it seemed like a place anyone would regret booking.

"It's not exactly busy," she said to Santos.

"It's been quiet for a while." He made himself a coffee, pulled a stool out and sat down too. "It wasn't going well to begin with, but during and after the pandemic, it's just been a downward spiral." He pointed in the direction of Paradise

Hotel. "They will survive, but I doubt we will. It's just not good enough."

"How long have you worked here?" Lisa asked.

"Five years. And I'm starting to get an itch," he joked. "But right now, I just feel lucky to have a job."

"What would you do with the hotel? If it was up to you?"

"I don't know. I'm a bartender, and a pretty good one. I just can't use my skills here." Santos fell silent as he thought about the question. "I'd do it up, for sure. But without sun, I doubt the hotel will ever be popular with tourists, no matter how fancy. It's okay for the staff, though; saves us from working in the burning heat."

Lisa nodded, pleased he'd given her the answer she was hoping for. "Do you mind if I take some pictures?" she asked.

"Of course not. Our guests take pictures here all the time." He narrowed his eyes at her. "Who are you? You don't look like you're on holiday here, with the clothes and all."

"My clothes?" Lisa looked down at her T-shirt, leggings and trainers. "I suppose you're right," she said absently. "I don't really fit in; I realised that when I moved into Paradise."

"You're staying at Paradise?"

"Yes." Lisa smiled. "It's not all that bad. The staff are lovely once you get to know them, and you get used to the food eventually, which I suspect is not much better here?"

Santos laughed. "I don't eat that crap, so I've never tried it but from what I've heard it's worse here. Anyway, the restaurant has closed. The kitchen didn't pass the last health and safety inspection and Paradise Group won't give us funding to buy new gear." He took a sip of his coffee and shrugged. "I have a bad feeling about Premier Sunset's future. One of my colleagues told me he'd seen potential buyers being shown around, so I've started looking at other jobs just in case."

"Buyers?" Lisa asked, pretending she knew nothing.

"Yes. They're obviously going to sell the place. No other reason they'd be here, whispering with the board. That means everyone will lose their jobs."

"Maybe they will keep the staff," Lisa said.

"It's unlikely. In the more upmarket hotels, they do that. They use the refurbishing period to retrain the staff, but not in the cheap hotels. I expect them to just get rid of everyone, patch it up, then rehire. It's just the way it works around here."

"Yeah..." Lisa's regretful look was heartfelt. Knowing how hard it was to find a job in this climate, she felt for Santos, and she wanted him to be okay. She wanted everyone to be okay. Snapping a couple of pictures, she made sure not to get any of the sleeping guests in.

"I hate to break it to you, but that's not going to get you any likes on Instagram," Santos joked.

"I know." Lisa laughed, finished her coffee and stood up. "Well, I hope it works out for you, Santos. And if you're right regarding the sale, I hope you get to keep your job." She glanced at the double doors that led into the reception area. "Is there a toilet I can use through there?" she asked, curious about the ground floor layout. The reception area would be the perfect spot to have a bar, so the terrace could be utilised as an extension.

"Yes. Straight on past reception. There are a couple in the first corridor on the left."

———

31

"Good morning, ladies." Stella stopped in front of Sheila and Tiff, who were lying on sunloungers, each with a cocktail, chatting to a couple next to them. She'd been on her way to speak to a group of women who had taken their drinks into the pool, but she saw Manuel was already on the case, gesturing to their plastic cups and telling them to keep them out of the water.

"There she is!" Sheila held up her cup in a toast. "I was just saying to Tiff, 'I wonder if we'll see Stella today. You haven't been around for the past few days.'"

"I had a long weekend off." Stella spread her arms and chuckled. "But here I am. Have you heard anything from the tattoo parlour yet?"

Sheila batted her long, fake lashes at her and shot her a beaming smile. Her shoulder was still covered with the bandage, but she was giggly and clearly in better spirits today. "Yes, I got a refund and another five-hundred Euros extra towards removing the tattoo. It was way beyond my expectations," she said. "To be honest with you, the police didn't seem that bothered when we were at the station, but I have to give it to them; they must have done something because I got a call from Beni Tattoo this morning and they transferred the money into my account shortly after. Just like that."

"That's great news. Let's hope they can remove it nicely."

"Nah." Sheila waved a hand as if she didn't care all that much anymore. "I've never had so much in my account; the money for that tattoo came from my savings and now that I've ended up with a profit, we're going shopping and partying tonight."

"Okay..." A little irritated, Stella needed a moment as she'd gone out of her way for these women to get justice so Sheila could have her tattoo removed. "So, you don't want to get rid of it?"

"Not right away. I'll have it done once I find a boyfriend with a proper job who can pay for it."

You're not going to find a boyfriend with that thing on your shoulder, Stella thought, but she kept that to herself.

"Anyway," Sheila continued, "it's not important anymore because there's even better news..." She took a big gulp of her cocktail, then paused for effect.

"Oh? More good news?"

"Yes, you'll never guess what happened."

"You'll never guess!" the man next to Sheila and Tiff repeated, glancing at his phone. "You need to see this, it's epic."

"Shhh... this is about me, so let me have my moment," Sheila said to the man, beaming as she took her own phone out of her handbag, opened Twitter and showed it to Stella. "I'm trending on Twitter and I got a reply from Keanu Reeves!"

Stella frowned as she took the phone and saw that the picture of the manky tattoo with the caption *'Asked for*

Keanu Reeves and got this' #benitattoo had over thirty-five thousand likes. "No..." She scrolled through the thread of remarks. Some were supportive, like: *'That's horrid. Sue them!'* and *'You poor thing.'* Others were less sympathetic. *'You deserve what you got for even coming up with such a stupid idea,'* someone said. The next one made her laugh. *'Could have been worse. Look at mine.'* There was a picture attached of a tattoo that indeed, looked worse than Sheila's, if that was possible. She couldn't work out who the full-coloured pink face belonged to at first, then read the caption underneath that said: *'Meatloaf forever.'* "I see you're popular. Where's Keanu's reply?"

"It's here." Sheila took the phone from her, scrolled down for a while, then held it up for Stella to read the tweet that was sent by Keanu Reeves with, indeed, a blue tick behind his name.

"Getting a tattoo of my face was probably not the brightest idea you ever had but I appreciate the sentiment and feel humbled. Good luck with getting it removed, assuming you will," she read out loud. "Okay, you really did get a reply from him."

"Amazing, right?" Tiff's voice was high-pitched with excitement. "We waited in front of his hotel for hours the last time he was in London. His fan club; the whole lot of us. Five hours we waited there, only to find out he'd left through the back entrance. And now Sheila's had personal contact with him." Shaking her head incredulously, she added, "I'm so fucking jealous. They're practically friends."

"Practically." Stella nodded, pretending to agree with that statement. She wasn't sure if a tweet counted as personal contact, let alone friendship, but she was happy for Sheila, whose spirits had lifted from zero to ten in a matter of three days. "Very cool. I get why you want to keep it for a while as a reminder. Anywhere special you're celebrating tonight?"

"Pit Stop!" Tiff shimmied her shoulders and laughed out loud. "Where else? Happy hour starts at five, which reminds me, we'd better get our outfits sorted." She turned to the couple next to them. "You guys coming?"

"Nah. You girls have fun. We'll just stay here and enjoy the free drinks," the woman said, flashing her all-inclusive wristband.

"Okay, well enjoy the rest of the day and have a lovely night, ladies. Make sure not to get any more tattoos," Stella joked as she walked off. She made a mental note to tell Lisa about it. It was funny how she felt the need to share everything with her, because Lisa just got it, and they had laughed so much together over the weekend. She missed not seeing her by the poolside today yet waking up with her more than made up for that, of course. Contemplating calling her, she decided against it. She didn't want to disturb her or come across as needy, and if she couldn't even wait a couple of days, then what was she going to do when Lisa moved back to the UK?

32

"What are you doing here?" Lisa asked, pleasantly surprised to see Stella as she opened her bedroom door. She was wrapped in a towel after a cold shower and was just about to get dressed for dinner. They'd waved at each other a couple of times in the past few days, and they'd talked a little in passing but other than that, they hadn't had any personal contact. Lisa hadn't wanted to message her, afraid she'd come across as too keen, and she felt silly about how much she'd been overthinking things. She hadn't been like this when she'd first started dating Sandrine, but with Stella, it felt like each action could have major consequences and that was daunting. Relieved to finally have her to herself for a moment, she opened the door wider, giving into the butterflies that made her weak in the knees.

"Hey. I'm on a break." Stella took off her mask and held up a pair of shades. "Are these yours?"

"Yes! Thank you so much, I thought I'd lost them." Lisa looked behind her to check the room, but it wasn't overly messy. "Want to come in?"

"Not sure if I can do that." Stella glanced into the corridor, then chuckled as she stepped in anyway. "But I have no willpower when a beautiful woman invites me in, so as long as no one sees me I was never here." She gasped and slammed a hand in front of her mouth as she looked around the small room. "What the fuck? Is this where you've been living all this time?"

"Yes, this is home for now. Why are you so shocked? Have you never seen the rooms?" Lisa asked. She followed Stella's gaze, mildly amused at how quickly she'd gotten used to her room. At first it had been her idea of hell but now it was... well, it was just her home, she supposed, and she didn't mind it anymore.

"No, I don't work in housekeeping, so I have no business wandering into the rooms." Stella closed the door behind her. "I shouldn't even be on this floor." Running a hand over a big stain on the wall, she shook her head as her eyes darted to the balcony and Lisa's 'nest'.

"That's where I sit, and sometimes even sleep at night because I like the breeze," Lisa said, opening the chest of drawers where she kept her underwear. "I only use the air conditioning for an hour before I go to bed because I hate the smell of mould with the doors closed." She rummaged through her lingerie and took out her nicest set, just because Stella was here.

"I can't believe it." Stella scanned the room once more, then looked at the bed. "Is it comfortable? It looks old."

Lisa laughed. "Why don't you try it for yourself?" When Stella got on the bed and lay down, she followed and straddled her. It creaked and the mattress sunk down in the middle, forming a U-shape. "Okay, maybe better not. It's obviously not built to hold two people off the ground."

Stella pulled Lisa back when she was about to get off the

bed. "Hey, where do you think you're going?" she asked with a chuckle. "I'm finally in your room and you're only wearing a towel. I'd be crazy not to take advantage of the situation." She took the white bra and knickers Lisa was holding and threw them across the room, then glanced at the door when they heard voices.

"No one is going to come in," Lisa assured her. "I've got the 'do not disturb' sign on the door and the cleaners have never been in before five." She opened the towel that was secured at the front, playfully flashing her body at Stella, then dropped it next to the bed.

"Mmm..." Stella ran her hands along Lisa's waist, then cupped her breasts when Lisa leaned in to kiss her. "Then let's make the most of my forty-minute break, shall we?"

"That sounds like a plan." Lisa shot her a wide grin. "And since you're the one on a break, why don't you lie back and relax?" She took off Stella's polo shirt and her sports bra, then nudged her, making her fall back into the pillows. Kissing her way down her neck, her collarbone and her breasts, she inhaled the delicious and intoxicating scent of warm, sun-kissed skin.

"Not bad for a lunch break," Stella said through heavy breaths. "I'd better not tell my colleagues I've been in the 'hot girl's' room," she joked when Lisa crawled back to unbutton her shorts. "You know that's what they call you, right?"

Lisa chuckled as she tugged down her shorts and briefs. "Is that so?" she asked in a sultry voice, then moved back up to meet her mouth. Arching a brow, she ran her tongue over Stella's bottom lip. "I thought they called me 'Miss Grumpy'."

"That too." Stella's breath hitched when Lisa lowered her hand between her legs. "But most of them..." Lisa's fingers circled her clit, and she moaned. "...call you the hot... Fuck!"

"A hot fuck, huh? I can do that," Lisa whispered. Her lips pulled into a smile as she slid her fingers lower and gasped at the wet heat she felt. She kissed Stella while she entered her, moved over her in sensual movements and fucked her slowly until Stella was writhing underneath her. She loved having her at her mercy; it made her feel wanted and desired and all those things she hadn't felt in such a long time. And she loved how the normally assertive Stella let go when she pleasured her, how she gave herself entirely. It blew her mind every time, and when Stella started tensing up underneath her and her moans grew louder, Lisa met her thrusting hips in a faster pace, stifling her cries with her mouth. She felt her contractions around her fingers, her quick breathing against her chest, the tremble in her limbs and the energy that coursed through them both as she stayed inside her until Stella let out a long, satisfied sigh. With Stella in her bed, she didn't mind her room one bit.

33

"*I* have to go soon." Stella glanced at her watch and jutted out her bottom lip. Her arms were wrapped around Lisa's waist, and it was so nice that she wished the last five minutes of her break could last forever. This was the best break ever, without a doubt. Even with the balcony doors wide open, it still felt like there was no oxygen in the room, yet she could happily stay here for many more hours. They were clammy and tired, both the heat and the thrilling satisfaction of after-sex relaxation sending them into a sleepy state.

"Can't you be late? You're the boss, right?" Lisa asked, trailing a fingertip over her breasts.

"Not sure if I can get away with that." Stella smiled and caught her hand. She was already getting turned on again, her breath quickening and her centre throbbing. "God, you're so distracting. I won't be able to keep my mind on my job after what you just did to me."

"I like being your distraction." Lisa batted her lashes and licked her lips seductively. "You can come up here any time you want. We could make it a lunch break tradition."

"As much as I like that idea, I think my team would be onto me." Stella stared at the shimmer on Lisa's lower lip and unable to resist, she pulled her in to kiss her, sinking into Lisa's hungry mouth that set her on fire. They were both insatiable around each other and that was something she'd never experienced with another woman before. When they finally broke apart, they were out of breath and Lisa's eyes were dark with desire. "Fuck, I really have to go now."

"I know." Lisa groaned, equally regretful. "Do you need a towel? You might want to have a shower before you go back out there."

"Nah, I like smelling of you." Stella glanced around the room again. "Listen, I can't let you stay here any longer. Frankly, I don't see how you managed until now; a student dorm room would have been better." She turned on her side to face Lisa and said something that surprised herself. "You can move in with me if you want."

Lisa stared at her quietly, and Stella could feel her heart pounding in her chest. She hadn't planned to offer her home, but after seeing Lisa's room and getting carried away in the afterglow of their lovemaking, she'd just blurted it out. Was it too much too soon?

"Are you serious?" Lisa asked in a whisper. A man and a woman entered the room next door and started arguing. The walls were so thin that it sounded like they were right there in the room with them.

"Come on; don't tell me you can sleep like this. Surely it must get worse at night," Stella said.

"I have earbuds." Lisa ran a hand over Stella's cheek. "I've already booked my additional month and they're keeping this room free so I don't have to move my stuff. It's not so bad at Paradise when you're around. I kind of like it here now."

"But this is a place to put up with for a couple of weeks at most, not months," Stella argued. Suddenly, she wanted this more than anything.

"It's very kind of you to offer but I don't want to be in your way and besides, I've already paid for it, not to mention I still have two weeks left on the initial period."

"Stop." Stella placed a finger on Lisa's lips, hushing her. "I can get you your money back, at least for the extra month you booked, and you wouldn't be in my way."

Lisa shook her head. "Well, I can't accept it, it's too much."

"I'm serious, Lisa. I'd love to have you around, and there's a spare room if you want privacy."

"I'm not worried about privacy. In fact, I like this very much." Lisa snuggled closer against Stella, sighing contentedly at the body contact.

"Then come and stay with me."

Lisa was silent for long moments as she looked at her intently. "You're really serious, aren't you?"

"Never been more serious. And it might seem a little much, but it's not like we're diving into a relationship. You need a place to stay, I have a room. It seems like a no-brainer." Stella grinned. "Plus, you're incredibly cute, so that's a bonus for me."

Lisa laughed. "You're not giving up, are you?"

"Nope."

"Okay, let's say I took you up on your generous offer. I'd pay you rent, of course, and I'd put all my stuff in the spare bedroom, so you won't have to look at my mess. And you must tell me what annoys you. Some people are really anal about their fridge for example, or maybe you won't like me cooking in your kitchen or you won't like—"

"Shhh... Chill out," Stella interrupted her. "We can talk

about stuff like that later but I'm sure it will be fine." She pinched Lisa's behind and smiled mischievously. "You know what the best thing would be about you staying with me?"

"What's that?"

"We wouldn't have to sneak around anymore. And I can kiss you anywhere and any time I like."

Lisa returned her smile, resisting the urge to pull her back in when Stella got up and gathered her clothes. "Hmm... that does sound appealing."

Stella got dressed and blew her a kiss before she left. "Think about it. It will be fun."

34

"*H*ey, babe, what are you up to? Working on your tan?"

"Hey, Ebs! One moment." Lisa put her phone on speaker and placed it on the bed, then continued folding her clothes into neat piles. After she and Stella had talked about it some more during a long walk last night, Stella had convinced her to move in sooner rather than later, as there was no point in Lisa staying at the hotel if she could be much more comfortable at her house. She felt excited, scared and nervous. What if they argued? She may have trouble finding another room at this price, especially now that high season had started. What if the opposite happened? If everything was wonderful... Both were a recipe for disaster because their lives were in different countries.

"Lisa?" Ebony paused. "Are you there?"

"Sorry, I'm back," Lisa said, pulled out of her thoughts. "I'm in my room, packing my things."

"Oh... Are you coming back to the UK? Do you have an interview?"

"No, I'm moving in with a new friend." On the one hand,

Lisa really wanted to tell Ebony about Stella, on the other, what Stella and she had going on wasn't serious enough to call a relationship and until she knew what to call it, she'd rather keep it to herself. But Ebony wasn't one to fool; she'd find out anyway.

Ebony chuckled. "Are you moving in with 'someone who works there?'"

"Her name is Stella." Lisa laughed too. "And yes, I am. I'll be in Spain for another six weeks. I'd still love you to visit but you might have to book a hotel nearby."

"Of course I'm coming. As your best friend, I want to be the first to meet your new girlfriend." She whistled. "Jesus, Lisa. Moving in already? Talk about typical lesbian."

"No, it's not like that, she's not my girlfriend. Stella has a spare room, and we really get along, so it made sense."

"So, you'll be sleeping in the spare room?" Ebony asked in a sarcastic tone.

Lisa smiled as she sat down on the bed. "I doubt it," she admitted. "But the option is there if I want to."

"Right. So, you'll be sleeping in the same bed for six weeks. Romantic dinners, waking up together, long walks on the beach... are you really so naive to think this won't get serious?" Ebony hesitated. "Are you exclusive?"

Lisa winced at the question because frankly, she didn't know what Stella was up to on the many nights they didn't see each other. She hadn't stayed over that often, worried that it would be too much, even though Stella had told her she was always welcome.

"Look," Ebony continued when Lisa didn't answer. "You're clearly head over heels with this woman because moving into someone's house on a whim is seriously out of character for you. And don't get me wrong, I'm so, so happy that you're finally having fun and having sex again," she added with a hint of humour, "but I'm just looking out for you as your friend. I don't want you to get hurt."

"I won't." Lisa cleared her throat and started piling her clothes into her first suitcase. "But enough about me. How's the new job?"

Ebony sighed, clearly frustrated she was changing the subject. "The job is good. Not as fun as when I worked with you, of course. But most of my colleagues are cool, and the senior position provides a fulfilling challenge. It took a couple of weeks to get into the flow but I'm starting to feel confident now."

"That's great." Lisa smiled, happy for her friend. "So, they're giving you time off?"

"That's actually why I called. I can come for three nights —a long weekend—at the end of August if you're still there."

"Yes, I'll be here. I'll send you some options for hotels. I'd ask Stella if you could stay with her; I honestly don't think she'd mind, but I just want to see how this goes first."

"No need. I'd rather not listen to you two getting it on at night," Ebony said humorously. "And at the speed you're moving, you'll probably have your wedding around that time, so I'll make sure to bring my bridesmaid's dress."

"Stop making fun of me." Lisa rolled her eyes and smirked. "I told you, I'm not moving in-in. It's just a practical temporary flatmate situation, that's all."

"Sleeping in one bed certainly seems like the most prac-tical solution." Ebony's full laugh roared from Lisa's phone speaker, and Lisa couldn't help but laugh along. "Okay, I'll stop teasing you," she finally said. "Tell me about her. What does she do? What does she look like? And most impor-tantly, how is the sex?"

"She's very cute," Lisa said, smiling as she pictured Stella's face. "Spanish, about my height, shortish dark hair, a dazzling smile... She's the poolside manager here, and she lives in a town about fifteen minutes from Benidorm with her five cats. She's kind and fun and she has serious charisma." She hesitated. "And the sex... My God, it's out of this world, like we were physically made for each other."

"Phew. It's getting hot in here," Ebony said in a high-pitched tone and Lisa imagined her fanning her face. "Happy to hear you're quite literally in good hands. And she sounds totally different from Sandrine, which is a bonus."

"You're the second person to tell me that," Lisa said, remembering her brother's comment. "Was Sandrine really that bad?" She zipped closed her case before she opened the next and placed it on her bed.

"Not really bad, just not good enough for you. I don't think she ever fulfilled you emotionally."

As Lisa shifted her attention to her underwear drawer and pulled everything out, she realised that Ebony was right. Sandrine had never made her laugh and smile the way Stella did. "No, she didn't," she said, hoping she'd made the right decision.

35

"Yo, Stella! What are you doing with that suitcase?"

Stella muttered a curse when Manuel walked up to her car as they were loading in Lisa's luggage. "Nothing," she said in a defensive tone, then reminded herself that they didn't have to sneak around anymore. She'd purposely parked around the corner where her colleagues rarely came as they tended to walk the other direction, into town or to the bus stop opposite Paradise Hotel after work but really, there was no need to be secretive. "Just moving Lisa out."

Manuel looked shocked to see Lisa appear behind the car after she slammed the boot shut. "Oh, it's you. Are you leaving? Going back to the UK?"

"No. Just moving out of Paradise." Lisa shot him a nervous smile, then glanced at Stella, leaving the decision on what to tell him to her. When Stella didn't answer, she put a large weekend bag on the back seat, closed the door and crossed her arms as she leaned against the car.

Manuel studied them both with a frown. "Sorry to hear

that." He hesitated, looking uncomfortable as he shuffled from one foot to the other, his hands deep in his pockets. "Before you go, I just wanted to say... Well, I guess I should have apologised for that night a long time ago, but Stella told me it would be best to leave you alone."

Lisa shrugged and shot him a small smile. "It's okay. Long forgotten."

"Thank you. I really am sorry," he said. "Which hotel are you moving to?"

"She's not going to a hotel." Stella impatiently tapped the bonnet of the car while she waited for Manuel to walk on. When he made no effort to move, she let out a long sigh and confessed. "Lisa's moving in with me for the remainder of her stay."

"Oh..."

"Yeah..." She shot Manuel a toothy smile. Now that she'd admitted it, she was enjoying his baffled reaction. He looked from her to Lisa and back, wide-eyed, no doubt speculating what was going on between them. 'The hot girl' was moving in with *her* of all people, and she knew he wouldn't be able to keep that to himself. It didn't matter all that much though, as Lisa was not a guest anymore and it was no one's business who Stella invited to stay at her house. "I just figured I have enough space, the cats would love some company while I'm at work and it beats Paradise, so why not?"

"The cats, of course," Manuel said with a hint of humour. "I'm sure the cats will be delighted." He turned to Lisa. "Well, you're lucky; Stella's got a nice place. I stayed in the guest room after one of her famous pizza nights on that amazing roof terrace."

Lisa nodded. "Yes. I love her place and I'm very grateful."

Stella chuckled at the cat comment and a silence

followed. A playful look passed between them as she met Lisa's eyes. There was no way Manuel hadn't spotted their electric chemistry, so she shot him a wink before she opened the door. *Fuck it*, she thought. Her colleagues were going to gossip anyway, so why keep secrets? "But Lisa won't be staying in the guest room."

Lisa got in the car too and they laughed as she drove off. "Did you see his face?" she asked, wiping tears of laughter from her cheeks.

"I did. I'm sorry but I just couldn't resist." Stella put a hand on Lisa's thigh. "You don't mind, do you? That was a little naughty of me; I probably shouldn't have said that."

"Are you kidding me? That was priceless."

Stepping on the accelerator, Stella felt on top of the world as she drove towards Altea. She had her crush next to her and they would be spending six weeks together. She couldn't even begin to imagine how nice it would be to wake up next to Lisa every morning. To see her beautiful face and cute smile first thing. "I think I've just made myself the most popular woman at Paradise."

"I gathered from the pizza night comment you're pretty popular already," Lisa said. "Staff parties?"

"Sometimes. The last time I threw one was just before you moved here. To celebrate finally getting back to work again. We never thought we'd actually celebrate being able to work, but God, we were so excited that week we got the news about the no-restrictions, full-house opening."

Lisa smiled. "You're a great manager. I've watched you with your team; they like you."

"I hope so. Because I like them." Stella turned onto the main road and opened her window. "Are you ready to put up with me?"

"I think the question is, are you ready to put up with

me?" Lisa retorted. Stella moved her hand further up her thigh, and it did all kinds of things to Lisa's body. Just a simple touch was enough to send her libido into overdrive; that was what Stella did to her.

"Trust me; I couldn't think of anything better."

"So, what about your lovers?" Lisa asked. The question came out of nowhere and startled Stella. "I should probably have asked you about this a while back, but are you seeing other women?" Lisa asked in a more serious tone. "I need to know because I'll get jealous if you do and…" Her voice trailed away, and she shook her head as if she already regretted bringing it up.

Stella glanced at her for a moment to gauge if she was serious and when she saw Lisa's uncomfortable expression, she shook her head. "Hey, I wouldn't do that. Why would you even think I'd do such a thing? Seeing other women while we've got this great thing going on?" Truth be told, perhaps it wasn't such a strange question after all. She hadn't been in a committed relationship in years, and Lisa knew that. Add to that the fact that Lisa was only here temporarily, it kind of made sense that it had crossed her mind. "I wouldn't do that," she repeated, shooting Lisa an earnest look.

"I'm sorry, but I had to ask. We never talked about it and I guess I just need to know what to expect if I'll be living with you."

"Well, I can tell you now that I haven't even as much as looked at another woman since that morning you came for a coffee with me."

"Really?" Lisa smiled.

"Yes. Have you been on dates with other women?"

"No, of course not."

Stella pointed a finger between them. "I don't want

anyone else, Lisa. You're all I think of." She paused, wondering how honest she should really be right now, then decided to just fess up. "So that morning when you came out for a coffee with me..."

"What about that morning?"

"I didn't realise it right away, but I think I fell for you then. I mean, I thought you were cute and sexy before that, but when you were in the car next to me, doing that thing with your hand... I watched your hair blow in the wind, and I had trouble keeping my eyes on the road. You've been on my mind ever since."

Lisa looked at her hand that was dancing on the wind and let out a shy chuckle. "What? This?"

"Yes, you have no idea how cute you are when you do that."

"Oh." Lisa bit her lip and grinned. "Well, I also have a confession to make. I googled you right after I came back that day."

Stella laughed. "Really? What did you find?"

"Not much. Just some information about you on the hotel's website. It said that you liked cats and flamenco. And then I tried to find videos of you dancing," she admitted.

Stella threw her head back and laughed. "I don't dance, I just like to watch. So, you looked me up..."

"Yes. I didn't want to admit that I'd been digging, but since we're sharing..." Lisa paused. "You've been on my mind too, since that day."

Stella turned into Altea and found a parking space close to the square. They should have had this conversation before today, and she was glad Lisa had brought it up. She turned off the engine but remained seated and shifted to face her. "Look, I'm not naive. I know you won't stay here forever, but I also want you to know that I'm serious about you for as long as you'll be here."

Lisa swallowed hard and a rosy blush appeared on her cheeks. She nodded slowly, then looked down at her lap. "Me too," she said in a soft whisper before lifting her chin to meet Stella's eyes. "And thank you again, for letting me stay with you. Not just because my room in Paradise is small and basic, but because I like to be near you."

"The pleasure's all mine." Stella's core filled with warmth as she leaned in to kiss her. There was so much more she wanted to say, but at the same time, anything else seemed pointless. They were drifting in a weird place, a temporary place, but she didn't want to think about that as it would only ruin the limited time they had. Forcing those thoughts away, she pulled away and smiled. "Welcome to Altea."

36

"Mmm... I could get used to this." Stella ran a hand up Lisa's thigh and gave her that lustful stare that made Lisa ache with longing again, even though they'd just made love.

"Me too." She shivered at Stella's touch and the intensity in her gaze. She was immensely physical, and Lisa loved that. No one had ever looked at her the way Stella did, and their need to constantly be all over each other was mesmerising. "Aren't you worried though?" she asked, then leaned in and kissed Stella's shoulder up to her neck and her ear, making her moan softly. Wrapped in white sheets, they were sitting up in bed, drinking coffee with the windows wide open. She loved waking up like this, to the sound of birdsong, Stella's cats and the Spanish music coming from the café on the square. A week in, and she hadn't slept in the guest room once.

"Worried about what? That we'll exhaust ourselves from having too much sex?" Stella chuckled. "Please specify."

Lisa grinned. "What I meant was, aren't you worried we'll grow too close? Because I'll have to return to London at some point. Even if I don't find a job to go back to, I'll run out of funds and besides, I can only stay in Spain for three months unless I work here."

"I know." Stella sighed as she turned to her, resting her temple against the headboard. "But I'd rather have you now than not have you at all. You British think too much." She took Lisa's hand and pressed it against her chest. "Feel my heart. You make it race, so why deny myself something good even if it might hurt down the line?"

"True." Lisa smiled as she put her coffee aside and scooted down under the covers, wrapping an arm over Stella's waist. "But you Spanish are overly passionate," she joked. "You throw yourselves into whatever you crave without thinking of the consequences."

"When it comes to passion, the consequences are usually worth it, good or bad. Otherwise, how would you ever feel alive?" Stella argued.

Lisa took a moment to think about that. She did feel alive. In fact, she hadn't felt this good in years. Not when she'd graduated, not when her relationship with Sandrine was running smoothly, not even when her career was at its peak. It was interesting that, right now, she should have been at her lowest, having nothing but an inbox full of rejections. But the truth was, she felt better than ever. "You make me happy," she finally whispered.

"You make me happy too." Stella smiled. "Do you like it here?"

"I do." Lisa hesitated. "I love it. This village is beautiful but getting to kiss you whenever I want is the main reason that I love it so much." She studied Stella, who seemed delighted with her answer. "Why do you ask?"

"Just curious." Stella's cheeks flushed, and she seemed nervous as she chewed the inside of her cheek. "Okay, I asked because I want you to come and visit me after you've moved back. Will you?"

"Of course." Lisa turned and straddled her, resting her arms on Stella's shoulders. She was adorable when she blushed. "Will you visit me in London?"

"At your parents' house?"

"If by that time I'm still in the same situation and don't have my own place, then yes. If you don't mind sharing a single bed with me and being quiet in that single bed."

"We've only used one side of the bed so far and you're the one who has a problem staying quiet," Stella retorted playfully. She wrapped her arms around Lisa's waist and shot her a teasing smile.

"Is that so?" Lisa arched a brow at her. "If I recall correctly, you weren't so quiet yourself twenty minutes ago."

Stella threw her head back and laughed. "You're right. I seem to have that problem too, and I wouldn't want to get in the bad books with your parents. The idea of meeting them sounds scary."

"They're not scary but Dad talks a lot, especially about his past. And he gets repetitive from time to time. He's not suffering from dementia or anything like that, he just likes to tell the same old stories."

"Let him. My dad loves to talk about the good old days too; it makes him happy." Stella smiled. "What do they do?"

"My parents? My dad is a retired naval officer, and my mum is the chief editor for a women's lifestyle magazine."

"Cool. That sounds fancy."

"Not really. They're just normal people. They separated when I was seventeen but got back together four years later and they've been happy together ever since," Lisa said, making a mental note to call them today. She hadn't picked up her phone last night as she'd been too busy in bed with

Stella, and it wouldn't be long before she'd get messages enquiring if she was okay. "What about your parents?"

"They're still together. In fact, they're together every hour of the day," Stella said. "They own a deli so they're constantly in each other's space and bicker all the time. It's just their way of communicating, I suppose. My younger sister works in hospitality too, and she lives not far from my parents in Seville." Stella pursed her lips, silently pondering over something. "I'm planning on visiting them soon," she finally said. "You're welcome to come along. It's a beautiful drive and I think you'd like Seville."

"To your parents' house?" Lisa asked, studying her. Of all the things she'd expected to happen when she arrived in Spain, meeting a woman was not a part of it, and meeting her parents even less so. Rowdy hotel guests? Yes. Sunshine? Yes. An underwhelming hotel? Yes, although reality had been worse. Meeting a woman who took her breath away like no one else ever had? Certainly not. And now this amazing woman had just asked if she'd like to meet her parents.

"Yes. They live in a lovely neighbourhood in Seville. They're easy-going and love to meet new people." Stella grinned. "Sorry, did I freak you out? It's just a suggestion, you don't have to come."

"No, you didn't freak me out." Lisa tried her hardest not to show how much Stella's question had affected her but inside, she was all over the place. She'd only met Sandrine's parents once, and that was after they'd lived together for four years. Ivana and Bruce had been polite and nice enough, but at the same time, she'd also felt terribly judged by them, as if their meeting was a test. Both being successful and wealthy New Yorkers with their own businesses, they'd raised Sandrine with a work ethic to match their own and that had rubbed off on her. 'What are your goals for the future?' and 'Where do you see yourself in two years?' Those questions had been fired off at her as soon as they'd sat down for dinner. Frankly, the whole conversation had sounded more like an interview than small talk between three people who were getting to know each other. No, Lisa did not have the best associations with 'meeting the parents', but the idea of meeting Stella's seemed intriguing. "Are you sure they wouldn't mind if I came along?"

"No, of course not. They'll love you." Stella took her hand and kissed it. "Who wouldn't?"

37

*R*ushing around the building, Stella internally scolded herself for being late. She was never late but having Lisa naked next to her in the mornings had changed that. It was the second day in a row that she was the last one to come in, because when Lisa threw her that look that told her she wanted her, every extra second in bed was a gift from heaven. Normally it wouldn't be a big deal—the poolside didn't open until eight-thirty anyway—but this was her own Saturday morning team meeting, and ten people were already gathered around the tiki bar, waiting for her. As always, she heard them laughing and talking but when she turned the corner everyone fell silent for a beat before smiles and greetings were cast her way.

"Hey, guys. Sorry, bad traffic," she lied, plonking her bag on an empty stool. Paradise Hotel did have a couple of meeting rooms, but they were a little depressing, so she'd moved the meetings to the bar three years ago. The smokers among them were happy as they could have a cigarette with their coffee, and in general, it was just much nicer to have their meeting in the sun. She walked around the bar, from where she normally addressed them and helped herself to a coffee. "What's up?" she asked, seeing the grinning faces. "I know you were talking about me, so you might as well admit it. Or not; I don't care either way."

Manuel held up his hands and confessed. "Okay, boss. Yes, we were talking about you. Apparently, I wasn't the only one who saw you move 'the hot girl' out of Paradise last week."

Stella arched a brow at him, then turned to the others. "Her name is Lisa and it's not what you think." *Another lie.*

"Sure, you're just friends, I've got it," Meghan, one of the newest but also most vocal members of staff, joked. "I didn't take her for a lesbian. She looks like one of those women on *Beverly Hills Housewives*. I imagined her with some tech tycoon or something but—" She stopped herself and winced.

"But not with me?" Stella asked with a chuckle as Meghan's cheeks had now turned bright red.

"No, I didn't mean it like that." Shaking her head, Meghan buried her face in her hands. "Oh, God, why do I always say the wrong things?"

"It's fine," Stella said with an amused smile. Sometimes it paid off to be amicable with her team, and sometimes, like today, the boundaries were too blurred for professional interaction, especially when she herself was the victim of team gossip. She glanced at her watch and cleared her throat. "But we're not here to discuss my love life, so let's get down to business. We have a full house again this week but only one large group to worry about. A group of fifteen is arriving late this afternoon, and they're all women, so I suspect it might be a hen party." Lisa didn't just make her forget about the time; she'd forgotten to bring her notes from her catch-up with reception yesterday, so she mentally scrolled through the bullet points she'd written down last night. "Eighty-five per cent of the arrivals are British, the others are European, apart from four Mexicans, so language shouldn't be a problem. The ratio of women to men is sixty-five to thirty-five which is unusual, so we've lowered the beer order and upped the wine. We're also expecting a larger attendance in the pool classes."

"Women," Florence said humorously. "That also means more fresh towels and a million requests for us to move those heavy parasols around."

"Possibly." Stella shrugged. She didn't like to stereotype but as things seemed to be incredibly predictable when it came to Paradise, she tended to go with her gut. Yes, women were generally more demanding, and they tended to get more emotional when drunk. They were also the ones to complain that hairdryers didn't work, or that the rooms weren't up to standard and that was totally understandable. Men didn't care all that much about amenities. All they wanted was to drink a beer in the sun. Stella could tell at first sight who were going to be troublemakers; she'd developed a sixth sense for it over the many years she'd worked in the hospitality industry. It was something about their demeanour on their day of arrival. Some men pranced around like dogs determined to establish their pecking order, talking down to the staff and flirting with other men's wives. Luckily though, their guests were generally just happy holiday makers, and serious problems were rare.

"As usual," she continued, "it will be busy until about midday, and then it will be busy again from around three pm after check-in, so try to plan your breaks accordingly. I'll put a schedule behind the bar, but feel free to swap break times if that works better for you." She took a sip of her coffee and looked at her team. "Anything you'd like to share? Questions?"

As everyone shook their heads, ten pairs of eyes stared at her curiously. Then Meghan spoke again. "Anything *you'd* like to share?" A mischievous wink, and then more laughter followed.

Stella tried to keep a straight face as she stared back at her. "No," she said in a neutral tone. Secretly, she felt a little smug, but no one needed to know that. It was time to focus and stop reliving her delicious sex-filled morning because today would be a very, very busy day and she couldn't afford to waste any more time.

38

Stepping out of the house, Lisa glanced to the left and the right, eyeing several cafés in the distance, then decided upon the café opposite Stella's house. The owner, who had spotted her coming out, waved her over and pulled out a chair for her.

"Buenos dias! English?"

"Please. I understand a little Spanish, but I'd probably confuse you if I tried to speak." Lisa smiled at him. "Sorry."

"No problem, I'm Carlo. Are you a friend of Stella's? I've seen you coming in and out of her house."

"Yes," she said, taking a seat. "I'm Lisa. I'm staying with her for a while." She pointed to her laptop bag. "Do you mind if I work here?"

Carlo shook his head. "No, no, go ahead and stay as long as you want."

"Thank you. Stella's got a great roof terrace but one of her cats loves to sit on my keyboard, so after several failed attempts to fight him off this morning, I thought I'd venture out."

"Pablo?" Carlo asked.

"Yes, Pablo. He's so sweet but he's also decided to be my right-hand man. Helping me type, clear my pens away, clean my screen—even my nose at times and—"

"And stir your coffee?" Carlo finished her sentence.

Lisa threw her head back and laughed. "How did you know about that?"

"Stella told me and then I found out first-hand when Pablo became more confident in his new habitat and started venturing into my territory. He got friendly with my customers; sat on the free chairs and all that, but I had to be strict and chase him away as he started making a habit of sticking his paws in the milk foam on the cappuccinos and stealing their cookies." Carlo's eyes narrowed into slits as he looked up at the thatched roofs opposite them and grinned. "There he is, the fat coño. I don't know what Stella feeds him, but he's still growing." He pulled a notebook and a pencil from his back pocket. "Anyway, what can I get you?"

"An iced latte, please. And anything sweet you recommend," Lisa added.

"Something sweet? Do you like walnuts? Have you tried casadielles?"

"No, I don't think I have."

"Okay, then you need to try it." Carlo went back inside, leaving Lisa in the blissful silence of the morning. She opened her laptop and saw there were another four emails from headhunters, but the subject lines did not look promising. A woman joined her on the table next to her, and she gave her a smile.

"Good morning. It's a beautiful day, isn't it?" she said in a Northern English accent.

"Yes, wonderful." Lisa turned to her. The woman was in her sixties, she guessed. Her dark hair was white at the roots and going on her tanned skin, she was a sun-lover. She wore a short, purple strapless dress and gold sandals, and her nails were painted in the same shade of purple. Despite her typical British appearance, Lisa sensed that she was part of the community here, from the way she interacted with Carlo when he approached her, and her fluent Spanish when she ordered an Americano. "Do you live here?"

"Yes, I live nearby and I love to have my first coffee here if the weather permits. I'm all for starting my day in the best possible way." The woman smiled at her and held out her hand. "I'm Delia. Are you local?"

"No, I'm just staying with a friend. I'm Lisa," Lisa said, shaking her hand.

"Nice to meet you." Delia's attention shifted to Lisa's laptop. "Are you one of those fancy bloggers?"

"I wish." Lisa laughed. "I'm job hunting, actually. No luck so far," she said. "But I was thinking of looking into some local opportunities today, just to keep myself busy until I find something long-term."

"Really?" Delia moved her chair away from the shade of the parasol and stretched her legs out. "I'm not surprised you want to stay. A lot of people who come here either return shortly after or never leave."

"Hmm..." Lisa didn't want to tell her it was desperation that had driven her to this point, so she gave her a beaming smile. And as she smiled, it felt real, like she meant it. Like she actually *did* want to stay here. "Who knows? I may be one of those people," she said in a tone that sounded way less loaded than it suddenly felt.

"What do you do?" Delia asked.

"I work in marketing. It's really hard to find a job at the moment."

"Okay. Well, I don't know anything about marketing but I'm sure there will be plenty of jobs going around here, if you don't mind working with small businesses, designing their websites and stuff."

Although designing websites had nothing to do with what Lisa did for a living, she nodded and smiled anyway. "Yes, I'll look into that. Do you work?"

Delia waved a hand and rolled her eyes as if that was a ridiculous question. "No, darling. Not really, anyway, but my husband does. He owns a construction business, and my daughter works for him; she's a builder and also his site manager. I just paint and drink wine, mostly."

"That sounds like a nice life," Lisa said in an amused tone. "Is your work on display anywhere?" She pointed in the direction of the street with all the galleries.

"Yes, I share a gallery with a friend." Delia rummaged through her handbag and handed Lisa a card. "Check out my website and stop by any time if you're interested in seeing my work. Or just for a chat and a glass of wine. I'm there every day from four pm onwards."

"Thanks, I will."

Carlo came out with their coffees and Lisa's pastry, and when he started a long conversation with Delia in Spanish, Lisa picked up her phone and looked up Diego Calvo's number that Stella had sent her. Perhaps today, she should start her morning differently and chase opportunities instead of reading the rejection emails first thing. There was no harm in making a call to see if Mr Calvo was open to meeting with her. What was the worst thing that could happen?

39

"*H*ey, beautiful. Are you still working on that presentation?" Stella ran a hand through Lisa's hair and leaned in to kiss her cheek. She'd just finished a late shift and it was almost ten pm by the time she got home to find Lisa behind her laptop on the roof terrace, surrounded by candles. She'd been working non-stop, three days in a row. "You must be a good talker since Diego Calvo agreed to meet with you."

"I don't know about that. I just pressured him, mostly," Lisa joked. "Anyway, I'm almost done." She turned to Stella with a beaming smile. "I've got two proposals. One teaser and the final one is close to perfect too, just in case he bites. Best to be prepared."

"That's my girl." Stella kneaded her shoulders, drawing groans of pleasure from Lisa's lips.

"I'm sure you're tired; I'll talk you through it tomorrow."

"I'm okay, actually. Have you eaten?" Stella glanced at the half-empty bottle of wine on the table.

"No, I got sucked into this and totally forgot about food or anything for that matter. I did feed the cats though; Pablo kindly reminded me." Lisa leaned back, rested her head against Stella's stomach and looked up at her. "Have you eaten?"

"A while ago, but I'm feeling hungry again. Want me to make a pizza?" Stella laughed at Lisa's reaction as her eyes widened.

"Would you do that? Really?"

"Of course. And I'm off tomorrow, so if you have energy left, you can show me your presentation while we eat."

Lisa stood up and fell around Stella's neck, surprising her with her enthusiasm. "You're the best, you know that?" She closed her laptop and took her hand. "I'll help you. Show me how you make those delicious masterpieces of yours. I'd like to learn so I can make them for *you* next time."

"Wow, with this reaction I'll make you pizza every day," Stella said as she pulled Lisa into the kitchen. She turned on the oven, opened her freezer, took out a Tupperware container with tomato sauce and put it in the microwave to defrost. Then she found a large bowl and poured in a generous amount of flour. She didn't even need to measure the ingredients anymore; she'd done it so many times that she could probably do it blindfolded. "Flour, a sachet of yeast, a pinch of salt"—she mixed the ingredients and made a hole in the middle—"And some good quality olive oil."

"You're quick," Lisa remarked.

"I am. I don't want to make a hungry lady wait now, do I?"

Lisa shot her a flirty glance as she washed her hands. "I take it you want me to get down and dirty with that?" She glanced at the bowl.

"I do." Stella stepped aside so Lisa could get in front of the bowl. It was sexy to watch her mix and knead the ingredients together. "Just a little bit longer," she said when Lisa turned to her for guidance. "Yes, that's perfect. Now make a ball, cover it with a wet tea towel and leave it on the counter to rest while we get the ingredients together."

"Is that all?" Lisa asked with a puzzled look.

"There's not much else to it, apart from my secret tomato sauce," Stella said, pulling the container out of the microwave. "I batch cook it and freeze it so I'm never out."

"Sounds intriguing. Why is it secret?"

"It's my grandmother's recipe for albondigas. Spanish meatballs in tomato sauce. Except I tend to put it on pizzas instead."

"Did she teach you how to make it?"

"Yes. Many, many years ago. She's not around anymore, bless her soul. Taste it."

Lisa opened the container, dipped a finger in the sauce and licked it off in a sensual manner, her flirty eyes meeting Stella's. "Mmm... it's good."

Stella closed the distance between them, leaned into her and took her hand. "I think I'll have to check too, just in case. Sometimes the flavour gets diluted after it's been frozen." She dipped Lisa's finger in the sauce again and sucked it off, causing Lisa to take in a quick breath.

"I like cooking with you," she said in a sultry voice. "What do you think?"

"Not sure. Let me try some more." Stella took three of her fingers now and dipped them in the sauce, then sucked them one by one, closing her eyes in the process. She knew she was driving Lisa crazy, the all too familiar sounds she made causing her to ache with longing. Unable to control herself, she grabbed her behind and lifted her onto the kitchen surface, chuckling when Lisa's whole hand landed in the sauce.

"Jesus, Stella! Do you intend to cover me in that sauce?" Lisa threw her head back and laughed, then spread her legs so Stella could step in between them.

"That's actually not a bad idea. But I'm going to clean this up first." After licking Lisa's hand clean until she was a heaving mess, Stella took hold of the hem of her top and lifted it over her head. Seeing she wasn't wearing a bra turned her on even more, and the hard nipples were so inviting that she couldn't stop herself from scooping a spoonful of the lukewarm tomato sauce and dripping it over them.

"Hey! What are you doing?" Lisa giggled, but her playful smile told Stella she liked it.

"Just enjoying my delicious sauce." Stella leaned over her and licked the sauce off her breasts, making sure she didn't miss an inch of her delicious skin. Folding her lips around the hard, pink nipples she'd been dying to caress all day, she sucked at them and tugged them between her teeth. The woman she adored was sitting on her kitchen counter, letting her devour her with her mouth. She thought of Lisa constantly, and she'd been distracted at work to the point that Manuel had made fun of her. 'I can see where your mind is,' he'd said, but she didn't care that people were talking.

Her mouth traced Lisa's belly down to the waistband of her denim skirt, and she lifted it up, then continued underneath it until her hot breath was between Lisa's legs. She tugged at her underwear with her teeth and could feel Lisa's wetness against her mouth as she wiggled and moaned in her grip.

"Dessert already?" Lisa asked, her eyes filled with anticipation. She lifted her hips so Stella could pull down her knickers. "We haven't even had pizza yet."

Stella shot her a mischievous smile as she threw her underwear behind her, then bent down again to trace her tongue over Lisa's folds. "Dessert first," she mumbled. "Always." A guttural groan escaped her when Lisa lifted her legs over her shoulders, pushing her pulsing centre against her mouth. She'd take dessert over anything, any time. The way Lisa moved, breathed, moaned was sensuality in its purest form, and it made her throb. She darted her tongue inside her, then moved to her clit, circling it until Lisa cried out loud enough for her neighbours to hear.

"Yes!" Lisa fell back, not caring about the flour or the splatter of tomato sauce on the surface. "Yes, yes, yes!" Grabbing a fistful of Stella's hair, she pulled her tighter against her and cried out, shaking all over.

"Mmm..." Stella kept her mouth there until Lisa came back to her senses and sat up to look at her, wide-eyed and bewildered. Licking her lips, she shot her a smirk. Pizza would never be the same again.

40

"**W**hat was it that you wanted to discuss, Miss...?"

"Walker. Lisa Walker." Lisa handed Diego Calvo her CV that she'd printed out on beautiful, thick paper in a copy shop she'd stopped by that morning. They were sitting in the local Calvo Group office that was situated in a tall building on the outskirts of Benidorm. Tastefully decorated in dark colours with deep, brown leather sofas, bold-striped, burgundy wallpaper and an antique drinks cabinet, it reminded her more of a gentlemen's club than an office. "I heard through the grapevine that you were planning on buying Premier Sunset and I had some ideas I thought might interest you," she continued and smiled as she folded her hands in front of her. "Ideas on how to change the hotel and make it work to its advantage." Diego was only half-listening as his phone flashed, and he took his time to type a reply before he even met her eyes. It was a little rude, but she supposed he was a busy man.

"Yes, I gathered as much but I'll be honest with you. If you hadn't been so persistent on the phone, I wouldn't have invited you over," he finally said. "Frankly, I don't know what there is to discuss, it's a straightforward job and we've done dozens of basic overhauls over the years. We don't need someone to advise us on how to change it or run it. We'll buy it, do some maintenance, cut down on staff, price it competitively and we're good to go."

"I was actually going to suggest the opposite," Lisa said carefully, studying his reaction to figure out if he was open to constructive feedback. She was not going to leave until he'd listened to what she had to say.

"Is this a joke?" Diego frowned. "And what makes you an expert on the hospitality business?" His gaze lowered to her CV for the first time, and he smirked when he scanned through it. There was no hospitality work on Lisa's CV. None whatsoever.

Lisa looked at him, unfazed. "I'm an expert in customer perception and experience and that's the most important thing when it comes to running any business." She pointed to her CV. "As you can see, I've worked for many big brands over the years and I've managed to make them even more successful by applying drastic changes on branding, marketing, PR, and as I mentioned, on customer experience level. I know what I'm talking about." For a moment, she thought Diego was going to laugh in her face, but instead, he nodded for her to continue.

"Go on."

"There is an opportunity for you here to change Premier Sunset into a very profitable business. First of all, the hotel name needs to change as it gives a false suggestion," she said. "Premier Sunset has no sun and suggesting otherwise will only result in complaints and low ratings." She paused as he let it sink in.

"Okay, but changing the name is not going to generate more income."

"It will if you give it an overhaul and triple the prices on the rooms."

As expected, Diego burst out laughing. "Why would they book Premier Sunset if they can get a room cheaper elsewhere? No sun and triple the price?"

"Because it will be tailored to a different market. Customers such as yourself." Lisa tilted her head and held eye contact to keep his attention. "Are you based in Benidorm? Is this your head office?" she asked, pretending she knew nothing about him.

"No, I'm based in Madrid. I'm generally only here one week a month."

"Right. And where do you stay when you come to Benidorm?"

"At the airport hotel in Alicante."

"Interesting." Lisa fell silent. "So, you don't even stay at your own hotels. And why is that?"

"Because I'd rather go camping than stay in a tourist-riddled hotel where I have to dodge drunk people and screaming children."

"Exactly. There are no hotels around here where you would even want to stay. And I'm not just talking about you. Tons of developers, hoteliers and other business people visit Benidorm both in summer and winter. And there's nowhere for them to stay because everything is tailored to tourists and focused on the holiday market. This is an opportunity for Premier Sunset to ensure occupancy all year round."

"Still not one bit convinced," Diego said. "I wouldn't want to stay at Premier Sunset. Not in a million years." He grimaced. "Everything about it is grim."

"I won't argue with that. So, my next question is, what do *you* need from a hotel?"

Diego's expression was more than sceptical now, but he answered anyway. "A bar with quality alcohol and wines, a restaurant with nice food and a decent room with excellent Wi-Fi and a good bed. A meeting space that doesn't look like a dentist's waiting room would be a bonus too."

"Your priorities are not sun and a buffet," Lisa concluded, pleased with his answer. "Premier Sunset is much smaller than most hotels along the strip. You could turn it into a boutique business hotel. Think lovely and simple rooms with a wonderful shaded outside seating area, a fantastic restaurant with good, Spanish food and a smart bar where you can enjoy a nightcap and meet like-minded people. A real Spanish vibe; understated and charming. A place to make valuable contacts."

"That will cost a fortune." Diego sounded stern, but Lisa could already see him wavering, allowing the information to sink in bit by bit. Now he would just have to sleep on it. Maybe a week, maybe a month. But sooner or later he would come to the conclusion that she was right, because it was just common sense. It was to her, anyway. She could see how people who had worked here for years got stuck in their ways, using the same formula over and over until the market was saturated. At that point, the only way to get guests in was to drop their prices and that wasn't a profitable strategy.

"It doesn't have to cost a fortune. Terracotta paint on the outside of the building, in the courtyard and along the pool-side, lots of plants—which are cheap here anyway—wooden tables and benches, traditional fabrics and simple things like cushions, lanterns and candles will go a long way. There's no need to splash out on ultra-modern design furniture; we're in Spain, so why not celebrate the country's heritage?"

"What budget do you have in mind?" Diego asked. "And how would we reach these business travellers?"

"I've put together a loose plan for you," she said. "Free of charge, of course. If you're interested, you can hire my services to do a more in-depth proposal that includes branding, name suggestions, customer experience et cetera. It's simple; if you keep the same formula, you may make a profit but if you invest and change the destination plan, your smallest hotel could generate the biggest profit."

"Right... I must say, you know how to sell yourself, Miss..." He stalled for a moment, realising he'd forgotten her name already.

"Just call me Lisa. Please have a look at the file and give me a call if you'd like to work together. My contact details are on the top of the first page." She stood before he had a chance to protest, dropped the file containing her presentation on his desk and let herself out. "Have a nice day, Mr Calvo."

41

"How did your meeting go?" Stella asked when she got home. She dropped her bag on the terrace floor and stroked Yeti and Pablo, who ran up to her.

"Not sure." Lisa looked up from her laptop, walked up to her and kissed her softly, then wrapped her arms around her waist. "It went okay, but it's hit and miss, I guess. He was more open towards the end, and I even think he might be interested in my idea, but he'll need some time to think about it, of course. If he doesn't want to work with me, then at least I've tried." She smiled. "And in the meantime, I'll look out for other interesting projects because I've had fun doing this."

"That's the spirit." Stella glanced at the table on the roof terrace that was laid out with a linen cloth and candles. "What's this for?"

"Just to say thank you for being so nice to me. I may not be a kitchen princess, but I went past the open market on my way home and got lots of tasty stuff and some nice wine."

"Babe, you're an angel." Stella wrapped her arms around Lisa in return and pulled her in. "I like having you here."

"Yeah?" Lisa grinned against her lips. "Well, I like being here."

"Mmm..." Stella grinned. "Let me just water the plants quickly."

"I've done that." Lisa pointed to the big palms in pots that provided a little privacy around the seating area.

"Oh. Thank you so much. Then all I have to do is feed the cats before dinner."

"Already done that too. Haven't you noticed there's only one still circling around your legs, hoping for a second meal?" Lisa's hands lowered to Stella's behind and slid into the waistband of her shorts. "Why don't you sit down and relax and I'll get the food out."

"How am I supposed to sit down if you're holding me like that?" Stella brushed her lips over Lisa's and moaned. "I've been thinking about you all day. You looked so fucking cute when you left for your meeting this morning, dressed formally and all business." She chuckled and lifted the sheer kaftan Lisa was wearing over her bikini. "But I think I like this even better."

"Oh, you do?" Lisa wiggled her hips and slapped her hand away. "Well, you're going to have to wait until after dinner."

"What if I can't wait?" Stella lifted the kaftan again and this time slipped her hand into the back of Lisa's bikini bottoms. "Oh my God, you're so delicious, I really want to fuck you right now."

Lisa laughed playfully. "What? You want dessert first? Again?"

"I do." Stella stared into her eyes and squeezed her behind, her libido firing at Lisa's firm bottom in her hands.

It wasn't a lie; she really had been fantasising about her all day. She'd struggled to keep her attention on the pool while she was on lifeguard duty and later on, in the office, she'd given up on finishing next month's rota.

"Okay, then. Come here." Lisa pulled Stella along to the sofa, pushed her down and straddled her. "I'll give you dessert."

Stella licked her lips as she looked up at Lisa, who took off her kaftan and tossed it behind her. She briefly glanced around to check if the neighbours weren't outside, then pulled at the strings of her triangle bikini and let if fall down, revealing her full breasts. "Fuck..."

"That sounds like a plan..." Lisa took Stella's hand and brought it between her thighs, into her bikini bottoms, gasping when her fingers skimmed her clit. "I want you too. I..." Her lashes fluttered and at the next stroke, she closed her eyes and moaned. "God, yes." Her arms wrapped around Stella's neck, her breath hitched as she leaned into her, then moved away and arched her back. She moved gracefully and rhythmically, chasing Stella's touch each time she pulled away. She was wet and swollen, her movements indicating she desperately needed more.

Stella held her breath as her fingers entered Lisa and as she watched her rise and fall she had trouble concentrating. Her hair wild and untamed from an afternoon on the windy terrace, her lips wet and glistening from a hint of gloss, her eyes hazy and so incredibly sexy each time she looked down at her. Yes, she'd dreamed of this and here she was. Lisa knew exactly what she wanted.

As she arched her back once again, her chest heaving forward, Stella's lips were drawn to Lisa's nipples, and she sucked one into her mouth, drawing another loud moan from her mouth as she fell back, only supported by Stella's arm that caught her.

Lisa moved faster, jerking her hips forward each time she thrust into her, and her hands were grasping Stella's shoulders tightly, then squeezing even harder as she climaxed with an intense shudder and a guttural sound that came from deep within. Her walls contracted fast and hard and her hand reached for Stella's, holding her fingers inside. "Fuck, Stella..." There was heavy breathing for long moments, and then there was silence.

Hearing her cry out her name slayed her, and Stella held her tightly, clutching Lisa close to her. Her body felt so right in her arms, her weight on top of her heavenly and seeing the smile on her face made her heart light up. Smiling from ear to ear herself, Stella slowly pulled out of her, then ran her hands over Lisa's cheeks. "Do you know that you're my ultimate fantasy?"

"You've told me that a couple of times." Lisa kissed her deeply, her tongue meeting Stella's in a passionate battle as her fingers raked through her hair and her hips moved into her belly. Finally, she shifted off her and kneeled in between Stella's knees on the tiles, grinning as she unbuttoned her shorts. "Did you know you're my ultimate fantasy too?"

"No." Stella lifted her hips so Lisa could pull them down along with her boxers, then gasped when she spread her legs apart. "But from what you're doing right now I can only —" She was silenced by Lisa's mouth kissing her inner thigh, slowly moving inward. Her fingers splayed wide, she squeezed her tensing muscles and ran her tongue over her skin. Stella rested her head against the cushion behind her and closed her eyes. Life had most definitely taken a turn for the better since Lisa had moved in.

42

"*Mr* Calvo?" Lisa's hand trembled as she plugged in her headphones to block out the noise from the beach and the promenade. A week after their first meeting, she'd ventured into Benidorm and had been hanging out at Sunset for most of the day, hoping to get more ideas, just in case he called, and she was just on her way home after a walk on the beach when he rang.

"Yes, it's me. Do you have a minute?"

"Of course." Fighting to keep her cool, Lisa scanned her surroundings for a quiet spot, then winced when she realised the only area not full of people was around a group of big commercial waste bins. Heading over there, she decided she could cope with the smell because everything depended on this phone call. A chance to put her brain to work again, and boost her drained bank account and her self-esteem.

"Well, myself and my team have taken a close look at your initial plans," he said. "And I must admit that we are quite impressed. We'd like to work with you."

Lisa grinned. "Excellent. What did you have in mind?" She held onto her chest as she waited for him to continue.

"We planned two months for Premier Sunset's turn-around but we've stretched it to ten weeks as it will involve more work. We work with a very good contractor, so we think that's doable, but we'll need you to present your in-depth plan as soon as possible. Once it's approved, we'll also need you to stay on during the implementation stage to ensure every aspect of the customer-facing experience is..." he hesitated. "I would like to say perfect, but as this will not be a five-star hotel, let's just stick with 'as good as it can possibly be'."

"Now, don't talk this down already, Mr Calvo. I always aim for perfection," Lisa joked.

"I like your attitude." Diego let out a chuckle. "This would be on a consultancy basis; our HR team will take care of the paperwork and your temporary visa. Would you be able to meet up with me to discuss salary and timelines at some point this week?"

"Absolutely." Lisa calculated that she was only a twenty-minute taxi ride away from his hotel, but not wanting to sound overly desperate, she said: "How about Monday? If we meet at Premier Sunset, we can do a walk-through before our meeting. That way, it will be easier for you to visualise the plans."

"Monday sounds good. I'll check if their meeting room is free. Would two pm suit you?"

"That is great for me. I'll see you then." After she'd hung up, Lisa let herself fall back in the sand. The area around her was riddled with empty cans and cigarette butts, but she didn't care. She was going to work again, and even if it was just a temporary job, it was a start. Half a year ago she would have snubbed a job like this, but now she was immensely grateful and incredibly excited.

"What are you doing there lying in the rubbish?" Someone towered over her, blocking the sun and when she looked up, she saw that it was Manuel.

"Oh, hey." They hadn't spoken since the day she'd moved, and frankly, she'd completely forgotten about his existence entirely. "I'm just chilling," she said, trying to keep a straight face. She got up and dusted off her denim shorts and top, so happy that even Manuel's presence felt like a welcome surprise.

"Strange place to chill."

"Exactly. So, what are you doing hanging out by the industrial waste bins?"

Manuel got on his tiptoes and looked into the giant, smelly container, then pulled out a football. "I've got a day off and was kicking a ball about. I hid it in here while I went to get a bottle of water. No footballs are allowed in the shops."

"Oh." Lisa arched a brow at him. "Gross, but also very clever."

"I'm not as dumb as I look," Manuel joked. "Are you still staying at Stella's?"

"Yes. I still have three weeks left." Lisa had no doubt he knew she still lived there, but perhaps he was just trying to make small talk. "But now I'll be staying for a while longer as I just got my first consultancy job." She gave him a beaming smile, wondering why she felt the need to share her big moment with Manuel of all people.

"Really? Congratulations. Stella told me you were job hunting. I didn't think Benidorm was somewhere you'd want to stay, but good for you." Manuel propped his ball under his arm and hesitated. "Can I buy you a drink? As I told you, I've been wanting to apologise for that night, so now seems like the perfect time."

He looked so uncomfortable that Lisa almost felt sorry for him. "Sure," she said, surprising herself. "And as I already said, it's long forgotten, but I'll take that drink." Stella was at work, and she really felt like celebrating. Since she didn't know anyone here, she figured she might as well take Manuel up on his offer.

"Seriously? You want to go for a drink with me?" Manuel's eyes lit up, and he seemed just as pleasantly surprised as she was that they were actually going to hang out together. "Pit Stop okay for you?" He pointed to the cocktail bar across the road from the boulevard.

Lisa shrugged. "Why not?" She didn't mention that she'd vouched to never set foot in the noisy and grotty bar because right then, she was in such a good mood that she had no problem with a cheap, sugary cocktail and rowdy clientele. "Is *Mr Ball* invited?"

"What? Who?" Manuel shot her a puzzled look.

Lisa pointed to his football. "Are you bringing the ball? Or are you throwing it back?"

Manuel laughed. "Oh, yes. I'd better bring it in case I forget to pick it up and they empty the bin in the morning. Wouldn't be the first time." He held out his arm and Lisa hooked hers through it. "Come on. I'm going to buy you the biggest, strongest drink they have on offer."

43

"It's quiet today, so I think I might head home early." Stella helped herself to a coffee and sat down at the tiki bar. "In fact, I think I might sign off right now and enjoy the last of the sunlight."

"You should. Days like this are rare." Dave, the bartender on duty made a coffee too, then pulled out a stool for himself and joined her. "How's that woman you've been seeing? I heard she moved in with you. Lisa, was it? She came to say goodbye before she left and gave me a tip. I thought that was very nice of her."

"Word travels fast." Stella laughed. "We're good, thank you, and yes, she's very nice. But it's not like she's permanently moved in with me; her life is in London."

"Well, London isn't that far."

"No, that's true." Stella managed a smile. She didn't like to think of Lisa's looming departure, and it got harder with each day that passed. "We'll see," she said, trying to sound casual about it.

"Is that your phone behind the bar?" Dave asked,

pointing to an iPhone that kept lighting up. "Looks like you have a ton of messages."

"Yes, that's mine, I put it on charge." Stella took it and narrowed her eyes as she opened a selection of pictures, then burst out in laughter. "What the..."

"What's so funny?"

"Lisa is at Pit Stop."

"Hmm... She doesn't seem like the kind of person to hang out there but maybe she's just waiting for you to finish work or—"

"She's there with Manuel," Stella interrupted him with an amused smirk.

"What? Wait, let me see that." Dave took her phone and chuckled. "Okay, this is seriously funny. Didn't those two used to hate each other?" Immediately after a message came in. '*Borrowed the hot girl for the night. Come join us!*' It was followed by a wink emoji and then another picture of Lisa dancing. "Are you going over there?"

"Of course I'm going. After all the times she's made fun of that bar, I have to see this for myself. Also, I can't wait to hear what the hell she's doing with Manuel."

"I wish I could come." Dave laughed.

Stella downed her coffee and patted his shoulder. "I'll fill you in tomorrow, how's that?" She went to the staffroom and swapped her Paradise polo shirt for a vest top but kept her work shorts on. Checking herself in the mirror, she wished she'd brought something nicer to wear, then decided she looked fine for the occasion. It was only Pit Stop after all, and she couldn't for the life of her imagine what Lisa was doing there with Manuel of all people.

The early night was balmy as she crossed the main road, the many bars along the strip already crowded. She vaguely recognised a couple of the hotel's guests and waved at them. It was noisy there, the different venues fighting with each other on volume, all playing different styles of music. There were a couple of English pubs where they played eighties and nineties hits, a karaoke bar where the patrons as well as the presenter—who sang medleys in between performances —generally had very little talent. The Mexican restaurant played mariachi music and the Dutch place next door had the same playlist of traditional Dutch songs on repeat all day. When she'd first moved here, she'd lived behind the strip, and it was even noisier there, so she'd spent years looking for the perfect tranquil spot to make her home. Buying her house in Altea had been the best move she'd ever made, and she counted herself lucky to have a quiet place to come home to at night after a long day's work. She didn't come here very often anymore apart from the occasional staff night out, but it was still entertaining to observe the happy holiday makers, all in their element and excited for a night of cheesy fun.

There were a couple of hen parties; the women all wearing matching pink feather boas or T-shirts with 'bride' and 'bridesmaid' printed on them, and a group of a dozen or so men on the terrace of the Mexican restaurant were dressed up as carrots. Stella had no idea what that was about, but she was amused by the streaks of orange face paint dripping down their necks as the padded fancy dress suits and green head pieces were way too warm for the Spanish summer.

She passed a Spanish restaurant, which was far from Spanish in her opinion. They served big plates of paella— the consistency more like risotto—and enormous jugs of sangria with sour freezer fruit. After that were a couple of shops that sold cheap tat, inflatables and souvenirs, a bar called '1 Euro Beer', a cabaret bar with a sign that announced the Michael Bublé impersonator who would perform there tonight, and a pizzeria with chequered white and red tablecloths and singing waiting staff.

And then there was Pit Stop, possibly the most unappealing of all. With its huge terrace, flashing neon signs, blue guaranteed headache cocktails and loud music, it wasn't somewhere she'd willingly go but the sight of Lisa dancing put a huge smile on her face. Stella stood there for a while, observing her. She looked so carefree and happy, so very different to when she'd just arrived. Dancing with Manuel and another woman Stella didn't know, they were singing along to the Spice Girls, and Lisa's long blonde hair was flailing around her as she moved. When she spotted Stella, her full lips pulled into a beaming smile, and she ran up to her.

"Seriously. You two?" Stella burst out in laughter when Manuel joined them. "I got your messages." She held up her phone.

"Come have a drink with us!" Lisa flew around her neck and grinned sheepishly. "We're having…" She frowned as she stared at her almost empty bulb glass that contained something white and foamy, then took out the umbrella and stuck it behind Stella's ear. "I don't actually remember what it's called but it's got coconut in it. Not real coconut of course," she added, rolling her eyes. "Just flavoured powder. The first one was horrible but I'm on my fourth now and they're definitely growing on me. Want one?"

"Why not?" Stella gave her a kiss, amused at Lisa's bouncy energy. "But let *me* get them." She pointed to Lisa's bare feet that were dirty all the way up to her ankles. "Babe, where are your shoes?" It was funny, to say the least. Lisa of all people had embraced the Benidorm lifestyle she hated with a passion in a bar she hated with a passion and was partying with someone she never got along with.

Lisa glanced down and wiggled her toes. "My feet hurt, so I took them off."

"They're over there! Your shoes are next to *Mr Ball*." Manuel, who was holding their female companion's hand, pointed to a table in front of the bar where Lisa's shoes and his football that had a smiley face drawn on it with Lisa's shades placed over the eyes, were on a chair in front of six empty cocktail glasses. "Want to sit down? This is Amy by the way."

"Amy is lovely," Lisa added, flinging an arm around the tourist they had adopted for the night. "She lost her friends and her phone is dead, so we're keeping her company."

"Hey, Amy. Nice to meet you. I'll make that four cocktails then." Stella shot them a smile and headed for the bar. As she waited for them to be made—hers without alcohol so she could make sure Lisa would get back safe—she watched them sit down and talk. Lisa was all kinds of adorable when she let her hair down. She wasn't completely hammered, but she was way past sober, her eyes widening as she discussed something she was clearly passionate about. Yesterday, she would have laughed at people who danced barefoot and drank ridiculous cocktails at the most unappealing bar in town. She'd even told Stella she'd felt intimidated by the holiday crowd on a couple of occasions. But tonight, she was one of them and that was too entertaining not to eternalise. Stella took a picture of her on her phone, making sure she got one of the many 'Pit Stop' signs in.

"So, why the party?" she asked as she joined them with four huge glasses that were jazzed up with umbrella's, sugar rims, glitzy straws, and anything else the bartender could get his hands on.

"Lisa got a job!" Manuel yelled, taking a glass and holding it up in a toast before Lisa had a chance to answer.

"You did?" Stella leaned in to kiss her. "Babe, that's amazing, I'm so proud of you. Congratulations." An intense rush of happiness coursed through her at the news she hadn't even dared hope for. "No wonder you're celebrating in the weirdest of ways."

"I know, I can't believe it." Lisa was bouncing in her seat as she took a sip of her drink. "Mr Calvo called me late this afternoon. I was going to pick you up from work and tell you in person but then I had one of these, and then a second and well... then Manual said he would message you to come here. Anyway, I'm meeting with Mr Calvo to discuss my contract on Monday." She tilted her head and locked her eyes with Stella's. "Come here and kiss me. I've missed you, you sexy woman."

Stella laughed and cupped Lisa's face as she leaned in to kiss her. "I've missed you too, babe." She pointed a finger from Manuel to Lisa. "And dare I ask how the two of you ended up here together?"

"We met by the bins on the beach," Lisa said as it that was nothing out of the ordinary. "I was lying next to them and Manuel was rummaging through one of them, so we got talking."

Stella laughed as she shot Manuel a quizzical look. "Bonding by the bins. Okay..."

"He's been teaching me how to blend in," Lisa continued. "We've been sitting in the full sun, drinking this crap, I've danced and talked to strangers and I've sang along to nineties boy band songs. I was surprised I remembered all the lyrics."

"She just needs to work on her appearance," Amy chipped in. "She could do with some extra make-up and a bit of glitz. I offered to give her smoky eyes, but she refused." She turned to Lisa. "You need to look like you're 'out', you know? Like out-out."

Stella frowned in confusion. "Out as in 'out of the closet'?"

"No!" Amy chuckled. "Out as in 'out on the town'. She needs a party dress. I have a couple of nice ones in my room at Sunset." She glanced at Stella. "You could do with a makeover too, if I'm honest with you. I can make you look really glam."

Stella shot her an amused look. "Thanks, but I'm—" She was silenced by the sudden increase of volume on the music and the cheering crowd who started singing along to some popular English song. "Oh boy, this is going to be a long night," she joked, laughing when Lisa pulled her onto the dancefloor and flung her arms around her neck. She wrapped her arms around Lisa's waist in return, lifted her up and spun her around.

Lisa laughed out loud, and when she put her back down, she pulled her in and kissed her fiercely. "Now we have more time; at least three months," she said with a beaming smile. "I have everything I wanted now. A job and more time with you. And you know what? This place isn't so bad either and the people are so nice. I think I can get used to this."

Stella kissed her and hugged her tight, and she realised then, that she had everything she wanted too. Happy people, happy music, a happy girlfriend... Life couldn't get any better.

44

"Here's your contract." Diego handed Lisa a file with a blue cover. "Once you've signed, we'll sort out your temporary visa. Have you read through the scanned version the HR department emailed you?"

"Yes, everything seems to be in order, so I'm happy to go ahead." Lisa took her time to check if the document was identical to the one she'd been sent, then signed on the dotted line. Now that she had the contract in her pocket, she didn't have to play it cool anymore. "Seriously, thank you for this opportunity. I won't let you down."

Diego smiled back at her. "I have a good feeling about you, so you'd better not," he joked. "Now, we've put together an initial team; a contractor for the refurbishment, a web designer, an interior designer and a landscaper who will report directly to you during the transition period. Their details are on the additional page in the back of your contract. You'll be responsible for marketing, branding and all other consumer facing aspects of the business, which means you will also have to work closely with the current general manager to set up programs to retrain the staff.

Someone from our group will liaise with you on budget and sort out local permits and such. Timelines are extremely tight, so you'll have to start yesterday."

"No problem." Lisa handed him back the contract and slipped her own copy into her handbag. "Then I won't have to bother you with anything at all, so I guess I'll see you in October for the big reveal." She held out her hand and he laughed as he shook it.

"I might sneak in now and then to see how things are coming along, but yes, I'll stay out of your way mostly; I'm heading back to Madrid in a couple of hours. Can't wait to get out of this dump."

"It's not so bad," Lisa said. "If you can't beat them, join them. That's what I've learned." She stood up and straightened the new, navy wrap dress she'd treated herself to on the weekend. "I won't keep you any longer. I'm sure you have a lot to take care of before you head back, so I guess we'll speak on our first debrief call."

"I'm looking forward to it." Diego stood up to walk her out. "You have a nice day, Lisa."

Outside, Stella was sitting on the bonnet of her car, waiting for her. She'd taken half a day off, insisting on driving her here for her big moment. It was warm today and she looked gorgeous and glowing, dressed in tiny jersey shorts and a white vest. "How did it go?"

"Perfect," Lisa said, waving the contract at her. When she reached Stella, she stepped in between her legs and brushed their lips together. "Apparently, I'm starting yesterday but apart from making phone calls to set up a ton of meetings tomorrow, there's not much I can do right now." She kissed her and moaned when Stella pulled her in and parted her lips to meet her tongue. The deep kiss set her on fire and neither of them wanted to stop, so they stayed there for long moments, kissing in the car park. "I love kissing you," she murmured against her lips.

"I love kissing you too." Stella caressed her cheek then ran a hand through her hair. "Can you make those phone calls over a long, celebratory lunch?"

"Absolutely. How about that little beach bar of yours?"

"Exactly what I was thinking. I've brought my newspapers in case you had to start right away."

"All done?" Stella tucked into the grilled squid with aioli, the fifth little dish they'd ordered. They'd been here for hours, ordering half portions so they could taste everything on the menu.

"Yes." Lisa slipped her phone into her handbag and sat back with a long sigh. "It's a lot. Tomorrow I have a meeting with the general manager first thing so he can brief the staff. By now, there will be a lot of speculation about redundancies, so I'm sure they'll be relieved to hear that they can stay on. It took a bit of convincing, but Mr Calvo agreed that loyal and trained staff makes for better service."

"Everyone?" Stella sounded surprised.

"Yes, the ones that pass the service training, but that shouldn't be too hard. The kitchen staff were already laid off months ago, so we're going to hire the new head chef early. That will give them time to put their team together and create a bespoke menu. Anyway, I won't have to worry about that too much; the general manager will take care of the recruiting. And then there's the interior designer, the contractor, a web designer and a Spanish copywriter who will translate all customer-facing marketing messages."

"That's a lot."

"Yes, it's going to be a long day tomorrow." Lisa chuckled. "It's going to be a hectic time, but I'm excited. The scale of the project is much smaller than the ones I've worked on in the past but it's also much more in-depth and there's a lot I have to figure out as I go along."

"But you have experts on board," Stella said.

"True. A big part of it is project managing and I have no problem with that. But I've never been involved with a physical overhaul, you know? This is new to me. It will be fun, though, doing something different for a change."

"I can imagine." Stella shot her a flirty wink. "I have a feeling you can do anything you set your mind to. How about your hours?"

"As long as the job gets done, my hours are flexible. The builders will be there Monday to Saturday, and in the first weeks, I'll mainly be working from home and just drop in now and then, apart from when I have meetings. Once we get closer to finishing, I'll be on-site mostly."

"That's nice. You'll be able to enjoy the rest of the summer."

"Yes, and I can even come to Seville with you. That is, unless I have to be on-site those days. I'll know more about my schedule this week once we've finished the planning." Lisa hesitated. "Do you still want me to come?"

"Of course." Stella's smile widened. "I didn't think you'd be able to make it with the job, so that's amazing news. I've already told my mum about you, and she can't wait to meet you. She even threatened to come over here and leave my father to run the business if I didn't bring you."

"Seriously?"

"Yes. Is that a bad thing?"

Lisa shook her head. "No, not at all." She felt herself

blush but kept her eyes locked with Stella's. "What did you tell her?"

"That I have a cute, beautiful, sexy, smart new girlfriend with a hot accent."

"Really?" Lisa laughed. "So, you told her I was your girlfriend."

Stella shrugged and shot her a smug look. "You are my girlfriend, aren't you?"

"Yes..." Warmth spread through Lisa's body, making her glow all-over. They both felt secure with each other, but they hadn't voiced it. She thought about her parents and her brother, and how excited they'd be for her if she too, told them she'd met someone special. "Yes," she said sweetly. "I'm your girlfriend."

45

"*How's* your new fridge, Dave?" Stella sat down on her usual stool and regarded the huge stainless steel unit behind the tiki bar.

"It's bloody perfect." Dave opened the industrial fridge that was twice the size as the old one, showing off his neatly organised stock. Now that the money from the sale of Premier Sunset had come in, there was budget for repairs and Stella had wasted no time requesting items they desperately needed. "Loving the new coffee machine too." He grinned and raised a finger to his lips as he slid a cup underneath it and pressed the cappuccino button. "Shh...Do you hear that?"

"Hear what?" Stella asked.

"Exactly! This one hardly makes any noise."

Laughing out loud, Stella took the cup from him. "If I knew it would make you so happy, I would have paid for it myself a long time ago." She gave him a high-five and sat back to enjoy her second coffee of the day. "God, this is so much nicer than the crap we had before."

"Isn't it just?" Dave smirked. "I got the fancy coffee beans too. Talk about splashing out."

"Talking about splashing out..." Stella turned to the poolside where Manuel was setting up for a new 'class' as he called it. "Have you heard what he's organised for this morning?"

"Yeah..." Dave frowned as he watched Manuel pull the speaker closer to the poolside before securing a banner between two palm trees. It said: *'Monday morning dive-bombing competition. Start your week with a splash!'* "Did you sign off on this?" he asked, lowering his voice.

"I did." Stella chuckled as she eyed the banner that looked a little amateurish in the graphic design department. It didn't matter; it was all about the fun. "I told him it would never work, that it's only something children would take part in, and we don't have any kids here. But he kept insisting our guests would love it, so I finally let him have a go." She turned back to Dave and sighed. "I doubt anyone will show up for it, but he works hard and he's so full of enthusiasm that I didn't have the heart to say no. He's convinced the first prize of a dinner at his cousin's restaurant will draw people in."

"So, he's basically promoting his cousin's restaurant. Is he even allowed to do that?"

"No reason why he can't. People are here all-inclusive, so it's not like we're losing money when they're not here. In fact, we're better off if they dine out."

"Good point." Dave turned when he heard voices coming from the back door. Five men walked out with their towels, all wearing matching yellow Speedos. "What the hell is that?"

Manuel shot Stella an 'I told you so' look, and she

gasped in surprise when a group of four women came out too.

"Where's that dive-bombing competition?" One of them shouted, and then there was an avid discussion about how they could easily take on the men waiting by the pool fence. More people followed and when Manuel finally opened the poolside, at least thirty people headed for the table he'd set up earlier. *'Sign up here!'* It said in clumsy handwriting on a sheet stuck to the front of the table. *'Biggest splash wins a romantic three course candlelit dinner for two in the heart of Benidorm. Including a bottle of wine.'*

"I guess I underestimated him," Stella said, shocked by the number of guests who had turned up.

"I have a feeling that bottle of wine may have something to do with it." Dave snickered as he watched the contestants stretch and warm up while they challenged each other. On the pool facing balconies, people were watching from their rooms, and more guests were settling on the loungers with cameras. "How can he even pick a winner when it's not determined by scale, measuring tape or stopwatch?"

"I have no idea. I suppose the audience will decide." If anything, this was the biggest turnout they'd had for an outdoor activity since she'd started working there, and Stella realised she wasn't prepared, so she put on her red lifeguard vest and got up. "I guess that means I'm on life-guard duty." She turned on her walkie-talkie and said: "Florence, please leave your current station and come over to the poolside. People have actually showed up for this ridiculous splashing competition, so I need an extra first aid officer just in case."

Florence's loud laugh made the device crackle. "Got you. I'll be there in two minutes. Don't let them start without me; I don't want to miss a second."

With an amused smile, Stella made her way to her life-guard chair where she perched on the edge and got her whistle ready. Convinced the event wouldn't take off, she hadn't even gone through the script with Manuel, and she regretted that now as he got up from his table and reached for the microphone.

"Ladies and gentlemen, welcome to the first ever adult Paradise dive-bomb competition. The only one in Benidorm! That means, if you win, you will be the official Benidorm champion for a week, and the honour to wear the crown is yours." Manuel held up a plastic crown he'd purchased at a toy shop. "You'll also get free drinks on Paradise for the remainder of your stay."

Stella rolled her eyes at his silly joke, but the audience was cracking up with laughter.

"And best of all," he continued, "you will enjoy the perfect dinner for two. If you've been planning on asking your spouse to marry you, this romantic venue will give you the perfect opportunity."

Stella wasn't convinced Manuel's cousin's restaurant was romantic enough for a marriage proposal but again, that wasn't really the point. The point was, that thirty or so adults had gathered and that for the duration of the competition, they would feel like a kid again and have great fun. And that meant good reviews. She winced at his next announcement but decided to let him off the hook.

"Extra points for a belly flop and a long and dramatic dead body float at the end!"

46

"It's looking good." Lisa followed Marcy, the contractor, through the poolside doors into the building where the reception desk had been taken out. They were building a circular bar. Half of it was inside and the other half was outside, accessible to staff through the sliding glass doors that opened fully.

"Yes, we're going full steam ahead. It's a great idea, extending the bar to the patio," Marcy said, then pointed to the pool that was drained now. "We'll start on the pool in a couple of days. We'll rip out the mosaic and replace it with a white liner. It's cost effective and it will look really clean." She kneeled and patted the rounded edge of one of the grey tiles that framed the pool. "And these will be replaced by simple terracotta tiles leading all the way around the pool and up to the bar. It will take a week, give or take. Once that's done, we'll move on to the kitchen, the lounge and the indoor restaurant."

"You're moving fast." Lisa had been surprised that the contractor was female, and she was grateful for Marcy who was easy going, efficient and reliable. Ten days in and she'd expected to find that they were already behind on the work as so often happened with refurbishments but instead, the bar was well on its way to looking finished.

"I have good people and I don't like to waste anyone's time. My whole team is on the job." Marcy looked her over. "You look familiar. Every time we meet, I keep thinking I've met you somewhere before..."

Lisa narrowed her eyes as she studied Marcy in return. "Yes, you look familiar too, actually. Do you live in Altea?"

"No, but my mother lives there, so I visit her regularly. She's got some of her work in a gallery and I often meet her there for drinks."

"Ah, that's where I recognise you from. Are you Delia's daughter by any chance?"

"Yes, that's my mum! You know her?"

"Not well, I only spoke to her once," Lisa said. "But we say hello in passing and I must have seen you hanging out with her, enjoying the red wine."

"Of course." Marcy chuckled. "Yes, Mum enjoys a glass of wine. So, how did you end up here?"

"Oh, it's a long story..." Lisa waved a hand. "I was only meant to stay for two months but while I was here, I met someone special and now I'd like to stay for as long as I can, so I'm grateful for this job, even if it's just temporary."

"How romantic. What's the lucky guy's name?"

"Her name is Stella," Lisa said with a grin. She aware of her love-struck expression, but she couldn't help herself.

"Ooh..." Marcy arched a brow, then looked Lisa over once more as if she was surprised to learn she was gay. "Stella Castillo?"

"Yes." Lisa laughed at yet another coincidence.

"I know her. Not very well, but we used to hang in the

same circles; it's a small world here if you're gay. But let's be clear on one thing; I have not slept with your girlfriend," Marcy added with a chuckle. "We should have a drink together some time after work. The three of us, I mean."

"Sure, that would be fun." Lisa smiled. She liked Marcy and felt a hint of excitement at the opportunity to make a new friend.

"Great, we'll set something up." Marcy continued around the pool and pointed to the high brick wall that surrounded the premises. "But let's get this over with first. You wanted these prison walls painted too, right?"

"Yes. The prison walls." Lisa laughed. "They're awful but I'm sure painting them white would make all the difference. It will make it feel like a little oasis instead of a prison court-yard. And the fact that they're so tall can actually work to the hotel's advantage as they block out the noise from the street. If we added some water features, the sound of running water would make it feel really tranquil." She gestured to the longest wall that ran parallel to the pool and into the courtyard. "And this back wall gets a small strip of sunshine in the middle of the day. Could you build some stone benches and paint them white, so it would look like they're part of the wall? I'll ask the interior designer to find some nice tables, so guests have the option for a late lunch in the sun."

"No problem, benches are an easy fix. Don't you want sunloungers there though?"

"No. The interior designer will create lounge areas and private pods in the courtyard. Once we've landscaped and added lots of plants, that will look really pretty."

"You seem to know what you're doing; a business hotel is a great idea," Marcy said, looking over her shoulder as she headed back inside.

"I hope I know what I'm doing. This is kind of new to me but I'm enjoying it."

"I'm enjoying it too. It's nice to do something different for once. Everything in Benidorm tends to be the same and frankly I'm bored with doing boxy rooms and sterile communal spaces."

"I've noticed they're all quite soulless." Lisa followed her to the lift. "Why are we going up? You haven't started on the rooms yet, right?"

Marcy pressed the button for the first floor. "Not really; but your interior girl was really keen to get started, so she asked us to prepare one room for you to look at. Two of my best men stripped it, painted everything white and put in a new bathroom before she sprinkled her magic over it. She wanted to be here today, but she had to go to a factory to look at some tiles, so she said she'd catch up with you later. I've worked with her before; she creates sample rooms so they're easy to sign off."

"Oh, wow." Lisa needed a moment when Marcy opened the door as the room looked so different from before. The patchy yellow walls were now flawless and white, and the floor was tiled with Spanish terracotta tiles. A simple wooden bed stood in the middle of the room, beautifully made up with white linens. The wooden bedside table held a rustic terracotta lamp with an off-white lampshade that matched the knotted rug on the floor. The blacked-out window had been replaced by normal glass and was wide open, letting in the daylight through off-white linen curtains. Opposite the bed stood a wooden desk and a chair, and someone had marked on the wall where the sockets would be. The built-in wardrobe was still there but now that it was painted white and given new handles, it looked fresh and contemporary. The alcove that was of no use before had been turned into a station for the coffee maker and underneath was a small fridge. Two big plants in woven baskets brought a splash of colour to the natural palette of the room that was neither too feminine nor too masculine; it was perfect. "I love it," she said, trailing a hand over the rattan headboard behind the bed. She'd discussed the plans with the interior designer in detail, but she hadn't expected it to look quite so striking.

"Good. In terms of man-hours, it's been very cost effective. Even the windows weren't too bad." Marcy handed her a cost sheet, then opened the door to the en suite bathroom. "In here, we stripped everything and kept it all-white like you requested, with basic materials and practical solutions."

"Fantastic. It feels like a different room entirely." The interior designer had added the black accents in the taps, the shower panel and the rain shower like they'd discussed, and she'd spruced it up with nice products, towels and a big, black-framed mirror.

"I agree." Marcy shot her a proud grin. "I have a very good team. Once they have a concept to copy, they can carry this over into the other rooms fairly quickly."

"Honestly, I couldn't be happier," Lisa said as they left the room and headed back to the ground floor. "And you know what? We should definitely go for that drink soon. I'll ask Stella when she's available." She waved at a woman she recognised from the picture on the CV the general manager had sent her. "I have to catch up with Zoe. She's going to be the head chef."

"Oh, God, that woman?" Marcy hesitated. "I spoke to her before you arrived and I'm afraid we didn't start off on the best foot." She chuckled uncomfortably when Lisa shot her a confused look. "Never mind, I'll tell you all about it over that drink. Thanks, Lisa. I'll see you soon."

47

*D*riving out of Benidorm, the landscape changed dramatically. They'd set off at seven am this morning to beat the commuter traffic and August heat. After following the coastline along golden beaches, dramatic cliffs and spectacular sea views, they were now driving inland, towards Las Alpujarras, an area of unspoiled landscape in the Sierra Nevada mountain range. Olive groves and Moorish whitewashed villages lay at the foot of the mountains, surrounded by wooded hills. Stella had planned a route to take Lisa past her favourite places; some on the way, some worth taking a detour for.

"You must have been in need of a break," she said to Lisa. "Since you've been working almost three weeks non-stop."

"I'm not complaining; I haven't had a job in months, but I must admit I was getting a little tired and I wouldn't have missed this for the world." Lisa gazed over the beautiful landscape. Ash trees, poplar and maple trees grew along the road, with wild rose bushes scattered in between. "Is that snow on the peaks?"

"Yes, there's snow most of the year, actually, but there's only a little now. I brought a couple of warm jumpers and scarves for us in case it gets chilly, but we're not going all the way to the top." Stella opened her window to let the breeze flow through the car. So far, there was no sign of a drastic temperature drop, and her back felt damp from the faux leather of her seat. Lisa was leaning out of the window, her long hair blowing wildly around her face, and Stella struggled to keep her attention on the road as she looked out for the next turning. "I booked a place in the village we're visiting. The accommodation is basic, but the area is stunning, so it will be worth driving the extra two hours for." She took a left at the narrow and steep road, hoping her car would make it. She hadn't driven here in a couple of years and the engine wasn't what it used to be. Her mother kept telling her she should trade it in for a newer, more reliable vehicle, but she couldn't bear the thought of saying goodbye to her good old friend. As she shifted into second gear and drove up, she felt a sense of pride for her country and immense excitement to show Lisa some extraordinary places.

"Do your parents mind that we're only staying two nights at their place, instead of three?"

"No, as long as we show up, they're fine and I really wanted to take you here. Besides, this will give us time to chill out before we set foot into my parents' chaotic household. My mother never stops talking."

The lush landscape turned rugged and untouched, with streams running down from the peaks and huge old trees scattered around patches of vivid green fields where sheep were grazing. Stella counted herself lucky they didn't meet any other cars in the hairpin bends that led to Pampaneira, a village that rested on secluded, steep slopes among rugged gorges, just above the foothills of the mountains.

Lisa smiled and inhaled deeply as she got out of the car and took in her surroundings. The white village before them, the green hills behind, and the bright blue sky made for a stunning palette.

"It's a no-traffic zone, so we'll have to leave the car here and continue on foot." Stella followed her gaze, rolling her shoulders that were stiff from driving. The views were exceptional and there were signs for several hiking routes that led higher up into the mountains, but despite the breathtaking beauty of the area, Pampaneira wasn't a very touristy town.

"Where is everyone?" Lisa looked around the pebbled parking area that was only half full. "I would expect this to be a popular destination."

"I suppose it's too far out of the way for tourists who stay along the coast, and conquering those narrow roads isn't easy if you're not used to it. Too much effort, maybe? It's mainly the hikers who come here and you don't really see them during the day as they're out walking." Stella took her bag out of the boot and Lisa took hers. As they walked into the town centre, she felt calm and happy at the serene scenes that played out around them. A group of elderly local women were drinking coffee on the terrace of a café, two men were playing a boardgame on the square at the end of the street and a couple of dog walkers were chatting while their dogs played together in the streets and alleyways that were safe for them to roam around as there was no traffic here.

With its white houses, serene lanes, flower filled stone beds and water springs twisting through the centre, it was an idyllic little town, and the handful of small churches in the quiet squares and a monastery that stretched around its outskirts added to the peaceful vibe. It was a little cooler here than in Benidorm, and the streets and squares were shaded by trees, canopies, parasols and the two and three-storey white buildings that were clustered close together. The facades of the town houses were well kept and presented with pride and love; little cast iron benches under the windows, wooden chairs and other small social areas where locals gossiped over their morning coffee.

"Thank you for bringing me here," Lisa said, squeezing Stella's hand.

"I just thought you should experience it. If you want to soak up Spanish culture, it doesn't get more authentic than this. The villages around here are so isolated from modern society that they don't even compare to the rest of Spain."

"I can see that." Lisa looked excited as they strolled through the high street that only held a couple of traditional crafts shops, cafés and restaurants. Without even asking, the women in front of the café spotted their bags and pointed out the direction of the only hotel in town. Stella chatted to them for a while and enquired about restaurant recommendations before they headed towards the converted farm at the outskirts of the village, where they would sleep tonight.

Walking out of town, a lush green landscape of fields and pastures greeted them, the walls of the monastery stretching over the hills in the distance. The old farm consisted of three two-storey stone buildings, clustered in a half-circle around a courtyard with a well in the middle. The six rooms on the second floor overlooked the courtyard and the mountains and there was a little shop and a breakfast area on the ground floor. Sheep were grazing in the field in front of them, a huge, hairy pig was sleeping in the sun—not in the slightest bothered by the visitors—and chickens were roaming around freely in the courtyard.

"This is lovely." Lisa gently nudged Stella, then planted a

soft kiss on her temple. "Why did you say it was basic? It's so incredibly romantic..."

"Well, I know you're used to the finer things in life. But I suppose after Paradise you may have redefined your standards."

Lisa laughed. "Hey, I'm not that bad."

"I know you're not, babe." Stella held open the reception door for her. "Let's check in and get some food, shall we? We can go for a hike tomorrow morning if you don't mind getting up early again? The best time for wildlife watching is during sunrise."

48

*T*he spread of regional food made Lisa's mouth water. The terrace tucked away in a courtyard on the outskirts of Pampaneira was lively, as if the whole town had suddenly awoken with a raging appetite. As the only non-locals in the place, they'd been the centre of attention when they arrived, subjected to both small talk and recommendations on what to order. The Alpujarran soup they'd tried as a starter had been superb, and now they were throwing themselves onto a variety of small dishes. The simple salad of thickly sliced local juicy tomatoes with a spicy dressing, the Jamón de Trevélez, the patatas a lo pobre 'poor man's potatoes' with black pepper, the chickpea stew and the manchego cheese with chutney and fig bread were a delicious fusion between Moorish and Andalusian cuisine. A guitarist was jamming at one of the tables, while patrons sang along to their favourite songs and bought him beers to keep playing.

"This is so much fun. I've been on many holidays, but I've never done something as adventurous as this," she said.

"Really?" Stella frowned as she took a sip of her ice-cold

beer. "But you had a really good job and the opportunity to travel anywhere you wanted."

"I know. But Sandrine preferred five-star hotels along the beach over off-the-grid places, and massages over hikes." Lisa shrugged. "I didn't blame her. She worked sixty hours a week and I wasn't far behind."

"And you? What did you want?"

"I guess I never put myself first," Lisa said. "Maybe I should have." She spooned more stew onto her plate and dipped the bread in its juices. "What about you? Have you travelled much?"

"Not as much as I'd like to. I mean, I used to travel regularly, but like most people, I haven't been away in the past two years," Stella said. "I used to jump at any opportunity to see new places. Although three weeks holiday in a year isn't much, I still managed to get away once or twice a year, aside from my trips to Seville for the holidays. Sometimes I explored Europe and sometimes I went further away but now, even a short trip through the region feels like a holiday. Or maybe that's just because you're with me."

"You're sweet." Lisa smiled and her stomach fluttered as their eyes met. "Or maybe you just needed reminding how versatile and beautiful your region is."

"That too." Stella reached over the table and traced a finger over Lisa's arm.

"Should we be doing that? Especially here..." Lisa glanced around, but no one was paying attention to them.

"I'm not worried. Yes, the average age may be over fifty here but it's still Spain, and Spain was the third country in the world to legalise gay marriage, after The Netherlands and Belgium. The Spanish are generally very open-minded when it comes to love."

"I like that." Lisa tilted her head and studied Stella. "And your parents? Are they as open-minded?"

"Seville is a very religious city, so I suppose their upbringing was slightly on the conservative side. It took them a while to get used to the idea, but overall, they just want me to be happy."

"You're lucky. So were mine. Have you ever brought a woman home?" Lisa asked.

"Once. I was dating this girl who really wanted to see Seville, so it seemed silly not to invite her to my parents' house, even though it wasn't very serious." Stella shot Lisa a reassuring look. "So don't worry; you won't be the first girl-friend to set foot in their house and they're long over the first shock of me dating women. But just like in your parents' house, we'll have to share a single bed."

"You know I don't have a problem with that." Lisa chuckled and glanced over the menu. "Want to share some strawberries with me?"

"I do. But maybe we should ask them to bag them up and add some whipped cream." Stella's eyes sparkled with flirtation. "What do you think?"

"I think that's a genius idea." Lisa sat back, creating some space between them so she wouldn't catch fire, because that was how she felt. Heat spread through her body each time they were together, each time they flirted, and each time Stella even as much as looked at her. It was quite puzzling how this woman was able to throw her off her game, erase her train of thoughts and turn her into a much younger version of herself in a matter of seconds. The younger version of herself that was curious and open to anything. The younger version of herself that was led by her intuition, rather than her brain. To just sit here and talk, not thinking about work, was refreshing and she was soaking up every moment with all her senses. "Dinner's my treat by the way." She beckoned the waiter over and ordered the strawberries, then looked at Stella to finish the order with the whipped cream as she had no idea how to say that. When she opened her handbag to find her credit card, her phone lit up, and her stomach dropped when she saw the name on the screen. *Sandrine.* She picked it up and read the message. *'Hi, hope you're okay. Please call me when you have a moment.'*

"Everything okay?" Stella asked. "You look startled."

"It's nothing, it can wait." Lisa didn't want to mention Sandrine now as they were having such a good time. There was no rush. She'd waited for Sandrine to call her for months, and now it was Sandrine's time to wait. It came as a surprise though as she'd never expected to hear from her again. Mentally calculating, she concluded it had been eight months since they'd last spoken. They weren't friends or even remotely close anymore and frankly, she didn't want to call her at all. Still, she was curious as to why she'd suddenly reached out. Handing her card to the waiter, she pushed the message to the back of her mind. *Not tonight. And maybe not even tomorrow.*

$\mathcal{L}$isa shot up at the knock on their door. She'd slept so deeply that she needed a moment to get her bearings. It must have been the effect of the mountain air, she thought as she put on her dressing gown and opened the door to find a member of staff with the breakfast tray they'd ordered for six am.

"Thank you so much," she whispered, and smiled as she inhaled the scent of the fresh coffee. Her new job and her road trip with Stella had already done her the world of good, and she felt rejuvenated.

She placed a soft kiss on Stella's temple and opened the curtains and the doors to the balcony. The breeze was cool and filled with the scent of pine, and the sound of birdsong and sheep bleating in the distance made her smile as she took in the view.

"Good morning, gorgeous woman." Stella sat up and yawned.

She was adorable in her sleepy state, and if they hadn't planned a hike, Lisa would have jumped right back in bed with her. "Good morning, hotness." She placed a coffee on

Stella's bedside table and leaned in for another kiss that was met with a longing moan. Biting her lip, she suppressed a grin as she pulled away. This, the hotel with the perfect view, and Stella smiling at her felt like a dream, like it was almost too good to be true. "Do you want your breakfast in bed?"

Stella shook her head. "No, let's go outside. We won't get a morning like this again any time soon, right?" She wrapped a large towel around her chest and followed Lisa outside. "I thought you weren't a morning person but you're doing pretty well for the second day in a row."

"And I thought you *were* a morning person," Lisa shot back at her, eyeing Stella as she rubbed the sleep out of her eyes.

Stella chuckled through a long yawn, stretched again and sank into one of the deep, wooden chairs. "Hey, give me a break; you kept me up most of the night." She patted her lap. "Come sit here with me. You're too far away in that chair."

Lisa gladly settled on Stella's lap sideways and buried her face in her neck. Every moment with her was heavenly and now that they were getting to know each other better, she was starting to feel an intense, almost seamless connection to her. The need to be close to Stella came from deep within and it wasn't just physical. No, it was way more than that, but she didn't dare go there. Not yet. "Mmm... you smell nice."

"I smell of sex."

"You do. I like it."

Stella laughed and snuck a hand into Lisa's dressing gown to caress her breasts. "I can't get enough of you."

"Same here." Lisa moaned and arched her back, pushing herself into Stella's touch. The first sunbeams were fighting their way over the mountain tops, casting a sensational play of light over the fields. Something was moving fast in the distance, making its way towards them. It looked like a cat, only much bigger, with long legs and a short tail. She narrowed her eyes, focusing as she pointed in the direction. "What's that?"

Stella gasped as she spotted it too. "Oh, wow. It's an Iberian lynx," she whispered when it came closer. "Andalusians call it the Spanish tiger. They're an endangered species and used to be extremely rare but the population is growing again."

"It's so beautiful." Lisa's breath caught as she eyed the heavily spotted creature with a bushy beard around its face and long tufts that rose from the tips of its ears. It stopped abruptly and looked up at them, suddenly aware it was being watched. For a moment, she was sure that it was looking right at her, and she kept still as to not scare it away. "It's not going to go for the sheep, is it?" she whispered, noting the sheep were getting restless and moving closer to the farm.

"No, they mainly eat rabbits. I don't know why it's here; maybe it's after the chickens."

"Oh, God, are we going to have a blood bath? I'm sorry but I can't let that happen." Lisa slipped off Stella's lap then and stood up, and the lynx disappeared as fast as it had come. "Sorry, I hated scaring it away but—"

"Yes, it's for the best. There are plenty of rabbits out there and I don't want it to get in trouble with the local farmers. We might see more of them on our hike." Stella took a sip of her coffee and got up. "I'm going to have a quick shower before breakfast."

Lisa laughed. "Okay, I'll go after you; the shower isn't big enough for two." The ping of her phone drew her to her bedside table, and she sighed when she saw she had another message from Sandrine. *'Hey, Lisa, I didn't hear from you, so I sent you an email. Please read it and get back to me asap.'* She opened the email as she walked back to the balcony, irritated that Sandrine wouldn't leave her alone for a couple of days.

Dear Lisa,

I'm not sure what your current situation is, but a vacancy became available in my department yesterday and I thought of you as you'd be perfect for it. Director of Marketing North America. The role is based in New York and the relocation package is very generous. You suggested perhaps looking for something in New York last year, so I know you're not against moving here. It would be nice to have you close again, I miss you and looking back, I finally see that we were very good together. Please think about applying. I can put in a good word for you and get you on the candidate shortlist if you're interested.

I'm sorry I hurt you and I'd like to make amends, perhaps see where we could go from here.

Love, Sandrine.

Lisa stared at the email for long moments, then read it again before she opened the attached job description. Truthfully, it was a dream job and a chance to re-establish herself in the industry without suffering from an enormous gap in her CV, and she felt a stir of excitement at the thought of being able to work for a big company again. Sure, she'd just signed a contract with the Calvo Group, but that was only for three months, and with relocation negotiations usually taking a while, it would probably line up nicely. With the job came Sandrine though, and Sandrine had hurt her. Why she wanted her back, Lisa had no idea. Now that she'd distanced herself from Sandrine it was clear that they were never actually that happy or even madly in love. She sighed, the dilemma already giving her a headache. And then there was Stella, of course. They'd promised each other that they'd still see each other when she moved back to London; that they would try to make this work from a distance. But New York was not London and flying to Spain every other weekend wasn't an option if she moved there. They'd only be able to see each other every two months or so and not only with the challenge of distance, but also the different time zones, she knew more than anyone how hard it could be. Ignoring the stab of guilt she felt, she sent a quick reply to make sure Sandrine wouldn't call her during their trip.

'Thank you for your email. You and I are over, but I appreciate the thought considering the job. Let me think about it.'

50

Following the sound of water, Stella and Lisa reached the top of the gorge and looked down to find a waterfall behind it. It clattered down from where the two little streams that spiralled through the landscape came together, creating a mesmerising natural mountain pool. The water was azure blue, shimmering in the sun, and surrounded by the green vegetation it looked like a little piece of paradise. Apart from a handful of sheep that were lazily grazing on the hills and a lizard that slid past them and disappeared behind a rock, there wasn't a soul in sight. It was an idyllic vantage point, and even Stella had never taken the effort to venture into the wilderness and appreciate the serenity of the mountains.

"Wow," Stella whispered, not wanting to disturb the peace. Lisa nodded in agreement and leaned into her as she caught her breath. It had been a tough forty-minute hike but now that they were here, it was so worth it. Stella had never made it this far and she wished that they had more time as the higher they climbed, the more their surroundings changed and there were beautiful surprises everywhere. An open patch in the strip of pine forest they'd walked through was like a natural stage, where the upcoming sun hit the stream and the ferns around it, making the water glisten like diamonds and the vegetation glow like gold. They'd seen birds of prey, another Iberian lynx, lots of rabbits and ancient ruins that had once been a village.

"This region was the last refuge of the Moors in Spain," she said. "That's why there are so many ruins. But the culture still rings through in the regional food and the architecture of the small flat-roofed villages." She pointed to where they'd come from, the outlines of the cubic buildings now clear from a distance. "The name 'Las Alpujarras' originates from Arabic and means 'land of pasture'."

"That it is. The landscape is so lush and untouched." Lisa took Stella's hand and smiled "Want to swim? I've always wanted to swim in a natural pool."

"It looks deep and it will be cold," Stella warned her, but Lisa was already kicking off her trainers and her socks. The sight of Lisa, now taking off her tight top and her running tights along with her lingerie made her forget about the freezing mountain water, and she stripped off too, then followed Lisa to the rocky edge. The woman was naked, so how could she not? Her perky behind was irresistible, her nipples erect in the cool breeze. "Nature looks good on you," she said, staring Lisa up and down. "God, I want you."

"Oh, yeah?" Lisa's gaze travelled to Stella's breasts in return, and she licked her lips as their eyes locked. "You'll just have to come and get me then." She dived in gracefully, but reappeared screaming and Stella laughed as she watched her frantically panic paddling in the pool that was much deeper than it looked. "Okay, that was probably not my most sensual moment," she joked.

"I told you it was cold."

Lisa wiped the water from her eyes and laughed out loud. "Come in, it's really nice." Her teeth were chattering, and she failed to keep a straight face as she said it.

"Sure it is." Stella shot her a sceptical look but dived in anyway. Although she'd expected it to be freezing, the temperature was still a shock to her system and she gasped as she swam towards Lisa, who was laughing even harder now.

"Come here, baby. Let me warm you up," she said, draping an arm around Stella's waist as she held onto a rock with the other.

"Thank you, that's better." Stella slowly got used to the cold, her body relaxing while the sun warmed her face. Lisa pressing against her was most certainly helping, and with her wet hair and shimmering water droplets trickling down her face, she took her breath away. This woman was everything she wanted and more and lately, the tight longing in her core she felt each time she looked at her came paired with something warmer and deeper. And Lisa was about to meet her parents. Stella had told herself that it was no big deal. After all, she wasn't the first woman she'd brought home. But she was the first woman she'd had such overwhelming feelings for, and it mattered to her that Lisa would feel comfortable around her family.

"This is perfect," Lisa whispered, gazing over the water and the mountains that towered over them. Now that they were closer to the top, the small patches of snow dotted along the peaks were clearly visible. "Don't you think?"

"You're perfect." Stella smiled and kissed her softly, then parted her lips to take the kiss deeper as her hunger grew. She steadied her foot on a rock so she could hold Lisa and pull her in as tight as she could. Lisa's chest was heaving but it wasn't from the hike, and the tremble in her thighs drew

Stella to slide a hand between her legs and cup her centre. Lisa's throbbing flesh was warm against her hand, her hips pushing into her as she moaned.

"What if someone walks past?" she asked through ragged breaths, her eyes darkening when Stella put more pressure where she needed it most. "Or what if—" Her lips were still parted as she stopped herself, closing her eyes.

"Small chance," Stella whispered, although she wasn't so sure of that. They'd met a handful of people on their way, and she suspected this pool was one of the destinations of the many hiking trails. She shot Lisa a mischievous smirk and raised a brow. "But if you're worried, I can be quick..."

51

"Wait... what's that over there?" Lisa was just about to get in the car after a comfort break on their way to Seville when she saw something moving in the field behind the petrol station. She walked back and approached it carefully, expecting a lynx or a fox, and she gasped when she saw it was a puppy sitting in the tall grass. It was tiny and yellow, and started trembling when she came closer.

"Everything okay?" Stella yelled from out of the car window.

Lisa nodded and placed a finger over her lips, beckoning Stella to be quiet, then bent down beside the puppy and slowly reached out to stroke it. The puppy winced and ducked down, as if trying to make itself invisible. "Hey, don't be afraid, I'm going to help you, okay? You're way too small to be on your own." Lisa had never had a dog before and wasn't even sure how to pick it up, but after a few failed attempts in which it shot from left to right, dodging her, she got hold of it and held it tightly against her chest. A couple of fleas jumped off it, and one of the puppy's eyes looked a little gummy. "You're a boy," she whispered, softly cradling him from side to side as she walked back to the car. "A tiny little boy."

"Oh, God." Stella stared at the fluffy creature and placed a hand on her heart. "Poor thing."

"He's got fleas," Lisa warned her when Stella took him to examine him. "You look like you know what you're doing."

"I know a thing or two; we used to have dogs at home. He can't be more than eight weeks old, and he looks skinny. Who knows how long he's been out here." Stella glanced in the direction of the petrol station. "I doubt he belongs to the owner. He's too young to be outside and he's not wearing a collar, so someone must have left him here." The puppy relaxed a little when she scratched him behind his floppy ears. "If there's one, there might be more. Will you give him some water while I have a look in the field? He must be really thirsty."

"Of course." Lisa rinsed her coffee cup with her water bottle and poured some for him. She could feel his heart rate slowing as she stroked him, but he was afraid of the cup. He refused to drink at first, so she dabbed his mouth with her wet finger, and he licked it off. "There you go. And a little more." She repeated the action a couple of times until he finally leaned over the cup and frantically started drinking. Whispering sweet words to him and covering him with a jumper so he'd feel safe, she waited for Stella to come back. Ten minutes went by, then twenty. Lisa was just about to get out and check on Stella after she'd disappeared behind the petrol station, when she turned the corner with another puppy.

"God help us," she said as she got in the driver's seat and handed Lisa the other puppy. It was a girl. She was bigger, a little darker and her ears were smaller, but they clearly came from the same litter. The two puppies squeaked as they were reunited and settled half on top of each other for comfort on Lisa's lap. The girl licked her brother's eyes and face, and the adorable sight stung Stella's eyes.

Lisa felt emotional too. They'd been in distress, possibly trying to find each other for hours, or perhaps even days. "You're together now. Everything is going to be fine."

"She's braver than her brother." Stella held out her hand and the girl sniffed it, then clumsily swung her paw at her finger while the boy hid under the jumper.

"Yes, you are. I'm glad Stella found you, so you can make your brother feel safe." Lisa held the water cup in front of her and while the girl drank, Lisa felt something warm spread across her lap. "I think he just peed on me."

Stella rolled her eyes and laughed. "Great. This is going to be an interesting journey; you'll probably be soaked by the time we get to the nearest vet."

"Is there one nearby?" Lisa asked when Stella scrolled through her phone.

"There's one eleven kilometres away. I'll call ahead to let them know we're coming."

"I don't understand how someone can just abandon helpless puppies," Lisa mumbled, using her jumper to clean the urine off the puppy.

"Don't get me started. It makes me so angry I can't even think about it."

"What are we going to do with them?" Lisa opened her window further. "After the vet, I mean. Can we bring them to your parents?"

Stella shrugged. "Sure, they won't mind. We can decide what to do when we're there. Maybe one of my parents' friends might want to adopt them, or someone in Altea, or one of my colleagues. If everything else fails, we could take them to a shelter." She bit her lip as she glanced at Lisa, who gave her a subtle nod.

"Yes. Let's just make sure they're healthy and fed first and go from there."

Stella typed in an address on her satnav. "Okay. They'll need flea treatment, worming tablets and jabs if they're old enough. I hope the vet sells puppy food as I'm not sure their stomachs will be able to handle real food yet." As soon as she turned on the engine, the puppies started to squeak and tremble in fear.

Lisa cradled them in her arms and held them close to her chest. "Shhh... It's going to be okay. I'll take care of you, don't you worry." She felt another warm, wet stain spread across her belly this time. "Fuck."

"What? Again?" Stella asked as she drove off.

"Uh-huh." Lisa carefully turned the jumper so the puppies would have something dry to lie on. "I think I might need a change of clothes before we get to your parents."

52

"*We're* here. Are you ready?"

"No," Lisa joked, eyeing the charming little street that wasn't far from the old city centre they'd driven through.

"Don't worry, babe. It will be fine." Stella parked along the road in front of the deli and spotting her car, her mother immediately came running out. The puppies had been a welcome distraction to stop her from worrying, but now she suddenly felt nervous.

"Madre!" She fell into her mother's embrace and then her father's, who followed only seconds later. "This is Lisa," she said, stepping away from them and taking Lisa's hand. "Lisa is from the UK so we'll have to speak English while she's here." As she uttered the words, they sounded strange coming from her lips. She'd never spoken English with her parents before and her mother grinned, clearly feeling the same awkwardness. "Lisa, this is my mother, María, and my father, Antonio."

"Of course, we'll speak English. We'll try our best, anyway. It's so nice to meet you, Lisa." María kissed Lisa on both cheeks and only then spotted what was in the basket she was holding. After the vet, they'd stopped off to buy something the puppies could sleep in, and after dozing off for a good hour, they were now curiously peering over the edge. "Madre de Dios. I hope that's not a gift." She leaned in to stroke them and cooed something in Spanish when the girl licked her finger.

"No," Lisa said with a chuckle, then greeted Stella's father. "I mean, you can have them if you want; we found them on our way here." She smiled widely and looked from Stella's mother to her father and back. "It's so lovely to meet you too. I've really been looking forward to it."

Stella noted her mother looked ecstatic today, as if her angelic girlfriend showing up with two tiny puppies was the best thing that had ever happened to her.

"Well, let's get these two inside so they're nice and cool." María took the basket from Lisa and studied them. "They're beautiful. I think they're a Labrador mix; they might grow quite big."

"That's what the vet thought too," Lisa said, following her into the deli. "The golden one is a boy, he's called Butters. The darker, chubbier one is a girl, and her name is Meatball."

María laughed. "You've given them names already? Oh my, you know what happens when you give puppies names..."

"We had a couple of hours to kill in the car, so it was hard not to." Stella loved the smell of the deli as she maneuvered through the narrow isle. The concoction of roasted garlic, stewed pork cheek and fresh herbs reminded her of her childhood. Nothing ever changed here; the old, rickety metal shelves that regularly fell over when kids ran into them, the worn-out terracotta tiled floor, the noisy freezers against the back wall, the deli counter filled with home-made dishes, cheeses and cured hams, and the TV that was mounted on the wall behind the counter so her mother wouldn't have to miss her favourite soap operas. She'd always thought it could do with an overhaul, but as the deli had been featured in numerous travel magazines and blogs —Condé Nast had referred to it as 'a refreshingly authentic deli serving moreish and delicious local delicacies'—and was popular with both locals and tourists, her parents didn't see the point of changing anything.

"What happens when you give puppies names?" Lisa asked, glancing at Stella over her shoulder.

Stella shot her a grin and pinched her behind. "You end up keeping them."

The narrow staircase in the back of the deli creaked as they went up to the flat and when they entered the living room, she noted the normally messy space was spotless. So was the kitchen, where her mother put the basket on the floor and filled a water bowl for the puppies. Even the kitchen table, that normally served as a desk and tended to be buried under paperwork, was free of clutter and there were no dishes in the sink. With her parents working long hours in the deli, the state of their flat was the last thing on their mind, but her mother had clearly prepared for Lisa's arrival.

They fussed over the furballs, who'd had their flea treat-ment after the vet had cleaned them up. At approximately eight weeks old, they were too young for their jabs, so they would have to take care of that later, but otherwise— although Butters could do with fattening up a little—they'd been assured they were both healthy.

"I have food for them," Stella said, taking the box she'd bought from the vet from her overnight bag. The puppies stayed in the basket, too scared to venture out, but Butters wasn't as shifty as he'd been a few hours ago.

"Let's put the food on the floor for them and leave them in peace for a while so they can get used to the space." María tutted as she stared at them lovingly, and Stella was hoping she might want to keep them. "Your father will be up later. He's minding the shop, so let's have a drink and a snack on the roof until he closes." She turned to Lisa. "I'm sure you're both tired after the long drive."

"Thank you, that sounds lovely." Lisa kneeled and kissed both puppies on their heads. "Don't be scared, okay? I'll be back."

"Oh boy, I foresee trouble here." Stella shot her a grin as she took the tray her mother gave her to carry up to the roof.

"Trouble?"

"Yeah. You're totally melting; you won't be able to give them away."

"So were you while I was driving," Lisa shot back at her. "You were telling them whole stories in Spanish in that cute, whispering tone. And need I remind you that *you* were the one who insisted on naming them?"

María laughed, amused by their playful back and forth, and she rubbed an arm over Lisa's shoulder, looking her over once more. "Such a pretty girl," she said, almost as if she were talking to a child. "How did my naughty daughter get so lucky?"

"Naughty?" Stella shouted from the staircase. "I've never been naughty."

"She's lying." Stella's mother beckoned for Lisa to follow Stella. "I will tell you all about the trouble we've had with Stella. Let me just heat up some food, I'll be five minutes."

53

*L*isa was enjoying herself, sipping sangria on the roof terrace that looked over the dozens of other roof terraces in the street. In contrast to María and Antonio's basic flat that clearly hadn't been given much love and attention over the years, their roof terrace was like an urban jungle, adorned with flowers and potted pineapple palms, quaint cast iron furniture and quirky little seating areas amongst all the green. The colourful Spanish tiles were polished, and the terrace-facing wall was painted bright yellow. Other roof terraces were equally green, she noticed. There had been some regular back and forth yelling between Stella, Stella's mother and the neighbours on the other side of the street, who wanted to know how 'little Stella' was doing and who her friend was. Her mother hadn't told them they were a couple, but she'd boasted about Lisa as if they'd known each other for years.

María was a short, voluptuous, happy and chatty woman with a grey perm, and her husband was taller and slimmer. Although Stella didn't look like either of her parents, there was no question as to where she got her optimism, humour and energy from, and Lisa really liked María, who had been curiously interrogating her for the past hour. *Where are you from? What do you do? Do you have siblings? Have you been to Seville before? How do you like Spain? Will you move here permanently?* The latter had been a painful question, not just because it was unlikely she'd be able to stay or even knew if she wanted to stay in Spain as that would be a drastic life change, but also because she hadn't yet discussed the New York job opportunity with Stella. So, they'd both skimmed around the subject, and Stella had told her mother to stop complicating matters as the UK was Lisa's home and it was only a short flight away; they would be fine either way.

The wooden table was filled with small dishes from the deli, all delicious and new to Lisa. Fried cazón; a tender white fish, salmorejo; a cold soup with crumbled egg, spinach and chickpea stew, snails in garlic and Iberico ham on fresh, grilled bread smothered in olive oil were spread over the red and white chequered tablecloth.

"It's so good. Did you make all this yourself?" she asked.

María nodded proudly. "Yes. Antonio and I make everything ourselves in the small deli kitchen. I usually cook and he mans the counter but when I don't feel like it, we swap; he's very capable. We generally sell the same things, apart from our daily specials. Do you cook?"

"A little, but nothing like this." Lisa looked up when Antonio came up to join them, holding the two puppies in his arms. María sneered something at him in Spanish, but he laughed it off and put them on the floor.

"They were howling, so I couldn't leave them there on their own," he said, laughing when Butters immediately ran to Lisa. "I guess he wanted his madre."

"Oh, he wants me to pick him up." Lisa held out her arms and lifted him when he clumsily got on his back legs, pawing her. She stroked him as he curled up on her lap and almost immediately fell asleep. "Could you be any more adorable?"

"That's going to be a crazy household, with five cats and two dogs." Antonio shot his daughter an amused look as she picked up Meatball.

"I was kind of hoping you might want them," Stella said carefully. "Or maybe Aunt Magda or one of the neighbours. I can't have dogs; I work all day."

"What about us? Don't we work?"

"Yes, but couldn't they stay in the deli?" Stella asked. "Blanco used to hang out there all the time."

Antonio shook his head. "Times have changed. People don't like dogs in delis or restaurants these days, we might lose customers. And as far as I'm aware, Aunt Magda is allergic and most of our neighbours are too old. You could take them to the local shelter, though. They're cute so I'm sure they'll find them a good home in no time."

"Hmm... Maybe we should take them back and ask around in Benidorm first. There are plenty of British pensioners who live there full-time who I'm sure would love a dog. Or Spanish locals," Stella said. "I want to make sure they end up in a good home."

"Yes, let's take them back with us," Lisa agreed, not liking the idea of letting them go so soon, especially not now that Butters had attached himself to her. She was in love with them both already and although the journey had been a hassle, and she'd had to write off her jeans and her jumper as they were drenched in urine, her heart swelled for the two puppies who had come into her life so unexpectedly.

Antonio helped himself to sangria and a piece of fish

and turned to Lisa. "So, have you been to Seville before? It's a very special city."

"No, never. It looked amazing as we drove through the city centre, and this neighbourhood is lovely. It seems so social, with everyone sitting on their roofs, talking to each other."

"I wouldn't mind doing without the nosey neighbours," Antonio joked. "But all in all, it's a very nice neighbourhood. We've lived here all our lives and the city centre has moved in this direction, so it's much more popular now."

Lisa smiled. "I love the view too. The town with all its churches in the distance, the pastel colours of the buildings and the smell..." She inhaled deeply but wasn't able to identify the pungent floral scent. "What is it?"

"Seville smells like the Garden of Eden," Antonio said. "It's jasmine actually, and in spring, the whole city smells of orange blossom. In those months it's hard to believe you're in a big city."

"Those are orange trees over there," Stella said, pointing in the direction of a tree-lined street in the distance. "There's nowhere else in the world where you can wander through random streets in the middle of the city and pick oranges from the trees. The orange season stretches between December and February, and in those months, the city smells of citrus." Stella refilled their glasses, her proud smile lighting up her face. "Seville is known for its aromas, but it's also known for flamenco and later tonight, I want to take you out."

"How exciting!" Lisa smiled. "So, I'll finally get to see what you're so passionate about up-close. Will you be joining us?" she asked, turning to Stella's parents.

"No, not tonight. You two go out and enjoy yourselves,

Stella is keen to show you the city. But we've arranged a family dinner for tomorrow when Stella's sister is here," María said. "Besides, flamenco is very romantic. It's not something parents should get involved with."

54

"Seville is the soul of Spain," Stella said as they wandered through the Barrio de Santa Cruz district. She felt at home in the ancient streets and effortlessly navigated through the maze of dark alleyways. Lisa's excitement was endearing, her reaction palpable in the way she squeezed her hand each time they turned a corner and faced another chapel, mosque, cathedral, synagogue or pretty plaza. "That's how I think of this city anyway." The night was steamy hot, but that was fitting here; summers is Seville were sultry and life passed at a slow pace.

"I couldn't agree more. There's so much culture and beauty, and it also feels mysterious, don't you think?"

"Yes, it definitely has an air of mystery to it. It's because of the gothic and baroque architecture, I suppose, and because there are so many places of worship here. The Easter processions are spectacular."

"I'd love to experience that." Lisa wandered into one of the dozens of courtyards they passed to admire the plants that were lit up from underneath, creating a shadow theatre on the walls of the white buildings. "I hear music. Is that where we're heading?"

"Yes, it's this way." Stella turned into another narrow alleyway that brought them onto a small plaza where locals were perched on the edge of a fountain, watching a woman in a long, red gypsy dress and a matching shawl with ruffles, dance and clap in the dimly lit square. The ruffled tail on her skirt moved gracefully around her, swaying with every turn. The sound of guitar music echoed off the tall walls surrounding them. High-pitched, sharp, percussive and painfully dramatic, it always pulled at her heartstrings. Sitting on a folding chair with his legs crossed, the guitarist picked at the strings and simultaneously tapped the instrument, the rhythm powerful, the music improvised. An old woman sitting beside him was singing, leading the performance with her hoarse and powerful voice.

"Oh my..." Lisa stopped in her stride and stared.

"They've played and danced for change here every night for as long as I can remember. Her grandmother and mother used to dance here, and now she's taken over the family tradition. The guitarist is her father, and the singer is her aunt," Stella whispered, pleased to see how much the performance affected Lisa as she led them to a free spot under a tree. "Do you mind sitting on the ground?"

"No, of course not." Lisa sat and leaned back against the trunk, and Stella beckoned her to wait while she walked to the hole in the wall that served tiny glasses of beer.

"There's no need to book some silly expensive touristy flamenco show in an air-conditioned building while you can sit out here where nothing is orchestrated," Stella said as she handed her a drink. "Here, it comes from deep within, it's passion in its purest form."

"It's truly beautiful. So intense." Lisa's gaze followed the dancer, her hand, leg and body movements intricate and her footwork percussive.

"It's a state of mind, an expression that connects with the audience on an emotional level." Stella put an arm around her, and Lisa sank against her, resting her cheek on her shoulder. She was glowing, intensely happy to be here and experiencing her favourite art form with the woman she was madly in love with. There wasn't a more romantic place in the world than here, on this plaza, a secret place that was hidden so deep in the labyrinth of the city that tourists rarely found it. This was her Seville and although she sometimes missed living here, it also meant that she appreciated it more than ever now. Lisa was looking gorgeous in her yellow summer dress, her skin damp and her cheeks rosy from the heat.

"I totally get your passion for flamenco now," she said, turning to her. "I wish I could understand the lyrics. I can pick up a few things, but the accent is so different to what I've heard in the past months."

"I'm glad you like it." Stella felt an urge to kiss her, but it was a little crowded for that here. "The songs are always sung in a very strong Andalusian accent, it's hard for outsiders to understand."

"It doesn't matter, I feel it right to my bones." Lisa snuggled closer to her and watched the performance, occasionally tapping her feet along. It was hard not to, Stella was tapping her thigh herself, the rhythm so entwined with her being. The members of the audience—even some of the regulars she recognised—were transfixed on the trio as if they were experiencing flamenco for the first time.

"Thank you," Lisa said when the song was over, and the dancer stepped away to take a break. "For letting me come along. This whole trip has been an amazing experience and I loved meeting your parents. They're so nice."

"They like you too. Honestly, you have no idea; they wouldn't stop gushing about you while you went to the bathroom and said you were always welcome, with or without me."

"Even without you?" Lisa laughed. "That's a good sign. So... it could have been worse."

"Yes. It definitely could have been worse." Stella lowered her gaze to Lisa's lips, the pull of longing stirring potently in her core. "You must be tired; we were up early and it's been a long day."

"If with that you're suggesting we sample that single bed of yours, then I'm all for being horizontal." Lisa shot her a flirty look. "But I hope you have a lock on the door because it's warm and I intend to sleep naked."

*a*fter a long day, nothing felt better than a cold shower followed by the privacy of Stella's small bedroom, even though it was small and warm and the bed creaked. Lisa was still on cloud nine from their romantic evening and felt lucky to be here, where she had the opportunity to get to know Stella on a deeper level. The window was wide open and the noisy fan on full blast was facing the bed, only redistributing the warm air. She had the impression nothing had been changed here in decades and was fascinated as she sat on top of the covers and looked around, studying the evidence of Stella's teenage years. The poster of Pamela Anderson made her laugh, and so did several centrefold pages, some only hanging on one corner, stuck to the wall with duct tape. There was an ancient CD player on a messy desk, CDs piled high next to it, and an old leather studded jacket was draped over the back of the office chair behind it. On a pinboard above the bed were pictures of Stella with friends on nights out, and she looked adorable in her failed attempt to look cool with a mohawk. Lisa found it hard to imagine Stella as a punk chick, then remembered she'd gone through a goth phase herself. Her mother had hated her heavy black eyeliner and her dyed hair, and it had taken her years to grow out her natural colour again.

"Pamela? Really?" she said when Stella walked in with a towel wrapped around her breasts.

Stella shrugged. "I was young, and I've always been a sucker for blondes." She reached out to caress Lisa's wet locks and grinned. "If my teenage self had known I'd have you in my bed one day..."

"And is that what you used to wear while you were hitting on girls?" Lisa pointed to the jacket with a smirk.

"Hey, don't make fun of my jacket. I happen to look really cute in it." Stella dropped her towel to the floor and put it on, her naked body on full display under the soft, black leather as she held it open and spun around.

"You're right; it's kind of sexy but I especially like what's underneath it."

"Yeah?" Stella sat down on the edge of the bed and cupped her neck, then pulled her in for a kiss.

Lisa closed her eyes and welcomed her. After hours of behaving themselves, she was more than ready for some alone time. "Then let me be your Pammie for the night," she mumbled against her mouth, parting her lips to let her in. She removed her own towel and heat flared inside her, the ache between her thighs growing as Stella pushed her back and draped herself on top of her.

"I'm not going to say no to that," she whispered, moving down to her breasts. "But you have to be very, very quiet."

"I can do th—" Lisa slammed a hand in front of her mouth when Stella sucked on her nipple, stifling a loud moan.

"Shh... My parents are right next door." Stella looked up and shot her an amused glance, then continued to feast on her while her hand disappeared between her thighs. "God, I love your body. You're so, so much sexier than Pam—"

Lisa muffled her words by pulling her tightly against her breast, bucking her hips in delight. Being in Stella's old bedroom was especially arousing for some reason, and she felt sixteen again herself. "Have you had lots of girls in this room?" she asked, keeping her voice down.

"Yes." Stella looked pleased with herself as she looked her over, clearly liking that Lisa was already starting to lose control. "And you know what we used to do back in the day?"

"What did you do?" Lisa's breath hitched when she saw the mischievous look on Stella's face.

"What every lesbian teenager did..." Stella turned around and straddled Lisa with her back to her, then bent forward and ran her tongue through her folds.

"Oh, my G—" Lisa held her breath and bit her lip, the delicious sensations it caused almost too much. Stella's mouth on her made her throb and having her wetness right in front of her turned her on like nothing else. She roughly pulled her in by her hips and did the same, sating her sexual appetite by licking and sucking at Stella's heated flesh until her thighs started trembling. It was exciting to keep quiet even though she felt like screaming her name and when she darted her tongue inside of her, Stella clearly felt the same, uttering a soft groan between her thighs.

Both shaking, they feasted on each other as silently as they were physically capable of. Lisa felt Stella tense first, her thighs clenching against her cheeks as she jerked back against her tongue. The moment was so erotic that her own orgasm ignited and spread like wildfire, quicker than she could fathom. She held Stella's thighs in a tight grip, and Stella held onto hers, undoubtedly leaving fingermarks on her skin as she was squeezing her so hard it stung. The delicious pain and Stella's skilled tongue that didn't stop stimulating her elevated her state, drawing her climax out for long moments and surprising her with aftershocks that made her whole body convulse.

Stella went limp and chuckled between her legs. "Mmm... It's been a while..."

"Let me assure you, you haven't lost your skills," Lisa whispered with a sigh. "Come up here, baby, and let me hold you." She took Stella in her arms and sighed in contentment. Warm wind blew over them through the open window and she smiled when Stella's breathing steadied before they fell into a deep, dreamless sleep.

56

Seville was—if possible—even more glorious by day and Lisa couldn't stop snapping pictures and gushing about how pretty the city was. Stella's heart swelled at how adorable she was, her enthusiasm infectious as she strutted around, taking everything in. They'd stopped to buy an ice cream to share and were sitting on the edge of a fountain on Plaza Doña Elvira, watching life go by. Surrounded by ceramic benches, orange trees and bustling restaurants, it was one of her favourite places, one she used to visit frequently when she still lived here. The sun shining through the trees created a slowly moving leafy pattern all over the square and the tables, and despite the crowd, the atmosphere here was dreamy and peaceful.

"This is the birthplace of Doña Elvira," she said. "The impossible love of Don Juan."

"How romantic." Lisa handed her the cone. "There's so much history here, it's—" Her phone rang and she looked irritated as she checked the caller ID and turned it off. It had happened a couple of times in the past days and Stella was starting to wonder what was going on.

"Everything okay?" she asked.

Lisa hesitated as she glanced at her phone, then let out a long sigh. "Actually, it's Sandrine," she finally said.

"Your ex?" Stella felt her heart sink. Was she back in contact with her again? And what did that mean for them?

"Yes. A job has come up at the company she works for in New York. She wants me to apply for it; she says I have a very good chance of getting it if she endorses me."

"Is it the right job for you?"

"Yes, it's an amazing job and it would be a step up for me but—"

"Hey, no 'buts'. This is what you wanted, isn't it?" Stella pursed her lips. "It's good news. For you, anyway." She didn't mean to sound negative. After all, Lisa had been job hunting all along and with her CV, she would be crazy to throw her career away by refusing such an opportunity. She'd always known this day would come; she just hadn't expected her to want to move so far away.

Lisa flinched, and she was silent for long moments. "Do you *want* me to move away?"

"No, of course I don't want you to move away, especially not to New York, but I don't want to limit you in your career either because that wouldn't do either of us any good."

"You're not limiting me," Lisa said. "You make me happy. That's more than any job ever could. I was actually going to discuss this with you when we got back but now that we're talking…" She took Stella's hand and gave her a shy smile. "I want to know exactly how you feel about me because honestly, I don't want to be so far away from you either."

"Oh…" Stella believed her when their eyes locked. and she slowly let out the breath she'd been holding.

"Your mother was asking a lot of questions while you were in the shower this morning," Lisa continued.

"Really? About what?" Stella frowned, confused at the random change of subject.

"Just about how we were going to make this work when I move back to London."

Stella groaned and raised her gaze skyward. "Oh, God, not again. I told her to stay out of it. Look, I know your life is not here; I've known that all along and although I'm delighted that you were able to stay for longer, I never expected you to move here because of me. Neither should my mother. She just likes you so much and she probably sees how crazy I am about you but that doesn't give her the right to get involved."

"Well, I told her how I felt about you," Lisa said shyly, avoiding her gaze.

"You did?"

"Yes. I'm not sure why but I found myself opening up to her. I told her you were the best thing that's ever happened to me. That meeting you was worth every agonising event that happened before I came to Spain because it led me to you." Lisa smiled. "It's true. I'd do it all over again. The break-up, the redundancy, losing my home..." She hesitated. "And to be honest with you, I can't stand the thought of going back to London, let alone New York because I don't want you part-time. I want you all the time."

"I'm..." Stella swallowed hard. "I'm not sure if I want to leave Spain now that it's going so well with my job and I have the house and the cats and—"

"No, that's not what I meant," Lisa said, cupping her face with both hands. "What I meant was, how would you feel if I moved here permanently? If I looked for a job in Spain? I've been doing a lot of thinking over the past few days; I had to because of the New York job but I don't want that job if I can be with you instead."

Stella opened her mouth to speak, but too stunned to answer, no sound came from her lips. Lisa's confession had caused a whirlwind inside her and she had to let it settle before she could think straight.

"Sorry. Is it too early for this conversation?" Lisa winced. "It probably is, but it felt like a good time to talk about it, since this job came up and I need to make a decision. It will take me a while to find something here if I find anything at all. But if you want me to stay, I'll try."

"No, it's not too soon. I just assumed you didn't want to stay in Spain, especially not in and around Benidorm."

Lisa pursed her lips as she thought about that. "Benidorm has grown on me, and I really like Altea," she said. "And now that I've been here a while and understand the language better, I think I could settle in Spain. I love the weather, the people, the culture and the food and I'm willing to give it a go, but only if you want that too."

"Are you kidding me?" Stella's eyes welled up as she pulled her into a long hug. "You don't even have to ask me that, silly. Of course, I want you to stay. I've been fantasising about you saying that to me, but I never thought it would actually happen." Swallowing down the lump in her throat, she laced a hand through Lisa's hair and held her as tightly as she could. "I want you with me all the time. I love you." She paused after the statement, but it only took a beat to realise that she'd never meant anything more. "I love you."

Lisa pulled out of the hug, their eyes meeting in a loaded exchange. "I love you too," she whispered, wiping a tear from Stella's cheek. She chuckled as she looked down at the ice cream Stella was holding; it had melted and was dripping all over her hand.

Stella followed her gaze and laughed as she placed it on the edge of the fountain for the pigeons to eat and rinsed her hand in the water behind her. "You," she said. "You really have a way of making me forget everything."

57

"So, here she finally is!" A slightly younger and more feminine version of Stella came to greet Lisa when they returned from their sightseeing tour through the city. Despite her legs being tired from walking for miles, she felt incredibly energetic and alive after their talk.

"Hey. It's so nice to meet you," she said, returning the hug when Eléa embraced her. "You look so much like Stella."

"I do? I thought I was much prettier," Eléa joked, throwing her head back with laughter when Stella nudged her. "Hola hermana! How are you?" She fell around Stella's neck, then mumbled something in Spanish before she stepped back. "How did you manage to find yourself such a beautiful girlfriend, huh? Is she blind or something?"

Stella shot a sharp reply back at her in Spanish, but she smiled and hugged her again. "You're just jealous," she said, taking Lisa's hand.

"Nah-ah. I like men." Eléa winked at Lisa. "I couldn't live without a big—"

"Hey, no dirty talk," María cut her off, and they laughed

as she ushered them to follow her up to the roof, where a spectacular feast and two overexcited puppies were awaiting them.

"They've been eating all day," Stella's father said, stroking Butters, who was sitting on his lap. He put him down when Butters wagged his tail at the sight of Lisa, and he immediately ran up to her.

"Hey, little one, mummy's back," she joked and exchanged a soppy look with Stella, who picked up his sister. "I've missed them."

"Yeah, me too. It's going to be hard to let them go," Stella said. They cuddled and kissed them before putting them down in the bed that they'd created from old blankets, and the siblings started play fighting, tumbling over each other.

"They're so, so cute. I wish I could have dogs in my flat," Eléa said. "You should keep them."

"We can't. It's too complicated."

"No, we can't," Lisa agreed, but she liked the 'we' part of Stella's answer. She was in such a peaceful headspace now as she didn't have to procrastinate over the job offer anymore. Her future was decided, it would be with Stella and that felt so good.

"That's a shame. I would have loved to see them grow up." Eléa gestured to the table. "Sit down, I hope you're hungry. Mum made me slave away in the kitchen all afternoon. I peeled gambas until my nails chipped."

"Oh no, that's the worst job ever." Stella chuckled and held up a hand. "But let's face it; fair is fair. I had to do it last time you brought a boyfriend over. Where is Sandro anyway?"

"I have no idea. I haven't seen him since last week when I threw a drink at him at that gypsy bar in Triana." Eléa let out a dramatic sigh. "I caught him cheating on me."

"Sorry to hear that. But I told you he was no good," Stella said, raising her hands in defence when Eléa narrowed her eyes at her.

"Hey, I know I'm the younger sister but 'I told you so' will still result in a fist fight if you're not careful; it's not helpful."

"Come on, girls, let's eat in peace," their father interrupted them. "Sandro is not worth spilling words over. He's good for nothing," he added in a mutter, pouring red wine for them.

"You're right." Eléa pulled out a chair for Lisa and took a seat next to her. "I just want to enjoy getting to know my new sister-in-law over a well-deserved dinner. I've worked hard enough for it." She sniffed her hands. "Fucking shrimp smell just won't fade."

Lisa laughed. "Sorry, I didn't mean to cause trouble. I would have helped if I'd been here."

"I'm kidding. It's so exciting to have another girl in the family." The way Eléa said it made Lisa think she'd already been accepted as part of the family, even though she'd only been here for two days. The warmth and love these people exuded made her feel so welcome, and the constant playful bickering, especially between their parents, was hugely entertaining.

"This looks amazing," she said, staring over the spread of tortilla, pickled carrots, grilled gambas with lemon and sea salt, fresh salads and a black rice dish that looked similar to paella. "I'd love to learn how to make all of this."

"Then we'll do it together next time." María took Lisa's plate and started serving up a generous portion with a bit of everything. "Make sure Stella brings you over again soon, she doesn't visit often enough."

Next time... Lisa smiled at her and nodded. "Yes, I would

like that." This wasn't just a trip to see the city; it was a very special visit, she realised then. The markings of a new beginning, of new relationships.

"Does your mother cook?" María asked.

"She's not great but she tries," Lisa said. "My mother has a busy full-time job so my father, who's retired, usually does the cooking and he's not much better either. My mother cooks a good Sunday lunch though; it's a tradition in the UK. Roast beef, vegetables, homemade gravy, roast potatoes, Yorkshire puddings and horseradish sauce."

"That sounds delicious. I'd like to try it, so make sure you're here on a Sunday next time." Stella's father said with an amused twinkle in his eyes. "And don't wait too long."

58

*L*isa was busy making a comfortable corner for the puppies on the roof terrace when her phone rang. She dropped the blanket she was folding and groaned when she saw it was Sandrine. She'd been ignoring her, putting off the conversation that was long overdue.

"Hey," she said, settling on the sofa in the shade. "Sorry I didn't call you back. I've been busy."

"That's okay, I gathered as much." Sandrine paused. "It's good to hear your voice. How are you?"

"I'm good. Really good, actually." Lisa took a deep breath, a little shocked to hear Sandrine's voice after so long. "What about you?"

"I'm good too. Missing you, though. Have you thought about that job? I have a big penthouse flat. I know it might be a bit presumptuous but if you get the job, you're welcome to move in here."

A sarcastic chuckle escaped Lisa's lips. "What about your new girlfriend? I bet she wouldn't be impressed if your ex moved in with you."

Sandrine chuckled. "We're not together anymore."

"Right." *Of course you're not, otherwise you wouldn't be pursuing me.* "I'm sorry to hear that." Lisa noted that there was no melancholy from her side. In fact, she felt nothing at all.

"It's fine. We weren't that compatible anyway. Not like you and me. We were—"

"Sandrine, it's not going to happen," Lisa cut her off. "I've moved on and I'm happy without you. I wish the same for you."

"But... I love you." The tremble in Sandrine's voice did not sound genuine and Lisa had a feeling she was putting on an act simply because she wasn't used to not getting what she wanted.

"Well, you hurt me, and I don't love you anymore." Lisa paused. "And if I'm honest, Sandrine, I don't think you love me either. You just love the idea of us, as long as I have a successful job and we can have the dream life you always envisioned. As soon as I hit rock bottom, you couldn't get rid of me fast enough. I don't want to be with you, and I'm sorry but I don't want to work with you either."

"So, you're not even going for the job?" Sandrine asked incredulously.

"No. I'm in Spain at the moment and I intend to stay. I'm going to look for a job here."

Sandrine cleared her throat. "You're joking, right? You can't possibly be serious..."

"I am serious. I like it here and life's not all about work. If there's one good thing that's come out of this whole disaster, it's that valuable insight."

"Then what is it about?" Sandrine asked.

"It's about love."

"Right." While Sandrine paused, Lisa imagined her doing an eyeroll behind her desk in her swanky office. She'd never been the sentimental type. "The Lisa I know is the most driven career woman I've met in my life. That's what I always admired about you." Again, there was a pause before Sandrine continued. "So, love, huh? That means you've met someone."

"Yes," Lisa said matter-of-factly. She didn't necessarily take pleasure in telling Sandrine she was in a new relationship—revenge was pointless in her opinion—but she did want to be very clear that she'd moved on.

"Who is she? What does she do?"

"She's the poolside manager at the hotel I was staying at when I first arrived in Benidorm." Lisa knew Sandrine's brain was churning as she waited for her reaction.

"First arrived? What does that mean? How long have you been there? And why the hell are you in Benidorm of all places?"

Lisa huffed. "What's with all the questions? You're awfully curious for someone who took zero interest in me when I needed you." She couldn't resist the dig and frankly, Sandrine deserved it.

"True," Sandrine admitted. "And you're right. I wasn't a good partner to you. I shouldn't have been unfaithful, and I shouldn't have ignored you the way I did. I'm very sorry."

"I appreciate the apology," Lisa said. "And I think we should leave it with that." She stretched out her legs on the coffee table, relieved to put an end to the conversation and leave the past behind her. Truthfully, it was the sincerest Sandrine had ever come across. Three months ago, she may have fallen for it, but she was a different woman now. She really, really wanted to move on and move forward, and Sandrine did not fit into that picture. She smiled when the puppies started barking; a sign that Stella had just come home from work.

"Are those dogs I hear? Don't tell me you have dogs."

"Yes, they're mine," she said, watching their tails wag in excitement. "Listen, I have to go but I wish you all the best, Sandrine, I really do. And good luck finding that perfect candidate for the job."

"Are you sure? You're not going to get another opportunity like this."

"I'm sure. I've been making my own opportunities for a while, and it's worked out pretty well, so I'm just going to have a little faith and go with the flow." Lisa hung up and smiled when Stella came through the door, getting down on her knees and holding her arms wide for Butters and Meatball who jumped up to lick her face. She played with them for a while, then picked up Pablo who wedged himself in between them.

"Come on, guys, give him a chance. Pablo wants some love too."

"Hey, what about me? I'm always going to be last now, aren't I?" Lisa joked, walking up to her.

"Last but not least, babe." Stella wrapped an arm around Lisa and kissed her while she held Pablo on her shoulder with her other hand. "I've missed you. How was your day?"

Lisa kissed her back and grinned widely. "Great. And even better now you're here," she said in a sappy tone, batting her lashes. "Want to take the kids to the beach? I bought them leads today. I think it's okay for them to go out as long as they're not around other dogs until they've been vaccinated."

"The kids?" Stella laughed, glancing at Butters and Meatball. "Is that what we're calling them now?"

"I just want to enjoy their company while I can. Now that you've put the word out, it probably won't take long until someone adopts them. I even took them to work this morning; the builders loved them."

"Why am I not surprised?" Stella shot her a loving smile and put Pablo down. "Did they behave?"

"Yes and no. Butters peed on someone's toolbox, but he immediately apologised by licking the man's face. Then Meatball went missing for about three minutes and I found her gobbling up someone's lunch behind the bar, so I had to go out and buy the carpenter a new sandwich. It was all a bit chaotic; I think I'll leave them home next time."

"You two..." Stella chuckled as she pointed a finger at the puppies. "Did you go to work with mummy? Did you misbehave? You did, didn't you?" They looked up at her, tilting their heads. "Do you think you deserve to go to the beach after that? Do you?"

Meatball barked, and they wagged their tails, making Lisa laugh out loud as she went to get their leads. "Right," she said. "I think that's a 'yes'."

59

"*H*ow was your trip to Seville? Lisa came along, right?" Manuel opened the poolside gate to let the first guests in.

"Great. Couldn't have gone better." Stella grinned. "It was eventful too; we found two puppies on our way there and brought them home with us. Any chance you want one? I've been asking around but no luck so far."

"Seriously?" Manuel laughed. "No, my friend. I don't have time for dogs."

"Too bad. They're incredibly cute." Stella opened a picture on her phone and showed it to him. It was a picture her mother had taken of her and Lisa, holding a puppy each.

"Who is cute? The pair of you or the dogs?" Manuel joked. "Why don't you keep them?"

"Can't do that. I don't have time for them either and I don't want them to be alone all day."

"What about Lisa?"

Stella shrugged. "We're not sure what will happen with her work situation, but she's going to look for a job nearby, so fingers crossed she's able to find something before her contract with the Calvo Group runs out."

"Madre de Dios." Manuel's eyes widened. "This is serious, isn't it?"

Stella nodded. "Yes, I love her." She realised her smirk couldn't have been wider. The past days had been a lot of fun. They'd spent hours getting the puppies accustomed to their new environment, then slowly introduced them to the cats who were far from amused with the new additions to the household.

"And where is 'the hot girl' now?" Manuel asked.

"She's over at Sunset. They've been finishing the outside space over the past days so she's checking it out."

"Ah! I saw they renamed it; there's an announcement on the banner surrounding the site. El Escondite. From the renderings underneath, it looks like it's going to be pretty fancy."

"Not fancy, just very Spanish and very welcoming. My girl knows what she's doing." Stella was close to bursting with pride. She'd listened in on Lisa's phone conversations on their drive back and she'd been impressed by her professionalism and leadership skills. She made herself an espresso behind the pool bar and handed one to Manuel. "So, what's been happening here?"

"Nothing much. They started some minor repairs in the building, which is good. Now that the group has money after the Sunset sale, there have even been rumours that they're going to spruce up the poolside."

"Excellent. I was hoping they'd do that." Stella checked her watch. "I actually have a meeting with Mr Avery in ten minutes. He never calls me in last-minute, so I'm sure it's got something to do with planned renovations."

"Make sure to pass on the info, I'd love to know what's in

the planning. Unless he's going to fire you for sleeping with the guests," Manuel joked.

"Not funny." Stella gave him a slap on his shoulder and knocked back her espresso. "Will you take over my lifeguard duty while I'm up there?"

Unlike his predecessor, Mr Avery wasn't a typical managing director. Never one to dress formally or even follow formal procedures very often, he was more of a hands-on type, juggling budgets and filling one hole by digging another rather than making his staff go through lengthy procedures if they needed something. Stella knew he hadn't had an easy time since he'd started three years ago. The pandemic had wiped his ambitious two-year upgrade plan out of the window, leaving him with huge problems rather than opportunities. When he started, he was full of optimism and energy, his glowing tan a testimony to his fun-loving life-style. Now, he looked like the average British man in his fifties; pale, slightly chubby, and his hair was thinning at the crown of his head.

Stella glanced around the office when his assistant, Kira, let her in. The strong scent of paint thinner hit her immediately, and she was pleased to see that one wall had had a fresh lick of paint. Carpenters were filling holes and cracks in the wall at the far end of the room, and the roof terrace was being cleaned. "It's looking better already," she said, smiling at him as she sat down on the opposite side of his big desk.

"Yes, it is. I needed something to give me my drive back." He smiled back at her. "It's not just the top floor that will be fixed, of course; we'll be working our way through the building, and that includes the poolside."

"That's great." Stella leaned in and folded her arms. "I assume that's why you wanted to speak to me?"

"Yes and no. We've got a pretty big team of contractors on this, and the hotel will be closed during the heavy work. The plans will be discussed with all the managers, but I can't go into detail until we have the final schedule. The poolside renovation is booked in for early October so we're not taking on any bookings during that period, and we've diverted all existing bookings to our sister hotels with an offer of a fifty per cent discount or a hundred per cent cancellation refund. So far, so good." Mr Avery thanked Kira when she poured them each a glass of sparkling water. "But more about that later. I actually wanted to discuss something else with you." He handed Stella a printout of an email exchange between a party organiser and the head of events for Paradise Group. "We've had a request from a British organisation. They want to block out the entire hotel for a three-day event. Their current venue has closed down, and they're in a rush to find an alternative. If we hold off on bookings the weekend after the poolside renovation, it would be great timing."

Stella took her time to read through the exchange, then looked up at him. "We've never done big events here, but you're right; it would be good timing. Simultaneously it's also a chance to get our ratings up. The hotel will look better right after the refurbishment, and people are generally very generous with positive feedback if they've had a good time." She looked at him quizzically. "So why are you asking me what I think? It's a no-brainer."

"Well, the thing is, it's not specified in this particular email but it's an LGBTQ organisation and they want to hold a long women's only weekend here. The event was supposed to be in July, as part of Pride month celebrations, but they moved it to later in the year as the rules on big gatherings were still too strict then. And then their venue closed down so they've been terribly unlucky." Mr Avery blushed and looked down at his desk. "I know nothing about this community, and neither do most people who work here, so I discussed it with Kira and she pointed out that you were…"

"Gay?" Stella finished his sentence with an amused grin.

"Yes, exactly. If we take on the booking, we'll need someone to liaise with the organiser and it may be best if that someone is part of their…" He hesitated again. "Community? Can I say that?"

"Sure, you can say that." Stella chuckled as she'd never seen him this crimson before. "And so you need my help?"

"Yes." He cleared his throat. "I know events is not part of your job description, but I think you might be the right person for this. You're good with people and you have great management skills."

"Oh. Well, thank you for thinking of me, it certainly sounds fun." Stella handed him back the sheets, excited to take on a new challenge. "You seem uncomfortable with the fact that this is a women only event. Am I right?"

"Not uncomfortable, it's just new to me." He paused. "I wanted your opinion and to see if you were onboard, I guess. Before we confirm the booking."

"Okay, in that case, consider me onboard. As long as I can do it within my workweek, I'm happy to take the lead on this from our side."

"Great." Stella could see his shoulders drop in relief. "Kira will put you in contact with the right people and you can take it from there. I don't think it will take up more than four hours of your time a week. Just follow up on their requests, they'll provide you with the budget."

"Thanks." She stood up and realised now was the time to discuss outstanding matters. She wasn't in his office very often and since she was doing him a favour, she should seize the opportunity. "Just one thing," she said, lingering by the door. "We need a new speaker for the poolside. It's started to crackle and—"

"Consider it done." Mr Avery smiled and stood up to walk her out. "And anything else you need. Within reason, of course." When he opened the door, a huge sweat patch was visible under his armpit. "Thank you, Stella. Kira will be in touch."

60

"*W*ow, look at the progress," Lisa said, glancing around the poolside that looked close to finished now.

"Yes, it's looking good." Marcy said, removing her tool-belt. "I had a couple of days off too, and I'm pleased with the result." She dropped it into her leather tool bag behind the bar and fished out her wallet, then slipped it into the back pocket of her jeans. "Been anywhere nice?"

"Seville." Lisa smiled and felt herself blush. "With Stella. Her family lives there."

"No way!" Marcy's eyes widened. "That's a bit soon to meet the parents, don't you think?"

"Maybe. But things are good between us and unlike you, I'm not a commitment-phobe," Lisa joked. She'd had fleeting conversations with Marcy over the past week and was baffled by how she'd hopped from one woman to the other.

"Hey, I'm not a commitment-phobe. I just haven't met the right woman," Marcy said in a defensive tone. "I've met at least forty women this year and I swear, none of them were a good match for me. We just didn't gel outside the bedroom, you know? They weren't my type."

"Hmm..." Lisa had her own theories, but she kept those to herself. Marcy was an attractive woman who many of her friends back home would have loved to go out with, and she could definitely see why she was popular with the ladies. "So, what is your type?"

Marcy was about to answer, then groaned when Zoe appeared and waved at Lisa from the doorway. "Anyone but her, that's my type. What's she doing here today?" she asked, lowering her voice.

"I have a meeting with Zoe and the general manager. We're going through the wine list." Lisa smiled and waved back at her. "Come on, be nice and say hello," she urged Marcy, who begrudgingly stuck up her hand for a split second. Zoe mirrored the uninspired gesture and headed back inside.

"The wine list... okay." Marcy stepped back and tapped her cap. "Well, I guess that's a cue for me to go and get lunch. Have a great day if I don't see you."

"Thanks." Lisa sighed and joined Zoe, who was waiting by the bar inside. "Hey, there. Would you not rather be outside?" she asked.

"No, the wine will heat up too fast outside and we need to taste it at the right temperature." Zoe produced seven bottles covered with temperature regulating sleeves from a big bag she'd brought and placed them on the bar. "Anthony will be here soon."

"We're tasting, are we? I thought we were just going through the list."

Zoe chuckled. "You've never worked in hospitality, have you? Everything needs to be sampled before it goes anywhere near a customer."

"No, I haven't," Lisa admitted. "And I don't know much about wine so I'm not sure how helpful I can be."

"That's even better." Zoe grabbed three wine glasses, three water glasses and a bottle of cold water, then started opening the wine bottles to give them some time to breathe. "Think of yourself as the average customer. Anthony is a trained sommelier, I'm confident with wines and food pairings and you can pretend to be a hotel guest. We're picking the house wines today. One white, one red, one rosé, and they need to appeal to a wide audience. And by the way, in my world, we don't spit the wine back out," she added with a wink.

"Good thing Stella is picking me up then," Lisa joked, studying the bottles. This meeting was turning out a lot more interesting than she'd anticipated. "Are you sure we don't need spitting cups?"

Zoe shook her head and laughed. "Nah. It's much more fun this way." She smiled over her shoulder when the door opened. "And here's Anthony, so let's get started."

An hour and a half later, Lisa was feeling a little light-headed. Anthony had just left but she and Zoe had decided to stay and polish off their favourite bottle; a local white Verdejo. When Marcy returned from her lunch break, she offered her a glass as she passed them, but Marcy kindly declined and mumbled something about checking on a bedroom.

"I usually don't pry so forgive me, but what's your problem with her?" she asked Zoe when the lift doors closed behind Marcy.

"Nothing. I already told you, I don't have a problem with

her." Zoe's finger combed her black bob behind her ears, avoiding her gaze.

"Come on, it's not just the bickering and disagreements about the kitchen layout in the past few weeks; you barely acknowledge her presence when she's in the same room. Are you sure nothing's happened?" Lisa didn't want to press on too much but at the same time, she was tired of the tension. When she saw Zoe flinch, she shook her head and held up a hand. "I'm sorry, I'm overstepping."

Zoe looked at her and shrugged her narrow shoulders. "No, it's fine. It's just that..." She hesitated. "I know her type and I don't like that type. They have no regard for other people's feelings and women mean nothing to them."

"I think she seems very nice."

"Yeah, well you're not dating her."

Lisa raised a brow. "Did you date her?"

Zoe remained silent for long moments, then shook her head. "No, I didn't. As I said, I just know her type and she's bad news." She finished her wine and stood up. "Sorry, I have to go."

Lisa shot her a regretful look. Marcy was clearly a much more sensitive topic than she'd anticipated. "I didn't mean to—"

"Don't worry about it, I actually genuinely have to go. My mother and I are cooking for my sister's birthday party." Zoe smiled. "I'll see you next week for the kitchen walk-through."

61

"Marcy, this is Stella, Stella, this is Marcy," Lisa said. "But I believe you two have already met." They'd agreed to meet at a bar in Altea so Marcy could drop by her mother's gallery later.

Stella gave Marcy a hug and looked her up and down as she stepped back. Out of all the people Lisa could have befriended in Benidorm, Marcy, the biggest player of all, was the last person she'd expected her girlfriend to invite out for a drink, and she wasn't sure if that was a good thing or not. "Yes, we've met a couple of times."

"We fought over the same girl once," Marcy said with a guilty grin. "Stella won and literally crushed my ego."

"God, please don't drag up old stories. I'm a good girl these days." Stella pulled out a chair for Lisa and sat next to her. Marcy wasn't wrong; she did get around before Lisa came into her life, and they weren't much different back then.

"Was Stella really that bad?" Lisa asked Marcy with a chuckle.

"Uh-huh. She was—"

"Hey, enough," Stella interrupted her. "No talk about my past antics with my girlfriend present, I don't want her to run off," she joked. "But it's good to see you again. How's life? Lisa told me you're leading the Sunset refurbishment."

"Yes, it's been fun. Business has been great in general and I love working with Lisa."

"That's great. Are you seeing anyone?" Stella asked, already knowing the answer.

"No, still single." Marcy let out a dramatic sigh and ran a hand through her short, blonde hair. "I'm bored with straight tourists, and I've just about slept with every available lesbian in the region."

Stella threw her head back and laughed. "Yes, it does get boring, I won't argue with that."

Lisa looked from Stella to Marcy and back. "Why do I get the feeling the two of you used to be the biggest woman-isers along the Costa Blanca?" She shot Stella a humorous look and added: "Should I be worried?"

"No, babe. Not at all." Stella put an arm around her and pulled her in. "I've only had eyes for you since the moment we met."

Marcy groaned. "God, you guys make me sick but it's also kind of endearing." She beckoned the waiter over. "Everyone okay with sangria?"

"Sure. I love sangria," Lisa said. "We're practically home so we won't have to worry about driving."

"Good point, I think I'll stay at my parents' house tonight." Marcy leaned back and crossed one leg over the other. "So, talking about parents, I heard Lisa met yours, Stella."

"She did. It was fun."

"I met her sister too. They're all lovely," Lisa added.

"And do your family know about Stella?" Marcy asked.

"Yes, I've told them. They're very happy for me, but they're also a bit worried that they won't see me as much anymore." Lisa turned to Stella. "And talking about meeting family, there's something I wanted to discuss quickly before I forget." She opened her messages on her phone and scrolled through them. "My friend Ebony—who is practically family—wants to come over next weekend and my brother the weekend after. I know it's a bit much but..."

"No, it's not a problem. I'd love to meet them." Stella was glowing, delighted that Lisa's best friend and brother wanted to meet her. She'd secretly hoped it would come to this, that she'd finally be able to welcome the people Lisa loved into her home. "I could take a day off, unless you want to spend time alone with them?"

"No, I'd love that if you don't mind." Lisa leaned in and kissed her cheek.

"God, just get a room already," Marcy said with a chuckle, then pointed a finger at Stella. "You'd better show your best side to her nearest and dearest, because this one is a keeper. Very talented too."

"I know she is." Stella moved back so the waiter could place a jug with sangria, three glasses and a plate with complimentary pinchos on the table. "I'm a lucky woman."

"So am I." Lisa helped herself to a tomato bruschetta and turned to Marcy. "Now tell me, what happened between you and the new chef? You've been arguing over silly, minor things for weeks now. I just don't get why you dislike each other so much."

"Zoe..." Marcy groaned. "That little girl is feistier than she looks."

"Little girl?" Lisa frowned. "She's thirty-one, hardly a little girl. It might seem young for a head chef, but her CV is impressive; she's worked internationally."

"Well, I just assumed she was a lot younger with her lean frame and big, baby eyes. Never trust a skinny chef is what my mum always says." Marcy poured them a glass of sangria and took a long drink before she continued. "Anyway, to answer your question..." She frowned and paused for long moments. "God, I don't even know where to start so I suppose I'll just start with our first meeting at the site. I introduced myself and she looked at me weirdly, like, not in a good way. She barely acknowledged me when I shook her hand. I said, 'it's nice to meet you' and she mumbled 'whatever', which is seriously rude, right?" Marcy raised a brow when Lisa didn't reply. "Right?"

"Sure, that is a little rude," Lisa finally agreed.

"Thank you." Marcy spread her arms in a dramatic gesture. "She said she wanted to discuss the kitchen layout with me before we started the work, and when we went through it, she criticised just about everything in the plans. I kindly reminded her that it wasn't *her* kitchen, that she was an employee and that showing her what we were doing was a courtesy from my side. We've been contracted to get the job done in the most cost-effective way and that certainly doesn't include rewiring and moving all gas and electric outlets and plumbing. And then she looked at me like she wanted to shoot me and stormed off."

"Okay, so that wasn't the best start," Lisa said with a puzzled look. "Zoe didn't mention anything to me but then we just talked about launch week and the menus. And you're right; she doesn't really have any say in the refurbishment." She hesitated. "Still, it might be useful to listen to her suggestions. She's an expert in her own field, after all."

Marcy groaned. "Ask the 'expert' and you'll have to cough up double. Do you have the budget for that?"

Lisa carefully considered that before she answered.

"Why don't all three of us get together and discuss it? You haven't started on the kitchen yet and I may be able to stretch the budget a little if certain changes will make the service run more efficiently."

"I'd rather you just shoot me," Marcy said. "And not because I'm not open to a change of plans; I'm the most flex-ible contractor you'll ever come across. But Zoe just has it in for me."

"Oh, come on. You're both adults; surely this can be resolved easily."

Marcy didn't seem convinced, but she nodded anyway. "Okay, let's talk. But only so you can see for yourself that it's personal. She hates me for no reason."

Stella laughed as she listened to their conversation. Lisa was good with people, and it was fun to see her in work mode. Sensing it was time to change the subject so the two wouldn't get into an argument over the new chef, she picked up the food menu and studied it. "Guys, how about we order some food?" she suggested. "If we're going to drink, we should probably have a little more than just snacks."

62

"It's not how I would have done it personally; we've wasted a bit of space, but I think it looks good and it works." Marcy inspected the kitchen that her team had finished over the past two days while she had some time off.

"It's not how I would have done it personally," Zoe repeated in a nagging tone. "Let me tell you something. You're not the one who will be working here in thirty degree heat, so it doesn't matter how you feel about it personally. It's essential that the dishwasher is under the window, or the poor kitchen porter will literally faint."

"Will you two stop arguing?" Lisa was getting annoyed with them now. Last week, she'd invited them out for drinks to talk over the plans in a neutral environment, but it had ended with Zoe storming out. She'd hoped they'd be calmer today as there were no discussions to be had. They just had to check they were happy with the changes Marcy's team had made so they could move onto the next job.

"We're not arguing, just disagreeing," Zoe said with a shrug.

"Well, I don't know anything about industrial kitchens, but it looks good to me." Lisa smiled and opened the cupboards to inspect the storage. "What's this?" She tapped a tall stainless-steel cube that looked a little like an oven.

"That's the rethermaliser I requested. To heat up food without drying it out."

"I see you got your way with the three-thousand Euro machine in the end," Marcy said cynically. "It meant we had to cut corners on the finishing in here."

"Quality is important," Zoe shot back at her. "Clearly not something you're familiar with. And what have you got to do with the equipment anyway? You're here to paint walls, not to get involved with the workings of the kitchen."

Marcy's eyes widened. "What did you just say? Is that what you think I do all day? Paint walls?"

"Hey, seriously, guys." Lisa got in between them. "Let's go outside and take a breather. I think we're done here anyway. Marcy, it looks fantastic, please give your team a huge compliment from me. Zoe, you've got your thingie..." She tapped the machine, already forgotten what it was called. "And you have your porter station under the window. If you're happy with everything, you can start hiring and training staff here."

"Yes, I'm happy," Zoe said, avoiding Marcy's poisonous stare. "Thank you very much, Lisa, I appreciate your flexibility. Unlike some," she added in a quiet mutter. "I'd better get going; I assume you don't need me anymore?"

"No, it's all good, thank you so much for coming in." Lisa waved her goodbye and grabbed her handbag.

"I honestly don't get what her problem is." Marcy gathered her things and swung her bag over her shoulder. "She's had it out for me since day one."

"And you love winding her up."

"I do not!"

"Come on, just admit it. You're constantly giving digs, knowing very well she's going to bite." Lisa arched a brow at Marcy. "She's extremely nice to your team and she's been nothing but friendly with me so it must be something personal."

"Bloody right it's personal. Except I haven't done anything wrong."

"Did you flirt with her by any chance?"

"God, no. Do you really think I just flirt with anyone? I have standards."

"But she's very pretty."

"She's hard work, that's what she is." Marcy groaned. "At least I won't see her again once the job is done. I certainly won't come here for dinner; she'd probably spit in my food."

Lisa laughed and decided to let it go as she wasn't getting anywhere with Marcy. "Have you finished for today?"

"Yes. I think I'll head home and get some rest. We're starting on the conference room tomorrow."

"Okay. Can I give you a lift or did you drive in?" Lisa said goodbye to the builders as they walked out, and Marcy followed her. "I borrowed Stella's car so I could get back early to walk the puppies; I'm picking her up from work later tonight."

"Sure, if it's not too much trouble." Marcy grinned. "Still not found a home for them?"

"No. It's actually more difficult than we thought. We've told all the local shop owners in Altea and asked them to pass it on to some of their customers who love dogs, and Stella's asked around at work but no luck so far."

"God, I imagine you'll have to keep them?" Marcy whistled through her teeth. "Five cats and two dogs... I bet you'll be running for the hills sooner rather than later."

"Nah, I love them all; it's actually fun with lots of animals around. And the cats are no trouble at all. They're so independent; we barely see them apart from mornings and nights when the wet food comes out." Lisa got in the car and rolled down all windows before she closed the door. "So, where am I dropping you off?"

Marcy was about to answer when a message came in on her phone. She smirked as she read it and shook her head. "Never mind, it looks like I have a date and it's so close that I might as well walk." She typed in a reply, then turned to Lisa with a smug expression. "I love a pleasant surprise, don't you?"

"A date? Right now?" Lisa pointed to Marcy's torn shorts, paint-stained T-shirt and the toolbelt she was still wearing. "Don't you need to get changed or something?"

"No, this woman just asked me if I can come around to hang up a picture for her. She's cooking me dinner in return."

"But every idiot knows how to hang a picture."

"Exactly." Marcy laughed. "I bet she needs it hanging in her bedroom."

63

"Hey, babe." Lisa had just sent her last email for the day when Ebony called. "Have you booked that flight yet?"

"I have," Ebony said in a cheerful tone. "And now that you're staying longer, it's much better timing with work, so they were happy for me to take an extra day. Are you sure Stella doesn't mind me staying with her?"

"No, she's really excited to meet you." Lisa paused. "But there's been a little hiccup..."

"What hiccup?"

"My brother was supposed to come the week after, but he booked the same date as you by mistake. Do you mind if he's here at the same time?"

Ebony laughed out loud. "That's so typical of your brother. Do you remember he asked me out for years and when I finally gave in and said yes, he never showed up because he'd lost his phone and couldn't remember where we were meeting?"

"I know. It's typical. But it is what it is."

"I don't mind as long as we don't have to share a bed."

Ebony paused. "And you know what? It will actually be nice to see him again because I'll finally be able to have a go at him for standing me up."

"I have no doubt you will." Lisa smiled, already looking forward to having them both here. Making fun of her brother was her favourite pastime. After his accident she'd refrained from it because she felt sorry for him, but now that he was getting better, the itch was starting to come back. "How's work?"

"Work is good. Very, very busy and messy at times; you know what it's like. How's your new job going?"

"It's going really well, I'm enjoying it." Lisa poured herself a glass of chilled, white wine and went outside. She sighed as she sat down on the ratan sofa and propped her feet up on the coffee table. "And I wouldn't mind doing more of this in future. It's refreshing to do something new; I'm learning so much."

"Good for you, honey. You sound so upbeat and happy. Are you even ever coming back?"

"I am happy." Lisa hesitated. "And no, I may not be coming back to London, at least not for good." She waited for Ebony to speak but there was nothing but a long silence, so she continued. "I've decided I want to stay here with Stella and I'm going to make it work one way or another. I might have to move in with my parents for a while until I find a job in Spain as I'm only allowed to stay until my contract runs out, but honestly, I'd take anything at this point as long as I can be with her. I'm not picky."

"Wow... This doesn't sound like you at all..."

"My priorities have shifted. A career isn't everything."

"No, it's not; you're right about that. But the Lisa that I know from a year ago would never say such a thing. Have you become all chilled and Spanish?"

"I guess you could say that." Lisa chuckled. "And we have two adorably cute puppies that we found on our way to Seville. They've just had their jabs and I can't wait to take them to the park to meet other dogs. We're not keeping them but I'm really enjoying having them around."

"Okay." Ebony burst out in laughter now. "Benidorm, job downgrade, dogs... I can't wait to come over now; I want to see for myself if this is actually *you* I'm talking to."

Lisa laughed too and picked up Butters, who was hopping on his chubby hind legs, trying to get on her lap. "I suppose I have you to thank for all of this," she said. "For everything good that's come into my life. If you hadn't pressured me to come here..."

"Aww..." Ebony cooed in a sweet voice. "You're welcome, honey. Not that I expected you to meet the love of your life and never come back, but I appreciate it. Just know that I'll always keep teasing you about that phone call when you said how much you hated it there."

"Fair enough," Lisa said with a grin. "So, what about you? Been on any more interesting dates lately?"

"God, no. I'm so sick of dating. Every man so far has turned out to be a bigger asshole than the previous. I've given up for now and I'm resigned to being single. Maybe I'm meant to be on my own."

"Maybe you'll meet a charming Spanish guy when you come to visit."

"Hmm... Does Stella have any cute brothers?"

"No, but she has a very handsome colleague. I couldn't stand him at first, but we've become quite good friends."

"Is he a player?"

"Yes," Lisa admitted. "He's a total player and only suitable for a fling if you ask me. But he is good fun, so I can invite him over if you want."

"Nah, just handsome and fun doesn't do it for me anymore. I'm looking for a decent guy, but they're all taken."

"That's not true. You meet the best ones when you least expect it."

"Like you?" Ebony asked in a sarcastic tone.

"Yes, like me." Lisa smiled. "I'm not ashamed to admit I've become a little romantic since I've moved here. Spain might do the same for you."

64

"*S*tella, this is Ebony. Ebony, this is Stella. My girlfriend," Lisa added with a smirk when Stella came down the stairs to greet her.

"Hi, Ebony! Welcome to Spain." Stella saw that Ebony was about to shake her hand, but she went in for a hug instead. It was just how she rolled; there was no way she was going to welcome Lisa's best friend without giving her a squeeze. Her first impression of Ebony was that she was hugely enthusiastic after she'd heard her and Lisa yell in excitement when she arrived. She seemed like a colourful character and Stella had a feeling she'd be in for a fun couple of days. She'd been nervous all morning, waiting for Lisa's brother, who'd booked an earlier flight, to arrive but once he was here, they'd immediately hit it off.

"Thank you so much for having me; I can't believe I'm here. Finally." Ebony gave her a wide smile, her eyes glistening with curiosity as she looked her over. "And what a wonderful place you have here. It's such a romantic setting right on that little square." She put her handbag down and wiped her clammy forehead with the back of her hand.

"Pleasure's all mine," Stella said, opening the door to the guest room. "This is your room; there's an en suite and a small courtyard through the door at the other end."

"Fergi will sleep on the sofa as he messed up his booking," Lisa added. "He's looking forward to seeing you again. It must have been at least five years since he asked you out at my birthday party."

"Yeah, and that date never happened." Ebony laughed as she glanced around the room and put her suitcase down. "It's very cool... so Spanish. Where is the troublemaker anyway?"

"Who, Fergi?" Lisa laughed when Ebony rolled her eyes. "Good question, I'm not sure."

"He's just gone to the shop to get something," Stella said. "He'll be back in a minute. Lisa and I made paella and there's a large jug of sangria in the fridge waiting for you."

"That sounds divine, I like you already." Ebony fanned her face in a dramatic gesture. "Do you mind if I have a quick shower? I feel so sticky after the journey."

Stella had learned a lot about Lisa in the past hours, just like she suspected Lisa had learned a lot about her when they'd visited her parents. Ebony had told her about Lisa's 'wild years' as she jokingly called them; a period of two years in between relationships in which she didn't have a single one-night stand, and about all the trips they'd taken together during the time they worked together. Lisa's brother had told her about how they constantly fought as teenagers and how it had been his mission to make her life miserable by breaking into her room, hiding her things and embarrassing her in front of her friends.

The puppies were delighted with the visitors, bugging Fergi, who had made the fatal mistake of bringing tug-toys that they were now obsessed with. The cats were curious too, especially Pedro, who had tried to steal food from Ebony's plate on several occasions. Now, it was getting dark, and Stella had turned on the fairy lights. The candles on the table were burning, and with music coming from the plaza below it felt cosy and intimate with her new friends. Yes, that was what it felt like, she realised. New friends. Feeling relaxed, she sat back and put an arm around Lisa, who leaned into her in return.

"You're adorable together," Ebony said, glancing at them. "I get it now but I'm not going to lie; I thought you'd lost your mind at first when you announced you wanted to move to Spain permanently." She smiled. "But it's lovely here, it truly is, and I can see that you're crazy about each other."

"I'm glad you can see I'm happy." Lisa frowned when she saw Ebony's eyes well up. "Wait... are you getting emotional?" She chuckled. "I'm sorry; I've just never seen you choke up before."

"Hey, don't make fun of me." Ebony laughed too. "It must be the heat and the drinks and this wonderful atmosphere. It's making me all mushy inside." She sighed deeply. "I need some romance in my life."

"Well, I'm single if you're in the mood for romance," Fergi said with a cheeky smile. "I might limp a little, but all my other limbs work perfectly fine, if you know what I mean." He winked. "We could share your bed if you want some company."

Ebony slapped his thigh, her eyes widening in shock. "No chance, Romeo. I'm drunk but I'm not that drunk. Besides, you had your chance years ago and you blew it."

"And I've regretted that every day since," Fergi shot back at her in a dramatic tone.

Ebony threw her head back and laughed. "Nonsense, that is so not true. A week later you had another girl in your bed. Lisa told me herself."

Fergi held up his hands in defence. "Okay, fair enough, but that was then, and this is now. I've changed."

"Sure, that's what they all say."

Stella refilled their glasses and kissed Lisa on her cheek. She was feeling a little tipsy herself, but she had the day off tomorrow, so it didn't matter. The banter between Fergi and Ebony was amusing, and she was sure there was some mutual interest there, even though Ebony claimed she wanted nothing to do with him in the romantic sense. The way they bounced off each other and kept glancing in each other's direction almost bordered on flirtation. It was something she never sensed between people before, but she did now.

65

"*T*hank you for being so nice and welcoming to Fergi and Ebony." Lisa was lying in Stella's arms, tired but happy after a long day of socialising. Stella's warm naked body against her own felt wonderful and the steady sound of her breathing was soothing. "They had a really nice time and I'm looking forward to tomorrow."

"You don't need to thank me. It's easy; I like them." Stella trailed a finger over Lisa's breast, then circled her nipple. She smiled when it rose to attention and moved down to run her tongue over it.

"Don't tempt me," Lisa warned her. "I won't be able to be quiet and I don't want my brother to hear me. That would be..." She moaned softly when Stella sucked it hard into her mouth, stinging her sensitive skin in the most delicious way. "That would be so awkward."

"He won't. I just went to get water and he wasn't on the sofa, which means he's downstairs in Ebony's room."

Within a split second, Lisa sat up. "I don't believe that," she said with a frown.

"It's true. He wasn't there."

"Then he probably went back up to the roof. Ebony has no interest in him; she'd never let him sleep in her bed."

Stella chuckled, got up and put on a dressing gown. "Want to come and check with me?"

"Sure." Lisa grabbed her own dressing gown and locked the bedroom door behind her so the dogs wouldn't follow them. They snuck up the stairs, past the living room where indeed, the sofa was empty, then continued up to the kitchen and saw the door to the roof terrace was open. When she heard whispers and giggles coming from the seating area, she quickly grabbed Stella's wrist to stop her from going outside. Ebony and Fergi were sitting close together, their silhouettes visible in the vague light of the candles that they'd relit.

"Mmm... You're a good kisser," she heard Ebony say in a sultry voice, and her brother mumbled something in return.

"Confession?" he said, a little louder.

"Go on." Ebony draped her legs over his lap.

"Let's go back to bed, we shouldn't be listening in." Stella tried to pull Lisa away from the kitchen, but she shook her head, wide-eyed with curiosity.

"No, I want to hear what he has to say."

"But it's—"

"Shhh..." Lisa placed a finger over Stella's lips and turned her attention back to the couple outside.

"I've had a crush on you for years," her brother said a little awkwardly. "But I never dared to tell you how I felt."

"Then why are you telling me now?" Ebony asked.

"I've had a lot of time to think in hospital and during my recovery," Lisa heard Fergi say. "I guess I've taken a good look at my life and realised I want to do things differently now. I like you and I've got nothing to lose, so what's the worst thing that can happen? You could laugh in my face, but I've survived worse things."

"Well, I'm not laughing." Ebony sounded emotional and Lisa knew she was in the wrong by listening in, yet she couldn't help herself. "And I'm glad you told me because I feel the same."

At that, Lisa and Stella exchanged surprised looks, and Lisa slammed her hand in front of her mouth to stifle a gasp.

"In fact," Ebony continued, "I've thought about messaging you a couple of times. Just in random moments, you know, after too many drinks. I don't know why I didn't. I suppose I did find you a little immature."

"I was. But I mean it when I say I've changed. My priorities have shifted." Fergi hesitated. "So, if I asked you out again, would you say yes?"

"Why don't you kiss me again and I'll think about it," Ebony said in a playful tone. When she straddled his lap, Lisa swiftly turned around and headed for the stairs.

"Gross, I don't want to see my brother like that," she whispered over her shoulder.

"So, you've seen and heard enough?" Stella laughed as they fell back into bed.

"Yeah, really I wish I could erase that last part from my memory."

"See? I was right," Stella whispered with a smirk. "Well, maybe not about the bedroom part, but they're most certainly hooking up."

"Good God, it sounds like it's more than just hooking up." Lisa needed a moment to let it sink in. Five years ago, Ebony had flirted with her brother, and he had asked her out. She'd never taken the situation seriously, and when the date never happened even less so. Her brother was a player, and he wasn't Ebony's type. Ebony liked successful men who had their shit together, just like Lisa used to lean towards successful women. But it seemed like her brother had indeed changed. He was a lot calmer, he drank less and he was more grounded. And now he was kissing her best friend. "I can't believe it."

"I can." Stella nuzzled her neck and pulled the covers over them. "You didn't even notice over dinner, did you?" She traced Lisa's curves, splaying her fingers wide as she dragged her hands down her body and inhaled deeply against her skin. "Now, where were we?"

66

$\mathcal{H}$eading to the beach with the dogs, Fergi, Ebony and Lisa, Stella was amused by Fergi and Ebony's interaction. They hadn't mentioned anything over breakfast and she and Lisa hadn't brought it up, but they had looked a little uncomfortable for the first couple of hours. It was a funny situation as Ebony treated him no different to last night; with playful rejection to his advances.

"Why are they trying to hide it?" Lisa whispered. "It's not like I care."

"You didn't go screaming it from the rooftops after the first night *we* slept together, did you?"

"No, you have a point there." Lisa chuckled. "And I suppose they might feel a bit awkward towards me. Brother and best friend and all that."

"Exactly. And it might not be anything more than one night. Maybe they just had to get it out of their system." Stella laughed too when she saw their hands brush in between them. "Although it doesn't look that way." Walking ahead of them; Ebony in an olive-coloured mini dress that was a little too glamorous for the beach and Fergi in shorts, an old T-shirt and his walking stick, they looked like a funny pair.

When Ebony turned around, Lisa and Stella pretended to look at a ship in the distance. "Hey, guys, the cripple is getting tired," she joked, and pointed to the nearest beach bar. "Shall we go and have a drink over there?"

"Sure. I'm sorry, Fergi, I wasn't thinking." Lisa ran up to him. "Are you okay?"

"Yes, I'm totally fine. I just haven't tried walking on sand since the accident and my leg is getting tired." He smiled widely. "To be honest, I wouldn't mind a cold beer either."

"Same here," Stella agreed. She turned around and called Butters and Meatball, who immediately came tearing up to her, their ears flapping in the wind.

"Oh my, they came back right away." Lisa looked impressed but laughed when she saw Stella was holding up their treat bag. "Never mind. I see bribery is still the only way."

"Hey, whatever works." Stella got down on her knees, ruffled a hand over their heads and gave them a treat so Lisa could put them on their leads.

Catching up with Ebony and Fergi, who had already grabbed a table, they ordered cold beers and water for the dogs. It was a nice Mexican-inspired bar with chilled music and a tranquil sea view. Stella had never been here before as she didn't tend to walk this way but with the dogs, it was fun to discover new places.

Ebony sighed in delight as she lifted her oversized shades onto her head and sipped from her beer. "I love it here. Please tell me we're good guests and that you'll invite us back." She twirled a lock of her curly hair around her finger and shot Lisa and Stella a pleading look.

"Of course you can come again. You're welcome to visit

whenever you want," Stella said, and she meant it. Lisa's people were fun, and she was having a great time with them.

"You usually invite yourself anyway, don't you?" Lisa joked. "But what's with the 'us'?" she asked in a teasing tone.

"What do you mean?" Ebony blinked and shifted in her chair.

"You said 'us'." Lisa grinned and looked from Ebony to Fergi and back. "Does that mean you want to come back together?"

"No, it was just a figure of speech," Ebony was quick to say, averting her gaze. She suddenly seemed very interested in her coaster and started peeling off the top layer with her long, manicured nails.

Stella nudged Lisa's leg under the table to stop her from interrogating them further, but Lisa ignored it. "Funny," she continued. "Our bedroom window was open last night, and I could swear I heard voices up on the roof terrace." She turned to Fergi. "Did you hear anything from the living room?"

Fergi's cheeks turned crimson, and he shook his head. "No, I was out cold from all that sangria. Didn't hear a thing." Picking up Meatball to stroke her, he skilfully changed the subject. "So, do you go to the beach a lot?"

"Yes, we take the dogs every morning before we start work, and if the sea is calm we'll go for a swim," Lisa said. "We're just enjoying the summer while we still can."

"At least the winters are short here. What a life." Ebony leaned in on her elbows, regarding them dreamily. "And best of all, you're not confined to a desk." She turned to Stella. "Any jobs going in that hotel of yours by any chance?"

Stella laughed. "If you're willing to take a massive salary cut by going into hospitality, sure, there are vacancies from time to time."

"Life is relatively cheap in Spain though," Lisa said. "And I've worked hard in the past two months but living here it doesn't really feel like work at all. Everyone is so chilled. It's just more balanced, I suppose."

Ebony nodded. "I could do with being a bit more chilled."

"Maybe I can help you with that." Fergi shot her a wink, unable to help himself. "I've recently been told I have a way of relaxing women."

"Ha ha, very funny." Ebony let out a long sigh of annoyance, but Stella could tell by her smile that she liked his comment.

"You're blushing, hun. I told you this was a place where romance blossoms, didn't I? And just so you know, I saw you two last night," Lisa teased, then held up her glass in a toast. "So, here's to romance."

Stella chuckled as she clinked her glass with theirs. "To romance," she said, amused by Ebony's stunned expression.

67

"It really wouldn't have been any trouble for me to drive you to the airport." Lisa handed Ebony's weekend bag to the taxi driver, then hugged her brother and Ebony goodbye.

"No way. I'm sure you're busy enough as it is, since you have that meeting with the big boss tomorrow." Ebony gave Stella a long squeeze and Fergi did the same before they got into the car.

"I'm not worried about it," Lisa said. "We've made great progress so I expect Mr Calvo will be pleased." She blew them a kiss. "Please come back soon, it's been so lovely having you here."

"Of course." Ebony closed the door, rolled down the window and smiled. "We will."

"*We* will?" Lisa leaned into the car and shot Ebony and her brother a smirk. "Does that mean what I think it means?"

"Yes, *we*," Fergi said, reaching for Ebony's hand in between them. "Take care, sis. I'll report back to Mum and Dad on how wonderful it is here, so expect a visit from them soon." The pair waved, and Lisa put an arm around Stella's waist as they watched the car disappear.

"Well, that's been interesting." She turned to Stella and cupped her face. "My best friend and my brother, all loved up."

"I'm feeling a little loved up too." Stella checked her watch. "It's early; I still have an hour before I have to leave for work. Want to have some fun?"

"Mmm... what did you have in mind?" Lisa asked, licking her lips as she leaned in closer.

"Why don't you come back to bed with me and I'll show you?"

Lisa laughed when Stella pulled her back inside, closed the door behind them and pushed her against the wall. "I'm not sure if we'll make it to the bedroom if you keep looking at me like that." Her eyes met Stella's fiery gaze and she brushed their lips together. Stella's hot breath against her mouth, her hips pushing into hers and the stare that lowered to her cleavage filled her with longing, and when Stella took her wrists and placed her hands over her head, her breath hitched. "You're so sexy when you take charge," she whispered, squeezing her thighs together.

"Oh, you like me being in charge, do you?" Stella asked teasingly, pushing herself harder against Lisa. "I can do that. Who needs a bed anyway?" She spun Lisa around so she was facing the wall, then made her lace her fingers together on top of her head. "Keep them there, hot girl."

Lisa chuckled but her heart was racing. Stella's mouth moved to her neck to kiss and suck at her flesh, and the sting it caused shot straight to her centre. Exhaling, she breathed seductively into Lisa's ear while her hands moved under her dress and over her behind. She slowly traced her curves over her underwear, squeezing her until she gasped.

Stella's possessive touch was thrilling, her sudden assertiveness arousing Lisa beyond control, and she pushed back against her.

"You have the nicest bottom I've ever felt," she whispered.

"Well, you've felt a lot of them in your time, so I'll take that," Lisa joked, her lashes fluttering at Stella's husky voice in her ear.

Stella chuckled as she moved her hands up to Lisa's breasts, hiking up her dress so she was wedged between the cold wall and Stella's warm body. "Don't be smart with me, hot girl. Or I'm going to make you wait..." She slipped a hand into Lisa's bra and pinched her nipple while she wedged her other hand into the front of her knickers. Cupping her centre, she rolled her nipple between her fingers, just hard enough to cause that delicious sensation again. "And wait..."

"Please," Lisa begged as her body screamed out for more. She wasn't sure what she wanted. All she knew was that she needed release, or she'd never be able to concentrate on work today.

"And wait," Stella continued, ignoring her plea and retracting her hand.

"Not fair." Groaning in frustration, Lisa moved her hands to the wall to keep herself upright. Unsteady on her legs, she felt elated with desire, and when Stella's hand returned to where she needed it most, she let out the breath she'd been holding and moaned.

Stella's mouth stretched into a smile against the base of her neck. "I can feel how turned on you are, hot girl. How about I take care of that?"

"God, yes." Lisa's head fell back against Stella's shoulder when she entered her, and already she felt her core tighten.

Dizzy and delirious, she gave into her as Stella's fingers filled her up over and over, slow and deep while she pulled her tightly against her with her arm around her chest. "More. Please." The words came out in a ragged whisper so soft she could barely hear her own voice, but Stella had heard her loud and clear and adding another finger, she found the spot that made Lisa's knees buckle.

"Let go, mi amor."

Climbing higher and higher, Lisa crashed with a loud cry. Her climax was intense and in need of an outlet, she slammed her hands against the wall as she buckled in Stella's grip. Even after months, she still couldn't grasp how good it was with Stella, how perfectly attuned they were both emotionally and physically. She felt as if she was drifting on clouds, wallowing in the embrace of the woman she loved. A bark coming from the top of the stairs pulled them out of their moment, and they both laughed at Meatball and Butters, who had ventured down from the roof terrace after hearing the noise in the hallway.

"It's okay," Stella said, looking up at them with an amused smile. "Mummy's fine."

"Yes." Lisa chuckled as she pulled down her dress and straightened it. "Mummy's very, very happy."

68

"So, what do you think? The rooms on the other floors will be more or less identical to these, depending on their size," Lisa said, walking Diego back to the lift after showing him five rooms and a suite on the top floor. "The photographer has been in to take pictures of the finished rooms and the rest of the hotel so we can start listing the hotel on booking websites early."

"Fantastic. I think it looks great." The normally stern man had a small smile on his face, and his smile only grew when they got downstairs and headed for the bar. Nine weeks in and El Escondite was well on its way to looking presentable, and the outside space was pretty and tranquil. Lisa could already imagine it filled with guests, drinking cocktails, attending meetings, or lounging in the courtyard or by the pool. "I see you're almost done here." He glanced around, taking in the dining area and the round bar. The sliding glass doors were wide open, bringing the outside in, and the white, embroidered cotton curtains to either side were stylishly draped and secured to the walls with heavy tasselled tie-backs.

"Yes, there's no water in the pool yet and the plants will need a little time to adjust to the new soil, but we're almost done. As you know, we had some requests from the chef regarding the kitchen, but I think the extra investment will pay off. The more efficient it's run, the less staff you'll need." Lisa had given the builders the afternoon off, so it was quiet and there was less mess to distract him from the new, clean layout.

"I agree." Diego tapped the leather covered barstools, then ran a hand over the Spanish-tiled surface of the bar. It looked authentic and brought a splash of colour to the space that was decorated in muted colours and natural materials. "This is very nice. It's all very nice."

"Thank you." Lisa had spent hours laying out the tables, just so he'd be able to envision it better. She'd also placed tables outside where the al fresco bar and dining area were situated, and dressed them less formally with herbs in Spanish pots and rustic water jugs the interior designer had ordered. Once everything was finished, the interior designer would spend two days going over each room and area, making sure every item was in the perfect position. "And in the back there, we have lounge pods, which offer privacy so they're perfect for meetings. They comfortably seat four, but they can also be placed together, to create bigger meeting areas." She pointed to the pool. "The pool has been relined and the new tiles make everything look fresh, contemporary and very Spanish. The kitchen will have a day and a night menu—both inspired by the local cuisine—and we'll also have a room service menu. The karaoke room on the ground floor will be transformed into a large meeting room with a folding divider to accommodate multiple smaller gather-ings, and the extra party room that was barely used will be a stylish business centre with printers, desks and a free coffee and water station. These will be done last as they're the least work."

"Excellent." Diego walked over to the built-in stone benches by the pool that were lined with waterproof cushions and sat down, resting his elbows on the table in front of him. "So, we're on schedule?"

"Yes, we are." Lisa handed him her iPad. "Here, have a look at the new website while I get you a drink; I've brough some beverages. I'd like you to sign off on the website and the booking system and I also have some interesting advertising options to show you." She glanced at the bar where she'd turned on the fridge, just for today. Nothing had been left unplanned and she felt pleased with her preparations for their meeting. "Wine, beer, water, iced coffee? I don't have normal coffee, I'm afraid. The machine hasn't arrived yet. And would you like an ashtray? I noticed you had one on your desk in your office, so I assumed you smoked."

Diego arched a brow at her. "You've thought of everything."

"It's all about the details," she said with a smirk.

"Let's have some wine while we go through this." He shot her a wink. "After all, it's five o'clock somewhere as you English say."

Half a bottle of wine later, most of Lisa's plans had been signed off. Apart from a few tweaks, Diego was pleased with everything she'd done so far and that felt really, really good.

"Thank you so much for your time," she said, straightening herself. "Next time you're in Benidorm you'll be able to stay at your very own hotel."

"That is good news, but I may see you sooner than that."

Diego finished his wine, looked something up on her iPad before he handed it back to her. "I'm thinking of acquiring a hostel in Sitges. It's about a four-hour drive from here."

Lisa scrolled through the pictures, studying them at length. "Sitges... isn't that the gay-friendly town close to Barcelona?"

"Yes. We've had a look around in the area; hotel prices are generally higher there and this came up for sale." He paused. "Would you be interested in going there and taking a look? See what you think?"

Lisa frowned, surprised that her opinion mattered so much to him. "You want me to assess the venue?"

"Yes, you're doing a great job with Sunset..." He cleared his throat. "Or El Escondite, as it's now called, and I thought you might have some ideas about the one in Sitges; see if you can find potential there. It's not exactly close, but it's doable in a day if you're driving."

Lisa smiled widely, excitement stirring inside of her. Was she reading him right? She wasn't sure where he was going with this, so she decided to just ask him outright. "Are you saying you'd be interested in using my services again?"

Diego tilted his head from side to side and smiled back at her. "Admittedly, yes. I think you're a valuable asset."

"Thank you. I'd be delighted to check it out." She felt like hugging him but stayed composed, frantically thinking on the spot now that she saw a way into a new life. "But if we decide to work together again, I'd like to become a part of your team. An employee."

Diego frowned. "Why would you want that? You'd make much more money as a consultant."

"I know, but I'd like to stay in Spain, so I need a sponsor. I've met someone," Lisa added, now unable to suppress a smirk.

Diego laughed. "Aha, so that was why you were so persistent with me in the first place."

"Not necessarily. Most of all, I was dying to work again. But now that I've been here longer and it's getting more serious between us, I really would like to try and build a life here."

Diego nodded. "I understand. I'll think about it, how's that? And I'll have to discuss it internally, of course."

"That would be more than I could wish for." Lisa poured them another glass of wine, pleased with how the day had gone and euphoric about the idea of a long-term opportunity with the Calvo Group. The man was warming to her. In fact, she was pretty sure he genuinely liked her too, and a little more alcohol while they shared some ideas wouldn't hurt.

"It's crazy what people do for love," he said.

"Are you married?"

"God, no, not anymore. Three times divorced." Diego waved a hand. "Never again but I appreciate your sentiment." He raised his glass. "So, what are we toasting to?"

"How about a fruitful long-standing working relationship?" Lisa said, pushing her luck.

He chuckled. "I have a feeling you're not one to take no for an answer, so yes, let's toast to that. It may not be long-term, but it could certainly add some time onto your stay."

69

"Hi." Stella opened the door to find a short, stocky woman in her fifties with bright red hair looking up at her. "Can I help you?"

"Yes, I believe so. Are you Stella Castillo?"

"That's me." Stella opened the door wider.

"I heard you found two Lab-like puppies who need a home. The owner of the café opposite told me, and I happened to be looking for a dog for myself, so I thought I'd just ring the bell."

"Oh..." Stella managed a smile but in truth she wasn't ready to let them go. The woman seemed nice enough at first glance, sweet even, with kind eyes and a genuine smile, and a couple of weeks ago she'd been delighted with someone like her enquiring. Now, all she felt was dread. "Sure," she said, hiding her discomfort. "They're upstairs. Why don't you come in for a coffee and meet them?"

"Thank you so much. My name is Mary. I live nearby, right at the top of the hill, close to the park."

"It's nice to meet you, Mary. Close to the park sounds

perfect for two hyperactive puppies." Stella led Mary up the two flights of stairs and onto the roof terrace where Lisa was working at the dining table. As usual, Butters was sleeping on the chair next to her—he always made sure to stay right by her side—and Meatball was fighting with a tug-toy, throwing it up into the air and shaking it between her teeth in between playful growls. "Lisa, this is Mary," she said when Lisa looked up from her laptop. "She heard about the puppies."

"Hi, Mary." From the expression on Lisa's face, Stella knew she felt the same. There was no enthusiasm whatsoever, but she smiled politely and stood up to shake Mary's hand. Butters immediately jumped off the chair and sat down by her heel. "This is Butters, my shadow, and that one over there is Meatball. She's a little more independent than her brother; he's not very brave."

"Oh my, they're so cute." Mary kneeled in front of Butters and scratched his neck. Meatball ran over to her too, her tail wagging so fast it was barely visible as she jumped up at Mary for attention.

"They're sort of toilet trained but they still have accidents now and then and we use a puppy pad at night. Their recall is good, especially Butters'; he wouldn't dare stray more than two meters from us," Lisa joked. "We've taken them out in the past two weeks as they've just had their jabs and although we tend to keep them on the lead when there's traffic, they're fine off the lead on the beach and in parks, and even on the promenade. They do steal food though, if they get the chance. Chubby Meatball here is quite greedy."

"Yes, you are a chubby girl," Mary cooed, fussing over them. "But you are the cutest chubby girl in the whole world. Look at that big, fat, pink belly. And so are you, little one," she said, turning to Butters. "You're such a sweetheart, I can tell already from those big eyes of yours."

Stella's eyes met Lisa's and they exchanged a knowing look. This woman seemed so nice, yet neither of them felt the relief they'd anticipated at finding Butters and Meatball a loving forever home. "Coffee? Tea? Something cold?" she offered.

"A coffee would be lovely, thank you. Can I pick them up?"

"Absolutely, they love a cuddle." Lisa looked defeated when Butters started licking Mary's face after she sat down and pulled him onto her lap. "I think he likes you."

"Well, guess what? I like him too. He's adorable." Mary then lifted Meatball up and their tails wagged rapidly with joy. And you, girl. And you."

Stella watched Mary kissing their little noses through the kitchen window and winced. "Damn it," she muttered under her breath, cursing herself for being so emotional about the puppies since they had only been with them for a month. Butters and Meatball seemed to like Mary just as much as she liked them. She made three coffees, placed them on a tray and added a sugar bowl, a jug of milk and some dulce de leche cookies, and her heart sank when she took it outside and saw the sad half smile on Lisa's face.

"I see you're getting along," she said, handing Mary a mug.

"Oh boy. Initially I just wanted to have a look but now I want them." Mary held up her hand in an apologetic gesture. "Sorry, I'm getting ahead of myself. You probably have tons of other people lined up but they're just so cute." She sighed deeply. "I just got divorced, my husband moved back to the UK, and I live on my own now. It would just be nice to have some company and a reason to go out on long walks every day."

"I'm sorry about your divorce," Lisa said. "And yes, I'm sure a dog would do you the world of good." She glanced at Butters lovingly, then picked him up from Mary's lap and held him close against her chest. "I love him. I love them both but he's my baby, for sure. God, I'm going to miss you, little one."

Stella swallowed hard as she watched Lisa with Butters. Since they'd found them, they'd been like a weird little family, training them and introducing them to the world. Lisa was smitten with the puppies and so was she, even though she hated to admit it. "The thing is, Mary," she said hesitantly. "You seem like the perfect person to adopt them, and I trust you already. My cats hate the puppies with a passion, the house is total chaos with seven pets and it's really not a good time for us to have dogs in the first place, but I think we've gotten more attached to them than we anticipated."

Lisa's face lit up and she gave her a subtle nod, letting her know they were on the same page. "Honestly, I thought I would be fine but now that the time has come, I don't want them to go."

"Oh." Mary smiled at them as she stroked Meatball's round belly. "I understand. It just happens, doesn't it? I fostered a Jack Russell twenty years ago. He was a total nightmare to be honest with you, quite a temper and it was only meant to be for a month, but I couldn't let him go either. He died a very happy old man at the age of seventeen."

"Yes, it happens." Stella took Meatball from Mary and kissed the top of her head, inhaling the scent of puppy that she'd grown to love so much. "I'm sorry."

"It's okay, don't be." Mary shrugged. "I can go to the shelter. Plenty of dogs there that need a home."

"That's true." Lisa turned towards the kitchen, then back to Mary. "Well, now that you're here, I was just about to fix some dinner. Would you like to join us?"

70

"I can't believe those two," Stella said after Lisa had filled her in on yet another meeting with Marcy and Zoe that had ended in an argument. They were walking along the shore of Altea beach with Meatball and Butters, who as always, were beside themselves with joy at being off the lead and free to roam. They rolled around in the sand and played; Butters always sure to run up to Lisa whenever they lagged behind. She felt good about keeping them now. They were more than a handful, but they were also incredibly sweet and entertaining, and it brought her pure joy to see them so animated. It was hard to believe that only five weeks ago they'd been weak, skinny and scared. Now, they were happy, chubby pups who trusted them blindly and they were even starting to obey a little. Just a little.

"Yes, I've given up on trying to have them in the same room, but there's no reason they need to talk anymore so I think that will be the end of it anyway. Good news is, Diego might have another job for me." Lisa smiled. "I didn't want to tell you at first because I have no idea if it's actually going to happen, but he wants me to have a look at a hostel in Sitges as he's thinking of expanding his portfolio there."

"Oh my God, really?" Stella slammed a hand in front of her mouth. "And he wants to work with you again?"

"Possibly, if it's got enough potential to make a decent profit." Lisa held up a hand. "But let's not celebrate just yet; it can go either way. I'm hoping this hostel will be suitable as that would work to my advantage, we'll see. It can be a hit and miss with any place but I want to be honest, not just go with it because it will give me a way in."

"Of course. I know you take pride in your job." Stella squeezed her hand. "When are you going?"

"I'm waiting to hear from the owner; he's coming down from Barcelona to walk me through the building and premises. Want to come along if you're free?"

"I'm off during the poolside renovation, so I'll definitely come. And I promise I won't get excited just yet, but it's a good sign, right?"

"Yes, I'd be so delighted with that job and hopefully more projects in future. It's quite a long drive, but I figured that if I do get the job, I can be there two to three days a week and stay at the site. I think I can cope with being away from you two nights a week." Lisa shot her a seductive smile. "Maybe."

"It's a fair compromise to have you close." Lisa's smile made Stella's knees go weak and the hopeful news filled her with excitement.

"How's work with you?" Lisa asked. "Is that upcoming event keeping you busy?"

"It's more work than I expected," Stella said. "But the organisers are on top of everything and they're very nice, so it's actually a lot of fun to do in between dealing with poolside drama. The event is sold out, but they gave me two day tickets in case you want to come." Stella turned to check on the dogs and called Meatball, who had decided to wander in the opposite direction. "There will be live music, games, speed dating... Just a bit of fun."

"I think I will. I'll have to keep an eye on you if there are going to be two-hundred ladies lusting after the poolside manager. I imagine you'll be very popular."

Stella laughed, put an arm around Lisa's waist and pulled her in. "Babe, you know you don't have to worry about that. But I'd love you to come. And maybe Marcy wants to come too, so you won't have to go alone?"

"Hmm... yes, I might ask her." Lisa shot her a sideways grin. "So, you trust me with Marcy now?"

"What do you mean?" Stella quirked a brow. "I've always trusted you."

"Come on. I know you weren't too keen on me hanging out with her at first, with her being such a womaniser and all. But I can assure you, there's no attraction whatsoever from either side. I've even dropped her off at her dates a couple of times after work. God, that woman has a new lady several times a week. Locals, tourists..."

Stella chuckled. "Yeah, she's quite something. And I'll admit I was convinced she'd hit on you at first, but I'm not worried anymore, I promise. In fact, I like Marcy and I think we should invite her over for my end of season barbecue along with some of my staff."

"That would be nice. Maybe we should invite Zoe too," Lisa joked.

71

Stella waited until her team members were gathered around the bar, then sat down with her coffee behind it. "Thanks for coming, everyone. I just wanted to fill you in on what's happening in the coming weeks."

"Yes, what *is* happening?" one of the animation team members asked. "I heard they're doing the pool."

"Yes, it's a poolside overhaul. Tiling work, mainly, and they're bringing in new furniture and sprucing up the tiki bars. As you know, we'll be hosting a women's weekend after the refurbishment; a three-day women-loving-women event. It's sold out and expectations are high." She shook her head and laughed when some of the staff started cheering. "You can all help set up three days before the event and you'll have full-time shifts during the event. Everyone okay with that?"

Her team mumbled their agreement, and there was some giggling coming from the female staff.

"Are we allowed to flirt?" Florence asked.

"I didn't know you were into women," Manuel said, arching a brow at her.

"I swing both ways." Florence shrugged. "Don't mind a cute girl at all."

Stella chuckled. "Okay, whatever way you swing, let's be clear on one thing. No, you are not allowed to flirt. Your shifts during this event will be no different from any other shift, so stay professional. That means no flirting and no personal interaction with guests."

"Says the pool manager who moved one of our guests into her home," Florence shot back at her.

"Don't be cheeky with me, that's different." Stella knew very well that it was no different and although she wished they would stop joking about it, she also felt a smug sense of pride. "Now, let's talk about the entertainment. There will be no aqua aerobics classes but instead we're having a welcome pool party with a DJ on the Friday and on Saturday there will be live music by the poolside and karaoke towards the end of the night. On Sunday we're having an outdoor brunch; the kitchen staff will prepare paella over an open fire, which will be served with fresh bread and salads. The event organisers have also arranged activities throughout the day which you'll assist with; I can update you on those once I have the final schedule."

"What about the bar?" Florence asked. "I've been asking for bar shifts for weeks and they're going to need help with so many thirsty women." She shot Dave a wink and grinned.

"Yes, I'm happy for you to help the bar team," Stella said. "The drinks menu will be limited, offering only three tailored cocktails, beer, wine, soft drinks, coffee and tea. That way we won't have to worry about running out of stock." She looked through her notes to make sure she hadn't missed anything, then added; "Oh, and you'll all get customised T-shirts or vest tops to wear; whatever you prefer."

"Can we keep them?"

"Yes, you can." She looked over the group and smiled. "Any other questions?"

"Can we join the party after we finish our shift?" Florence asked.

Stella laughed. "No, you cannot. It's for ticket holders only, I'm afraid. Does anyone have a problem working at this event? For religious reasons or whatever other reasons? If you do and you're uncomfortable speaking up, come talk to me in private."

Heads shook and small talk picked up, the staff keen to use their last ten minutes to catch up on gossip. She hadn't expected anyone to have a problem with it; her team was young and open-minded, most of the women quite possibly bi-curious after a couple of drinks.

"Okay, thanks, everyone," Stella finally said. "It's going to be overcast today, so it shouldn't be as busy as usual. If you feel like you're twiddling your thumbs and you can make it work, feel free to ask for a longer lunch break." She opened the pool gate to let in the handful of guests who were keen to top up their tans and was surprised to see Lisa walking up to the bar.

"Hey, babe. Mind if I have a coffee here?" she asked, flicking a blonde lock over her shoulder.

"Not at all." Stella resisted the urge to kiss her but came up as close as she could get away with. Aware of her staff staring at them, she felt herself blush. "What a nice surprise."

"I had an early meeting and my next one isn't until ten. I thought I'd come and sit here so I can admire your legs while you're working." Lisa looked up and blushed when she heard someone chuckle. "Sorry, I shouldn't be flirting with you while you're working."

"I don't mind," Stella said playfully. "And I have ten more minutes, so I'll join you for that coffee."

Before she'd had the chance to order, Dave put two cappuccinos in front of them. After moving out of the hotel, Lisa had been here a handful of times while she waited for Stella to finish her shift, and he knew exactly what she liked. "On the house."

"Not again." Lisa sighed and handed him a five Euro note, which he refused. "If you keep giving me coffee for free, I'll stop coming here. I know you're not allowed to do that, and I don't want to get you in trouble." She patted his arm and put the note in his chest pocket instead. "Keep the change, darling."

"All right. Thank you." Dave leaned over the bar and narrowed his eyes at her. "You're looking very polished today. Special occasion?"

"Yes, actually. We have a pre-opening dinner across the road tonight. For the new buyers of Sunset, now renamed El Escondite."

Dave's eyes widened. "Is it finished already?"

"Almost. Our deadline is today. There are still some outstanding finishing touches and plumbing work which will take a couple of days, but we're a week away from officially opening so we'll just have to get all hands on deck."

"That's impressive." Dave glanced at Stella, who was beaming.

"Yep, that's my girl," she said, pulling Lisa in for a peck on her cheek.

72

"Thanks for coming to Sitges with me."

"Hey, I had the day off, so why not? I've actually never been here, even though it's supposedly the gayest town in Spain." Stella put the puppies on a tighter leash as they navigated through the busy streets of the picturesque coastal town, headed for the hostel Lisa was viewing. They'd passed packed beaches, mainly filled with men and now they were passing countless gay bars, also mainly filled with men. "So, you've suddenly become a hotel expert now, huh?"

Lisa laughed. "I hardly know what I'm doing but Diego doesn't know that and so far, it's worked out."

"Well, let's hope this one works out too. It's nice here, don't you think?"

"Yes, it's way more sophisticated than I thought it would be." Lisa checked the route on her phone and pointed to a narrow street that led up a hill. "It seems like a great town for a more upmarket hotel."

"The pink pound is powerful," Stella agreed. "Those women who have booked for the women's weekend are paying double what we normally charge for the rooms and that doesn't even include the event tickets. It felt like a rip-off, but Mr Avery assured me that it's perfectly normal to charge more if there's a special event on. What do you think?"

"He's right. Holding the rooms for three days is a risk— you're lucky it's sold out— and you'll have to be fully staffed, so it makes sense." Lisa glanced at the antique shops, delis and gay novelty shops and made some notes on her phone. "Culture, tick. Proximity to Barcelona, tick. Pride presence, tick. Great cuisine, tick. Good beaches, tick." They reached the top of the hill and caught their breath as they glanced over the beach and the town below. "View, tick." She looked pleased with herself as she pointed to the cream coloured boarded up three-storey building. "It's old and slightly worn out, but it has character and lots of potential. I love all the climbing plants on the facade."

"It's certainly charming but it looks like it's been closed for a while." Stella followed her around to the side of the building, where the entrance was.

"Two years," Lisa said, looking up at the sign that said, *'Welcome to Sitges Hostel.'* "It would look lovely painted in pale pink and price-wise it's a steal, considering the central location and the view. The front borders on the edge of the hill so it's nice and private and apparently there's a small pool too."

"Miss Walker?" A man approached them, dangling a set of keys in his hand.

"That's me. Please call me Lisa. And you're Rad?"

"Yep. Nice to meet you."

"Nice to meet you too." Lisa shook his hand. "This is Stella, my girlfriend."

"Hello, and welcome to Sitges." Rad looked down at the

puppies and chuckled. "Hello, guys. I see you've brought the whole family along."

"I figured as the building is closed, it wouldn't matter that much." Lisa smiled. "Is it okay if they come in with us? If not, Stella can grab a coffee somewhere with them."

"No, that's not a problem. It was always a dog friendly hostel to begin with anyway." Rad unlocked the door and switched on the lights. "We've turned the electricity back on this week as it's too dark for viewings with the windows boarded up. I was actually planning on reopening after the pandemic, but it just dragged on and eventually I decided to sell as I was losing too much money on it."

"Sorry to hear that," Lisa said.

"It's okay. I have two other hostels in Barcelona so it's easier for me to centralise my business and look at other options there. Sitges was never ideal for the backpackers' market; it's a little more upscale here and that's not my expertise."

They took in the reception area that was basic but spacious. It led to a communal dining area from which doors opened up to a back terrace with a spectacular ocean view.

"This is nice," Lisa said, continuously snapping pictures on her phone. "I like the unobstructed view. Have you ever tried to get planning permission for ocean facing balconies?"

"Yes, they were already in place when I bought the building, but with it being a hostel I figured one communal outdoor space would be sufficient so we could keep the prices down." Rad pointed up to the second and third floors as they walked further out into the garden. "There are six large sleeping dorms, three on each floor, and there are also six shared bathrooms so the plumbing can easily be extended should you want to create separate rooms." He turned to the pool. "It looks a bit sorry for itself now that it's empty and filled with leaves, but it's only five years old and still in good condition."

"It's a lovely outdoor space," Stella said, hoping her enthusiasm would rub off on Lisa. Sure, she genuinely liked it, but most of all, she wanted Lisa to convince Diego to take it on.

"Yes, it's great. Lots of opportunity to put in a swanky bar and a barbecue area. I'm thinking high-end but charming with romantic touches and lots of flowers. With plenty of entertainment options, this will be perfectly tailored to the LGBTQ market. After all, people come here for fun and to mingle, not for a solitary spa break. Lots of communal areas would be good, maybe a big hot tub..." Lisa walked to the edge of the cliff and stared down over the hedge. "Replace the hedge with a glass wall and it will be even more spectacular," she continued. "It's incredible how secluded it feels back here considering it's only a five-minute stroll from the bars."

"I get the feeling you're into this," Stella said with a grin.

"I am. And from the look on your face, I think you are too." Lisa turned to Rad. "Could we have a look upstairs? I'd like to see the view from up there."

73

"*H*ere's to El Escondite being a huge success."
Marcy raised her glass and clinked it with Lisa's.

"Let's hope so." Lisa let out a long sigh. She was exhausted and hadn't been able to sleep in the past few nights. They had rushed to get everything ready for the Calvo Group's pre-opening dinner, but now the relief of seeing how everything had come together was giving her a buzz. "I'd better not drink too much; they'll be here soon."

The interior designer had just left and the hostess, a bartender and three waiters were getting dressed in the staff room to serve Diego and his team.

"We still have some time to enjoy the calm before the storm. And it's been fun. I've enjoyed working on this project with you."

"Same here. If you're interested, there will probably be another one to come." Lisa lowered her voice to a whisper. "But this is off the record; nothing's been set in stone yet."

"Seriously?"

"Yes, Mr Calvo is talking about revamping a hostel in Sitges. They're just waiting to finalise everything with the bank. In fact, I have a feeling there may be an announcement tonight."

"Cool. I'd love to work with you again. Building the same blocks of flats was getting a little boring so this has been a breath of fresh air. I do have a project booked in right after this one though, so I'll have to see if I can make it work, should it come to that." Marcy rolled up the sleeves of her blue shirt and opened the top two buttons, fanning her face with her hand. "God, I hate formal wear."

"Is that what you call formal wear?" Lisa laughed, glancing at Marcy's faded jeans and shirt. She was dressed smart casual herself in white linen trousers and a navy boat-neck top as it seemed fitting for a poolside dinner, and she'd been to the hairdresser for a cut and blow dry and splurged on new heels.

"It's as formal as it goes for me," Marcy said with a grin. "Is Zoe stressed out of her mind in there?" She pointed in the direction of the kitchen. "I bet she is."

"Not at all, actually. She's calm and composed and she promised everything is under control." Lisa smiled. "They're playing classical music in the kitchen. That's quite unusual, don't you think?"

"It's weird if you ask me." Marcy turned when Zoe walked out with a small tray.

"Did I hear my name?"

"We were just saying that it's unusual to have classical music in a kitchen," Lisa said.

"Yes, it is, but I find it very useful. It keeps my team calm, and it helps us get into a certain flow while we're working; it's almost like dancing through the courses."

"That sounds fascinating." Lisa looked at the canapé

spoons filled with a sauce and topped with octopus and a sprinkle of paprika powder. "Wow. Is this for us?"

"Just a little amuse-bouche while you wait for the party to arrive." Zoe smiled and even managed to acknowledge Marcy's presence with a subtle nod. She was clearly on her best behaviour today. Dressed immaculately in a white short-sleeved chef's jacket and a white headband pushing her dark bob back, she looked spotless, like she'd just walked in. "It's octopus stew. Traditional for the region."

"I love this, I've had it before." Lisa ate the spoonful and moaned. "Mmm... That's really good."

"Yes. It's delicious," Marcy begrudgingly admitted, avoiding her gaze.

"Excellent. Let's hope the others like it too." Zoe looked Marcy over. "Well, don't you scrub up nicely?" Then she took the empty spoons, turned and headed back to the kitchen.

"Am I going mad or was that a compliment?" Marcy stared after her until she disappeared out of sight.

"It sure sounded like one." Lisa was baffled too; it was the first time she'd heard Zoe say anything to Marcy that wasn't insulting or cynical. "Maybe she secretly fancies you."

"That's ridiculous." Marcy rolled her eyes. "That girl's not even gay."

"I'm not so sure about that. She was wearing a vest top from a pride event under her chef's jacket the other day; I saw it when she unbuttoned it before she left. She also has a rainbow key ring attached to her locker key," Lisa added. "That doesn't necessarily mean she's gay, of course, and I didn't ask, but there have been other clues too. Just passing comments about cute actresses and stuff like that."

"Well, shoot me." Marcy looked puzzled. "I thought my gaydar was flawless but clearly I was wrong." She took a long drink of her champagne and held it out for Lisa to refill. "Well, it doesn't matter. It doesn't make her any less of a downer."

"Not tonight, you promised." Lisa shot her a warming look.

"Okay, okay. Let's change the subject. Are the guests staying over?" Marcy asked.

"I don't think so, but we do have the rooms ready for them in case they change their minds. You know how it goes... dinner, drinks, then probably more drinks. I'd be surprised if at least not some of them want a room."

"Yes. I expect it to be a late one; it's not my first rodeo with the Calvo Group. Diego's quite close to my father; he's hired our company for overhauls several times now." She looked over her shoulder when she heard voices by the reception desk. "Oh, there they are." She straightened her shirt and put on her most charming smile. "How do I look?"

"You look very nice. And very formal," Lisa joked. She got up and headed for the door to greet Diego and his business partners. "Hello, everyone, welcome to El Escondite."

74

"*How* did it go?" Stella yawned and rubbed the sleep out of her eyes.

"It went really, really well." Lisa got into bed and turned to her. She'd just had a shower and smelled like coconut and lime. "They were still there when I left. One of the waiters volunteered to stay on, the general manager is with them, and Zoe is coming in tomorrow morning to make breakfast, so they really didn't need me there." She smiled and cupped Stella's face. "And I got some good news tonight."

"More good news? Is that hostel in Sitges going ahead?"

"Yes." Lisa grinned from ear to ear. "And not only that. They've offered me a contract."

"Really?" Stella sat up and stared at her, her heart suddenly racing.

"Yes. It's only a year contract for now, but if they keep expanding, they'll extend it, possibly to an indefinite one."

Stella suppressed a gasp, then let out a cry of joy. She suddenly felt wide awake as adrenaline rushed through her veins. Her love would stay and that was more than she could have ever hoped for. "Lisa, that's..." She shook her head and laughed, wiping away the tear that rolled down her cheek. "Sorry, I'm feeling a little emotional right now. Please pinch me; I'm not dreaming, am I?"

"Baby, are you crying?" Caressing her cheeks, Lisa kissed her temple and her forehead, softly stroking her hair. When their eyes met, Stella saw she was teary too.

"I'm just so happy, I can't believe it."

Lisa smiled and rolled on top of her. "Does this feel like a dream?" She pushed her hips into Stella's and kissed her hard.

"No..." Stella moaned and wrapped her arms around Lisa, then laced her fingers through her long hair. She loved her hair, she loved everything about Lisa, but right now, she especially liked her naked body draped over hers and knowing she'd be able to feel this for a very, very long time to come. The way she grinded into her—her body rolling so sensually—was making her crazy and she cupped Lisa's behind and pulled her hips towards her. "Come here. I want to taste you."

"Oh, yeah?" Lisa's eyes darkened with desire, and her breathing became ragged as she shifted up, steadying herself over Stella with her knees to either side of her shoulders.

Stella groaned at the sight of her wet and swollen centre, and overcome with lust, she tugged her down and started feasting on her.

"Oh, God!" Lisa held onto the headboard, her hips jerking with each stroke of Stella's tongue. "You always know exactly what to—" Her words faded into sounds of pleasure when Stella's tongue darted inside her. Moving faster, Lisa's moans turned louder, her back arching as her head fell back.

Stella smiled against her throbbing centre, her fingers digging into Lisa's thighs. She could do this every day for the rest of her life and never get enough of the sweet noises she made as she brought her to the brink of an orgasm.

Lisa peaked with a loud cry, shaking as she lowered herself further against Stella's mouth. "Fuck, fuck, fuck!" Breathing fast, she stayed there while aftershocks coursed through her, causing Stella to shiver in bliss. "Fuck," she said again, then laughed at how noisy she'd been. "This might be the best day of my life."

"I'm with you on that." Stella grinned at her when Lisa crawled back, bringing them face to face. "You're staying..."

"Uh-huh." Lisa smiled back at her and licked her lips. "As I said, this must be the best day of my life."

"It's crazy that we only met in June." Stella's eyes met Lisa's and she was delighted to see that they were filled with joy. "You were so sad back then."

"I was a mess. It's amazing how love can change everything." Lisa took her phone from the bedside table and showed Stella her screensaver. "Look. I just remembered this was on here, I didn't register it anymore."

"What does it say? I can hardly read it through all the apps you have on there."

"It's a wish list of things I wanted to accomplish. I wrote it before I came to Spain." Lisa held it up and read it out. "One – Find a job. Two – find a flat in South West London. Three – Make new friends. Four – Be healthy and happy."

"It looks like you managed to get three out of four and that's not bad," Stella said, then kissed her softly. "So, I assume you'll scrape that flat off your list?"

"I think it's time to delete the list altogether." Lisa curled up against her and held her phone above them. "Smile."

Stella stole another kiss as Lisa took a picture of them,

then reached for her phone. "Cute," she said, studying their happy faces. The Spanish sun had kissed Lisa's skin and she had a golden tan now. Her eyes were bright and clear, and her smile was so infectious that she cheered up everyone around her. She was confident and calm within herself, the restlessness replaced by a drive that had surprised them both. And Stella had changed too, she noticed. She was glowing, her eyes loving and affectionate as they focused on Lisa. Her hair was a bit longer, but it suited her and she too looked radiant. "I think we should hang this on the wall of your new permanent home." She pointed to the wall opposite the bed. "Right there."

"Yes, let's do that. And it's going to be my new screen-saver too." Lisa fiddled with her phone until the picture appeared on her home screen. "This is my new list. Just you and me. It's all that matters."

75

———————

"My God, I've never seen so many rainbows in my life." Lisa laughed as she sat down at the bar with Marcy. The women's weekend at Paradise was in full swing, the outdoor premises decorated with rainbow flags, balloons and banners. The guests were clad in colourful outfits too, in rainbow striped sarongs with leis around their necks. She'd returned from Sitges last night and had missed the first night, but that was a good thing, she supposed. During events people tended to loosen up on day two, after getting the first awkward acquaintances out of the way. The atmosphere was happy and celebratory, many dancing and singing along to the band that was playing on the stage by the poolside.

"Fuck the rainbows, I've never seen so many cute women in my life." Marcy chuckled as she glanced around. "Thanks for bringing me. I tried to get tickets but failed."

"You're welcome. Thought you could do with a break after all the hard work. You never seem to stop." Lisa studied the drinks menu and laughed. "How about a unicorn?"

"A unicorn sounds good. I may need some liquid

courage to approach that hot girl over there." Marcy pointed to a woman with a short black bob who was dancing on the other side of the pool. Her hips were swaying to the beat, her fit body on display in only a pink bikini and a tiny matching sarong.

"She looks cute indeed, at least from behind. But there's someone even hotter here." Lisa winked at Stella, who walked past them with a hand full of inflatables.

"Hey, sexy." Stella surprised Lisa by kissing her full on the mouth.

"I don't think you're supposed to do that here," Lisa mumbled against her lips.

Stella shot her a mischievous grin. "I know, but how can I resist when you're dressed in a bikini and those tiny shorts?"

"Hmm... you're looking pretty good yourself." When their eyes locked, Lisa felt her core flutter. Stella was most definitely the hottest woman here, and she was all hers. The rainbow vest top showed off Stella's toned shoulders and her legs looked endless in the denim shorts. "It's a shame you can't join us."

"It is, but even working here is fun today." Stella smiled. "The atmosphere is amazing, I don't think I've ever seen so many happy, flirty people together." She turned to Marcy. "And I bet you're feeling like a kid in a sweet shop."

"I sure am." Marcy was still staring at the dancing woman, but her expression dropped to utter shock when the woman turned around. "What the fuck..."

Lisa followed her gaze and burst out laughing. It was Zoe, and she was clearly just as surprised to see them from across the pool. She waved at her, then nudged Marcy to do the same. "Go on, don't be rude."

Marcy gave her a brief wave, then turned her attention back to her drink. "Damn it. Of all the people."

"Is that the one we don't mention?" Stella asked her.

"Yes, that's Zoe." Marcy sighed. "What a way to ruin my day."

"She's pretty. Maybe now is a good time to kiss and make up." Stella shot her an amused look and turned on her heel. "Well, have a lovely day, ladies. Let's have a drink somewhere after I finish."

"Here you go." The bartender put two huge bulb glasses in front of them, filled with layers of colourful alcohol that were impossible to identify, topped off with a strawberry, rainbow parasols, rainbow straws and a glowstick.

"There's your liquid courage." Lisa held up her glass in a toast and winced as she glanced at the drink, remembering her night at Pit Stop. "Oh boy, that's strong," she said, then lowered her voice as she saw Zoe heading in their direction. "She's coming over. Be nice, okay?"

"Hey, I'm always nice. It's her that's being a b—" Marcy stopped herself when Lisa shot her a warning look. "Hey, Zoe," she said with very little enthusiasm. "What a surprise to see you here. I didn't know you liked to party."

"How could you? You don't know anything about me." Zoe gave Lisa a hug. "Are you having a good time?"

"Yes, we just got here. Want to join us for a drink?" Lisa knew it wasn't one of her best ideas, but it felt wrong not to ask.

"Sure, why not?" Zoe pulled a stool out and sat next to Lisa, then arched a brow at Marcy when she caught her staring. "Are you seriously checking out my breasts?"

Marcy frowned and was silent for long moments as if digging through her memory for something. "It's... it's your tattoo," she said, referring to the dragon tattoo on Zoe's cleavage. "It looks so familiar."

"It's beautiful." Lisa studied the ornate, fluid dragon that grew larger over her left breast, its tail curling around her ribcage towards her back. Some might think the dragon was crushing her, but to Lisa, it looked more like an embrace. It was unique; she'd never seen anything like it. "Did you have that done while you worked in Hong Kong?"

"No, I've had it since I was seventeen." Zoe looked down at it. "I did it as a nod to my heritage, but nowadays I tend to forget it's there. I'm just so used to it, I suppose. It's become a part of me." She looked at Marcy, whose eyes were still fixed on it. "And you're right to say it looks familiar. Funny that you remember my tattoo, but you don't remember me," she continued in a sarcastic tone, then ordered a beer for herself.

Marcy swallowed hard and met her eyes. "Have we slept together?" She fiddled with her straw, clearly uncomfortable. "If we have, I suppose I owe you a big apology for not recognising you." She groaned when Zoe didn't answer. "We have, haven't we?"

"You still don't remember..." Zoe took her drink and stood up. "Not only have we slept together, Marcy. You..." She dropped a dramatic pause. "You took my virginity."

76

"Jesus, what a fuck up," Stella said, staring at Marcy in disbelief. Even after midnight, the promenade was still filled with crowds, and she felt a good kind of tired after being on her feet all day. Propping her legs onto another chair, she sat back and took a sip of her beer. After Marcy and Lisa had filled her in on what had happened, she totally got why Zoe didn't like her one bit.

"Yeah. I'm starting to remember her now. She just looked so different when she was younger. She was kind of boyish and I prefer more feminine women so the memory never stuck. Anyway, I was drunk, I think, otherwise I would have surely remembered her sooner." Marcy was drowning her sorrows in tequila and was on her third shot of the night after knocking back unicorns at the women's event. "I really fucked up and I feel so bad. I actually think I gave her a fake phone number that night."

"You were young, and it was a long time ago," Lisa said in an attempt to make her feel better. "People make mistakes." She rubbed Marcy's arm and smiled. "At least now you know why she was so angry. Just apologise. That's probably all she wants; a simple apology."

"Maybe." Marcy looked at her empty shot glass and beckoned the waiter over.

"Why don't we get you some water instead?" Stella suggested. "You're starting to look a little cross-eyed. Or do you want me to drive you home?"

"No, I don't want to go home. But I suppose water would be good. Don't feel like you have to stay here and keep me company though; I can just call one of my..." Marcy pulled her phone out of her back pocket and frowned as she scrolled through a long list of female names. "Hmm. I could call Celine, or Debs..." She paused and grinned. "Or Abby. She'll be able to distract me from my guilty conscience for a while."

"Who's Abby?" Stella asked.

"My mum's friend. They share the gallery."

Stella laughed. "You're sleeping with your mum's friend?"

"Only when her husband is away for work. And she just messaged me to tell me he left this afternoon."

"Does your mum know?" Lisa asked.

"Of course not." Marcy chuckled. "She'd kill me if she knew." She ordered a large bottle of sparkling water and rested her elbows on the table, rubbing her temple. "Anyway, as I said, you don't need to stay for me. You've got another long day tomorrow and I'm sure you're looking forward to curling up in bed together."

Stella nodded and yawned. "I actually wouldn't mind getting some sleep."

"Come on then, babe. Curling up sounds like a great idea." Lisa took her hand and pulled her up. "Marcy, have fun with your mum's friend and let's meet up soon. Don't worry about Zoe too much; it's not like you're going to run into her again. But if it bothers you, I really think an apology would do the job."

"I'll do that." Marcy waved them goodbye, then turned back to her phone, looking defeated.

Stella pulled Lisa in as they crossed the road to the taxi rank. "I'm so glad I'm not living that life anymore."

"What? Hopping from woman to woman?" Lisa asked with a grin.

"Yes, I don't think I realised how lonely I was until I met you." Stella glanced at the long queue before the taxi rank, shook her head and pulled Lisa towards the beach instead. "It's too busy right now. Want to sit on the beach while we wait for the line to die down? It's nice here at night."

"Okay." Lisa followed her down the concrete steps and they walked towards the shore, where they sat down. She snuggled up next to Stella, resting her head on her shoulder and inhaled the sea breeze. "You're right. I never thought I'd say this but it's actually quite pretty here at night. That is, as long as you don't look behind you," she added with a chuckle.

Stella laughed. "There's nothing like the horizon." She ran a hand through Lisa's hair and pulled her closer. Nothing felt as good as Lisa's body against hers and even after months, she still felt that almost violent flutter each time she was near. "You don't regret anything, do you? Now that you're staying here you may never be a big shot marketing executive again."

"No, I don't regret a single thing." Lisa smiled. "I have the most amazing girlfriend in the whole world, and everything is good in my life. I'm going to London to sell my car and pack my things soon. Want to come? Meet my parents?"

"Are they not going to hate me for stealing you away from them?" Stella asked.

"No, they're very happy for me. But it would help if you came so they can get to know you."

"Of course, I'll come. I'm sure I can arrange some time off; high season is over so we're only on sixty per cent occupancy. Shall we ask Mary to look after the animals?"

"Yes, I think she'd love that. She did say she wanted to socialise the new dog she got so it would be good timing."

"Perfect." Stella pulled Lisa closer and softly kissed her temple. "It will be nice for you to have all your stuff here. Two big suitcases and a weekend bag is not much to go on for so long."

"Honestly, I haven't missed anything at all, but I suppose I'll need my winter wardrobe." Lisa closed her eyes and sighed with contentment. "When it comes down to it, you're all I need. I love you, Stella."

"I love you too," Stella whispered back, her eyes swelling with emotion at the sincerity in Lisa's voice. "And I want to spend the rest of my life with you."

EPILOGUE

*M*eatball and Butters were racing up and down the terrace, chasing each other. They were getting big now but were still full of puppy energy, leaving a trail of destruction whenever they were in play-mode.

"Meatball, come here," Lisa called. "Stop running around the plants, you keep knocking them over and I've already cleared up after you five times today. There's soil everywhere." She snapped her fingers and the chubby, dark Lab ran up to her. "Stay here, honey. You have to set the right example. If you calm down while we finish this, your brother will too. Can you do that?"

Stella laughed when Meatball looked skyward, already distracted by a seagull that flew overhead. She was panting and her tongue was hanging out. "I'm not sure she got that, babe. Short commands usually work better than long monologues with dogs."

Lisa chuckled. "I know; I just had to vent." She knelt down to scratch Meatball's ears and when Butters joined his sister, she kissed the top of their heads and gave them a cuddle. It had been a sunny, early November day, and it was still warm enough to sit outside without a jumper. They were setting the terrace table for Stella's end of season barbecue. Soon, Stella's team would be there to celebrate the quieter months ahead, and Lisa had invited Marcy, Marcy's mother, Delia, a couple of people she'd gotten to know through work and after much consideration, Zoe. She figured it had been a while since Marcy and Zoe's run-in and was hoping they'd be okay in each other's company. She'd grown close to them over the past months, and she really wanted them both here.

"How many are we? Twenty-seven?" Stella asked, counting the plates piled up on the table. "We should have enough glasses as long as everyone keeps the same one throughout the night."

"I think we're good. And we're twenty-eight, actually. Marcy's bringing a date."

Stella's eyes widened. "What? Marcy?"

"Yes. She was a little vague about it; she mumbled something about bringing a woman and didn't really give me an answer when I asked her if she was a friend or something more."

"That would be a first. I thought she never mingled with women outside the bedroom."

"Exactly my words." Lisa shrugged cheerfully. "I guess we'll see." She came up behind Stella and wrapped her arms around her waist. "It's so nice to have some time off together. I had fun cooking with you today." Burying her face against Stella's shoulder, she inhaled her familiar scent and felt grateful for their life. She had everything she never knew she wanted. The days were getting shorter, and she loved the change of seasons in Spain; the colours of the landscape changed, and the streets became quiet with the absence of tourists. Beaches were often deserted in the mornings, and Altea belonged to the locals again. It wouldn't be long until they'd light the fireplace at night and snuggle up on the sofa, and she was looking forward to hosting Christmas for their parents and siblings, who would meet here for the first time.

"Me too." Stella turned around and ran her fingers through Lisa's hair. "Anything else we need to do?"

"I don't think so." Lisa's eyes fluttered closed when Stella caressed her cheek. "I just need to dress the salads, that's all. Oh, and the flatbreads should be ready by now." She inched closer, pressing her forehead against Stella's. The sun was setting and it was cosy up here with the candles dotted over the dining table, the fairy lights fixed along the terrace railing and the smell of barbecue and freshly baked bread. This was her home now. She'd said goodbye to her life in London and hadn't missed it for a minute. As far as her parents were concerned, she suspected she'd probably see more of them now that she lived here as they'd already planned multiple trips to Spain.

"I'll get the breads out," Stella whispered against her mouth, pulling her closer. Their lips met, and Lisa moaned softly as they fell into a kiss. She felt an immense fire every time they were intimate, and an overwhelming sense of love every morning she woke up next to Stella. Life had been a string of unexpected events, both good and bad, but everything had led her here, to Spain. To Stella.

A familiar voice coming from the street below pulled them out of their moment, and Stella reluctantly stepped away to look over the railing. "I think it's Marcy," she said. "And her date, it seems."

Lisa joined her and followed her gaze. From the top, she only saw the crown of their heads. She immediately recognised Marcy's messy, blonde do, but there was something familiar about the woman on her arm too. "Wait, is that..." When the dark-haired woman looked up, she gasped in surprise.

"Oh my God." Stella laughed out loud and waved at them. "Hey, guys, what's happening here? Give me a moment and I'll buzz you in; you have a lot to explain."

IREADINDIES

This author is part of iReadIndies, a collective of self-published independent authors of women loving women (WLW) literature. Please visit our website at iReadIndies.com for more information and to find links to the books published by our authors.

AFTERWORD

I hope you've loved reading *Welcome to Paradise* as much as we've loved writing it. If you've enjoyed this book, would you consider rating it and reviewing it on www.amazon.com? Reviews are very important to authors and we'd be really grateful!

ACKNOWLEDGMENTS

A big hug to everyone who has supported me throughout the process of writing Welcome to Paradise.

Camilla, thank you for a fun time in Benidorm. I've rarely laughed so much! Also, I've never felt so hung-over.

Antonia, thank you for letting me write at your beautiful family home in Spain and showing me around. It was truly inspiring.

Claire Jarrett, thank you for putting up with me while writing the first book in this . Series do not come naturally to me, I've been super chaotic and stubborn as always. I hope you know how much I appreciate everything you do.

I also want to thank my proof/beta reading team. Laure Dherbécourt and DJ - you guys have done a great job as always!

ABOUT THE AUTHOR

Lise Gold is an author of lesbian romance. Her romantic attitude, enthusiasm for travel and love for feel good stories form the heartland of her writing. Born in London to a Norwegian mother and English father, and growing up between the UK, Norway, Zambia and the Netherlands, she feels at home pretty much everywhere and has an unending curiosity for new destinations. She goes by 'write what you know' and is often found in exotic locations doing research or getting inspired for her next novel.

Working as a designer for fifteen years and singing semi-professionally, Lise has always been a creative at heart. Her novels are the result of a quest for a new passion after resigning from her design job in 2018. Since the launch of Lily's Fire in 2017, she has written several romantic novels and also writes erotica under the pen name Madeleine Taylor.

When not writing from her kitchen table, Lise can be found cooking, at the gym or singing her heart out some-where, preferably country or blues. She lives in London with her dogs El Comandante and Bubba.

ALSO BY LISE GOLD

Lily's Fire

Beyond the Skyline

The Cruise

French Summer

Fireflies

Northern Lights

Southern Roots

Eastern Nights

Western Shores

Northern Vows

Living

The Scent of Rome

Blue

The Next Life

Under the pen name Madeleine Taylor

The Good Girl

Online

Masquerade

Santa's Favorite

Printed in Great Britain
by Amazon

21069689R00212